UNBROKEN

UNBROKEN

KIM PRITEKEL

SAPPHIRE BOOKS

SALINAS, CALIFORNIA

This and other Sapphire Books titles can be found

at

<u>www.sapphirebooks.com</u>

Kim Pritekel Books

Standalones
1049 Club
After Shadow
Blinded
Connection
Control – with Alex Ross
Damaged
Shadow Box
Swann Song
The Gift
The Plan
Wild – with Alex Ross
Zero Ward
Unmasked Desire

Dance with Me Series
Curtain Call
Encore Performance

The Traveler Series
The Traveler: The Hunted
The Traveler: The Huner

The Wynter Series
Finding Faith
Taking Liberty
Justice Won
Keeping Hope
Showing Mercy
Having Honor

The Destiny Series
She Who Would be King
Daughter of Ankou
Doors
She Who Dreams

Chapter One

Denver, Colorado – 1945

The yellow taxi drove up the long, winding road to the house. The curvy car had driven beneath the wrought iron gate, once so grand and ornate to the onlooker. But to the woman who sat in the back seat, it no longer held the magic it once did. No, now those ornate letters spelling out *Greyson Manor* made her feel uncomfortable, trapped.

Taking a deep breath, Jessie Lowrey forced herself to look at the house. It was massive, a monstrous silhouette against the heavy, pregnant gray clouds of early spring above. How appropriate, she thought. The long cobblestone approach wound its way to the circular drive in front of the house, its impressive portico shadowed the two large front doors which were reached from the curved set of stairs.

The taxi driver pulled the big car to a squeaky stop in front of the stairs and turned to her, telling her the amount she owed him. Jessie took one last look at the house before she reached into her pocket to grab the little coin purse she kept there. Digging out the correct coins, she handed them to him before climbing out of the car.

Standing alone, part of her wanted to run after the taxi and beg the driver to take her back home, that there had been a terrible mistake. She didn't, though. Nope, she stood her ground, no idea why she'd agreed to come. Hooking her thumbs into the belt loops of her trousers—men's, though she'd tailored them down to fit her frame—she looked up at the house.

Three stories of windows and sixty years of history looked down at her. Part of that history was her own. Eighteen years of it, in fact. Considering she was only thirty-three, that was a good chunk of it. Bringing up a hand, she ran it through her light brown hair, kept short since she'd cut it all off as a teen. Her bangs were longer, long enough to tuck them behind her ears, which she did. Yes, to get them out of the way, but also a nervous tic, and she was nervous.

Blowing out a breath, she gathered her courage and began to walk up the stone stairs when one side of the double doors was pulled open. She was stunned to see the butler, Terry, standing dutifully beside it. He'd been there since the very first day she and her parents had walked up the very same stairs when Jessie had been six years old. She was pretty sure he was wearing the same black suit, too. Strange thing was, this Terry looked like the grandfather of the Terry she first saw.

"Miss Jessica," he greeted with a slight bow.

"Hey, Terry," she responded, giving him a tight smile, which he didn't respond to. She always thought that man had the best poker face ever. "Where am I to go?"

"The great room," he said, closing the large door once Jessie had passed through it and now standing in the grand entryway. "You'll be met there."

Marble floors were polished to a mirrored shine, the family crest inlaid. To the left was the sitting room where basic chitchat took place. To the right, the great room, which was an expansive space with the biggest fireplace Jessie had ever seen, still to this day.

A mammoth maw of a firebox that could easily fit four grown men standing shoulder to shoulder inside.

An intricate stone mantel set it off, a mountain scene of a hunter and his hounds along with their mighty and glorious bounty on full display. It was an homage to an earlier time before Denver had become the busy, congested city it was today.

The furnishings that peppered the room were expensive, beautiful, and, to Jessie's estimation, as cold and lacking in personality as most of the house was. It was more of a museum than any sort of home. But then, that had all changed on that cold, tragic Tuesday when they were just sixteen. Before that, the large house had been filled with laughter and silly tricks and games of hide-and-seek. An endless maze of hallways and rooms for two young girls to play. She smiled at the thought, but it was quickly wiped off her face when she heard her name.

Turning, she saw the tall and well-dressed man that she'd known for a brief time standing in the wide archway that led from a hallway into the great room. His hair, once dark brown, now had gray in it, though was still slicked back from a handsome face. The pencil-thin mustache he used to sport was gone, leaving him clean-shaven.

"Hello, Mr. Russ," she greeted, walking over to him. She took the hand he held out to her, his fingers cool to the touch and his hold much like that of a limp fish. She squeezed the fingers in a firm hold, assuring him she wouldn't break. "Nice to see you."

He looked her over, a heavy eyebrow raised. "You as well." He released her hand. "I see you still dress… for the occasion."

She looked down at herself. "Well, sir," she said,

meeting his disapproving gaze. "I had to work this morning. With my father and I working on the grounds of the school, the church, and the cemetery, I gotta dress for *that* occasion. Not yours."

"So, your father isn't with you, then?" he queried, turning and leading the way back down the hallway that sported a bathroom and then his large office. She'd only been in the office once before, but it looked basically the same. Bulky, masculine furnishings and lots of wood accents in the wainscoting and coffered ceiling.

"Uh, no," she said, taking the seat he offered with a light touch of his hand to the back as he made his way around the large desk to sit behind it.

The office was dimly lit, as the wood shutters were partially closed, only allowing in minimal light from the dreary day beyond the window. He switched on the Tiffany lamp that sat upon the expanse of the desk. This illuminated his face into eerie, buttery patches of light and shadow.

"He had to finish the work at the cemetery," she explained. "So I left early to get here at the time you stated in your letter."

He nodded, lacing his fingers atop the leather blotter on his desk. "Understood. You can fill him in later, or he can come at another time to speak to me himself."

"What is this about, Mr. Russ?" She felt uncomfortable sitting there across from him, even now, so many years later.

"Alright, I'll be blunt," he said. "My wife has asked for you. She's suffering a terrible illness. Cancer."

"Mr. Russ," Jessie said, shaking her head. "I'm not a nurse, nor a doctor."

"No," he said with a little smirk in his deep brown eyes. "You beautify tombstones."

"Okay," she said, pushing to her feet. "It was nice seeing you again, Mr. Russ." She headed for the door, ready to walk back to town where she could call a damn taxi.

"Eliza is dying, Jessica," the man called to her, still seated. "Her wishes are to be surrounded by those she cared about most in her life. Apparently, that includes you and your father."

Hand on the doorknob, Jessie stopped. She turned to look at him. "What about her own children? She does have two."

He nodded. "Yes, but I'm simply following her wishes."

Shoving her hands into the deep pockets of her trousers, Jessie said again, "I'm not a nurse."

"Eliza has all the medical professionals she needs for her condition," he assured. "This is more about her mental and emotional health. Making sure she can find her way out of this life with some peace."

Jessie wasn't entirely sure what to say, or even what to think. She made her way back to the chair but didn't reclaim it. Instead, she stood behind it, her hands resting on the wood back, padded with dark green leather framed by brass studs. "What *exactly* are you wanting from us?" she asked. "To go sit with her? Visit?" She shrugged. "What?"

"I'm asking you and your father, Dobbs, to return to the property. You both will be paid handsomely for your efforts but will have jobs, of course, outside of simply playing chess with Eliza when she's up to it."

"We have jobs, sir," she reminded. "And a house."

"Indeed. I'll pay you both three times the amount

you're currently making for the entirety of your stay here." He reached into the pocket of the vest in his three-piece suit and retrieved a gold pocket watch. He flipped it open and glanced at it before snapping it shut and replacing it, the gold chain hanging in a loop outside the pocket. "I must go soon," he announced, rising to his feet. "Her doctors have said she may last out the month or the year. They just don't know."

Jessie chewed on her bottom lip, no idea what to think. She certainly needed to talk to her father about it. She cleared her throat and met his gaze as he walked around the desk toward her. "I need to think about this, Mr. Russ. And talk to my father. In the meantime, can I borrow your phone to call for a taxi?"

"Do you one better," he said, placing a light touch to her shoulder to urge her to turn around so they could leave the office. "We'll give you a lift to where you need to go."

❧ ❧ ❧ ❧

The house Jessie shared with her father was a small two-bedroom with one bath, small living room and small kitchen. It was plenty for their needs. It had a tiny yard, ironically neither of them wanting to deal with much yardwork at home. Their days were spent caring for properties all over town, so at home, it was about staying inside out of the hot sun or cold weather.

"Dad, you want water or iced tea to drink?" she called out from the kitchen, her father in the bathroom washing his hands after he'd arrived home from work.

"Ain't we got any of that lemonade left?" he responded.

"You finished that last night," she said, placing

two loaded plates on the table. Dinner was served.

"Iced tea, I guess." He appeared a moment later, running his hands through his hair, which had wet bangs as he'd clearly washed his face, too. He pushed them back from his face and took a seat. "Looks good."

Jessie said nothing as she placed her father's iced tea and her own water before their respective plates. "I need to talk to you about something."

Dobbs began to cut up his meatloaf before spooning more homemade ketchup over the pieces from the canning jar it was still in, despite Jessie having put a good amount atop the meatloaf before it went into the oven. "George Russ meeting?"

"Yeah." She scooped a bit of mashed potatoes on her fork and said, "Eliza is dying." She put the food into her mouth and chewed, allowing her father to absorb what she'd said before she continued.

He eyed her, sipping from his tea before he spoke. "That's a real shame. What from?"

"Same thing that got Mama," Jessie responded. "Not sure what kind, though."

He nodded, looking down at his plate. Jessie knew her mother's death, eight years before, was something her father had never gotten over. Four years ago, she'd finally fished him out of the booze he was drowning in and moved him in with her. "What does he want with us?"

"Wants us to come work for them again," Jessie explained. "Not sure on all the details, but she's asking for us to be there. Help out, that sort of thing."

He was taking a drink from his iced tea and looked at her over the rim of the glass. "You don't say," he muttered, finishing his drink and setting the glass back down on the round wooden table. "But, we got work to do."

She nodded. "I told him that. He offered to pay thrice what we're making now. At least, for the duration we're there. Would give us the money to buy a second truck." She shrugged. "Might make things easier."

Dobbs said nothing for a long time as he ate his dinner. Honestly, Jessie thought maybe he was done with the conversation until finally he wiped his mouth with his sleeve. He met her gaze. "I don't know, Jessie. We got us a good thing goin' here. Don't ya think?"

"We do," Jessie agreed. "Alright. Tomorrow I can go down to the diner down the street from the park and use the pay phone to call Mr. Russ and let him know."

ॐॐॐॐ

Later that night, Jessie lay in her bed, hands tucked up behind her head. She stared up at the ceiling of the small bedroom she'd called her nocturnal home for the three years they'd had the house. When she'd pulled her dad in to live with her, she'd been living in a small apartment above the pharmacy. Not at all feasible for the two, they'd gotten the house instead.

Her bedroom was fairly basic, like the rest of the house. Simple, functional furniture, nothing all that personal on the walls or even knickknacks on tabletops.

Truth was, there wasn't anything really to put on them or hang on the walls. Jessie's entire life had been about working from the moment her parents had stepped into Greyson Manor. Six years old, immediately given a job. Granted, her job had changed by the year, by the day, and sometimes, by the minute.

She smiled at that. At times it could be exciting,

and admittedly at times it could be unsettling or overwhelming. Her parents had always done their level best to give her a stable existence, so to essentially be at the whim of a living hurricane named Heaven had been an eye-opening experience. Soon enough, however, she'd learned how to not only anticipate the turbulence but to sometimes even hold it back or bring it down to the level of a tropical storm.

She quickly pulled herself from those thoughts and the direction they were headed, and turned them to her current life. Her father had been the groundskeeper for Greyson Manor for nearly all of Jessie's childhood. He'd left his post the year Jessie's mother had gotten sick. He'd been crushed and wanted to spend every moment with her that he could. The family, for the most part, had been gracious, paying for Louise Lowrey's medical bills during that time. Jessie knew that had been all Eliza's doing, as George Russ was a controlling, stingy son-of-a-bitch.

After she'd died and Jessie had gotten him back on his feet, no longer working for the family, he'd used his incredible green thumb skills to get hired on with the city. A steady job, and with Jessie working as his helper, they both were assured work. In a time when women were being forced back into the kitchen or often getting pregnant, as the men were coming back from the war in droves to reclaim their jobs, Jessie wouldn't have a chance for employment any other way. So, together, they'd built a little life for themselves.

Jessie turned to her right side, the bedsprings squeaking softly with the move. She tucked her right arm up under the pillow her head lay on. She now faced the window, her gaze taking in the night beyond. Their little house was out in an area that hadn't been as developed, so the houses were farther apart. Word was, developers were buying up the land hand over fist, so it was just a matter of time before neighbors began to pack in. She wasn't looking forward to that.

So, overall, they had a good thing, yes. But then the pendulum of her mind swung back to Eliza McGovern-Russ. She'd been good to Jessie, overall, though they hadn't been particularly close. She honestly had no idea why she was asking for her.

She and Jessie's mother, Louise, had been very close, but it had nothing to do with her and her father. Heck, Dobbs was rarely even in the main house, and while Louise worked as Eliza's personal maid, she and Dobbs had lived in the gardener's cottage on the property. Jessie had initially bounced back and forth between the main house and the cottage. Ultimately, however, she'd stayed in the main house with her own charge. She was to be Heaven McGovern's playmate, hired bestie, or whatever else her little entitled heart desired.

She growled when again her mind began to lead her thoughts to where they didn't want to go. She hadn't allowed it to since the last time she'd seen her, eight years ago. The image forced itself into her mind's eye.

"Damn it," she whispered, rolling to her back again.

Her hands came up and covered her face as she tried desperately to get the image to go away. Unfortunately, as that image began to fade, others drifted in. Giggling as they tried to climb the many trees on the property. Laughing as they built the fort beneath the grand piano in the music parlor, only to get yelled at and shooed away by Terry.

She saw wide, curious dark eyes watching her as she took the first bite of ice cream, making sure it was good. Once Jessie had made her pronouncement, the bowl had been snatched away—as well as her spoon, even though a second one lay available on the table—and Jessie had watched in wonder as Heaven gobbled the whole thing up, every single drop of the sundae made for them to share.

She smiled at that, remembering how hurt she'd been, only to find it quite amusing later to hear her companion's moans and groans from a tummy ache. Too much, too fast. That night, at eight years old, she'd learned a new term from her father—karma. Needless to say, that hadn't happened again.

Well, Jessie thought, her taking the entire bowl or dish, that is. The practice of Jessie testing her food for her had continued. Again, those wide, expectant dark eyes watching Jessie's every move, every expression as she tried the new piece of fruit they'd been given. If Heaven wasn't so sure about the juice at first sniff, she passed it on to Jessie.

"How on earth were you so damn uncertain about some things when you plowed head-long into others?" she whispered into the darkness.

What she especially didn't want to see flashed before her mind's eye anyway. The dark eyes, so damn dark yet so expressive. Her hair, dark as her eyes, painted by midnight with the mischief of the stars reflected in those eyes.

In the twenty-five years that Jessie had her mother in her life, the one and only time they'd ever argued over anything substantial had been over Heaven. She could still see her mother's surprised eyes at Jessie's sudden appearance and hear the disappointment in her voice.

"What are you doing here?" Jessie's mother demanded, looking from where she stood at the sink washing dishes in the gardener's cottage.

Jessie set her large knapsack on one of the kitchen chairs. She spared her mother a glance. "I just can't do it anymore, Mama."

"Can't do what?" Louise removed her hands from the dishwater and dried them on a towel before they went to her hips as she faced her daughter and only child.

"Be there," Jessie said, feeling her emotions once again start to well up. "See that. See..." She looked away, unable to finish the sentence.

"You can't just abandon her, Jessica," Louise said, voice hard. "She needs you."

"And what about what I need?" Jessie exclaimed, whirling on her mother. This time the emotions rose to the surface and welled in her eyes. "Why is that never part of anyone's calculations?"

"Don't you think you're being a bit dramatic?" Louise said, her green eyes, so much like her daughter's, fiery. "You made a promise to her, Jessica. You pick up that bag and you march your butt right back there!"

Jessie stared at her, deeply hurt. "No. No, I can't." She used the sleeve of her jacket to swipe angrily at the tears that began to trail lazily down her cheeks. "I can't, Mama. I can't watch her with him."

"I did not raise a coward nor somebody who goes back on her word. You're going to make your dad and I look bad to Eliza. Don't you care about that?"

All Jessie could do was just stare at her mother, stunned. She sniffled and grabbed her bag and, heaving it on her back, turned away. "Forget it. You'll never *understand, you refuse to even try."*

She'd left that day and had never returned to the gardener cottage again—until her mother got sick, four years later.

Chapter Two

It was a chilly morning, yet again, the clouds pregnant with threatening storms. It had rained off and on all night and clearly wasn't finished. It was that strange time in Colorado where the harshness of winter wasn't quite ready to hand things over to the new life brought on by the warmth of spring. So, cold rains or even snowstorms weren't uncommon.

Jessie made her way to the area of the cemetery that she visited every time she worked there, which was several times a week. It was so big, it wasn't possible to get it all done in one go.

"Good afternoon, Mama," she greeted, squatting in front of the simple gravestone with her mother's name as well as birth and death dates. "Sorry I'm a bit late today. Storms are comin' in and look to be a real gully washer. So," she continued, looking up into the sky that was beginning to grumble. "Got everything done before I came to see you and Molly. Not a lot of time today." She reached out and dusted off a few fallen leaves on the top of her mother's headstone. "Love you, Mama. Hope you know that."

Placing a quick kiss to the stone, she pushed to her feet to walk over to the stone of Molly Steele, a woman whose last name she didn't even know until she died. To her knowledge, she was the only person who visited the grave, Molly now dead more than eleven years.

There'd only been about a dozen people at her

funeral, including the two grave diggers waiting to go to work. Molly Steele had been about as alone in life as a soul could be. Maybe that's why she'd been so gracious and kind with Jessie, literally let her in. She knew what it meant to feel thrown away or alone.

Sometimes Jessie still had nightmares of that day, coming home from work at Mr. Beason's store just down the way. "I'm so sorry, Molly," she said, resting a hand on the simple stone. Just Molly's name and the day she'd died, not even a birthdate. Nobody knew it, including Jessie. "I'll never forget you and your friendship," she added. "You were there for me when I really did need a friend." Her smile was sad. "You sure did teach me a lot."

She lowered herself to the ground to sit, knees pulled up to her chest and arms wrapped around her shins. She looked up again, watching as the clouds grew darker and more menacing. There was also more rumbling, and it was getting closer overhead.

"Gonna have to go soon." She looked back to the headstone. "You know, you were the only one I ever told the whole story to." She snorted. "Isn't it funny how we end up telling our stories, divulging our souls, to virtual strangers rather than those closest to us?" She let out a heavy sigh. "But then, she was the one who was closest to me. Guess I couldn't very well go to her, now could I?"

She let out a heavy sigh and ran her fingers through her hair just as she felt a raindrop land on her forehead. Looking up again, she chuckled. She uncurled herself and got to her feet.

"It was raining cats and dogs the day we formally met. Remember?" She smiled and again touched the top of the stone. "I need to go before it really starts to downpour. See you Tuesday, Molly."

As if offering its own salutation, the sky fully opened up with a loud *CRACK*. The storm was in full swing. Jessie sprinted through the cemetery and to the wrought iron gate, letting herself out before she dashed across the street, deciding to take refuge in the store across the way. Clearly she was not alone in her thinking, as the small general store was nearly packed to capacity as she pushed through the door.

She ran her hand through her bangs, which hung limply in her face as the rain had hit when she was about halfway across the street. Pushing them back, she took a quick inventory of herself and those around her.

Some folks were clearly trying to shop, making their way around those who were standing or meandering around, wasting time until the worst of the storm passed. She tried to stay out of the way of those who were actually shopping, as she could see some were irritated as they clearly intended to pay for their purchases and leave the store.

She found a place to stand near the counter where large, clear glass jars were lined up, each one filled with a different type of candy. Small paper bags were stacked nearby for customers to fill with the penny candy of their choice and pay for at the cash register down the way.

As she leaned against the wall a couple feet away, she saw the most adorable little boy run up to the counter. He had medium-brown hair and big blue eyes and looked to be no more than four years old. His short hair was damp, as though he'd just escaped the storm. And, by the looks of it, he had escaped whoever he was in the store with.

He ran to the counter, far too little to see the jars

of candy, though he was trying oh so hard as he lifted himself up on his tippy toes, his neck craning. A little pink tongue poked out, though Jessie wasn't sure if it was in anticipation of a sweet treat or the exertion of trying to grow another eight inches to see over the counter.

"Hey, little fella," she said, smiling down at him. "Wanna lift?" At the boy's enthusiastic nod, Jessie reached down and picked him up, settling him on her hip as she stepped up to the counter. "What's your favorite kind?" she asked, meeting big blue eyes before they flicked to the sweets in front of him.

"There you are!"

Jessie turned to see a relieved and very wet young woman push through the door and approach them. She looked to be around thirteen or fourteen, her long dark brown hair in wet strands hanging around her lovely young face and shoulders. Grass-green eyes met Jessie's with a question in them.

"I guess this big boy belongs to you?" Jessie asked, handing over the bundle of cuteness. "He's a bit too short to see the candy he was looking at."

"You know better, Ronin," the girl said. "I told you not to do that. I only have money for what Mom told me to get." She looked shyly up at Jessie. "First time my mom is letting me go off on my own to get stuff."

Jessie nodded but was concerned. "Are you okay? Do you have a ride?"

"Oh yes," the girl assured her. "She's just down the way." She hitched a thumb toward the sidewalk beyond the store.

"Okay. Well, hey, as a celebration of your first go and because of the storm, how's about you two pick five pieces of candy each and I'll treat you, okay?"

"Oh no," the girl said. "You don't need to do that. Ronin knows better than to run off like this. I don't want to reward that."

Jessie eyed her, impressed. She nodded approvingly. "You've got a good head on your shoulders, young miss."

The girl smiled shyly. "Thank you. My mom says that, too." She shrugged a shoulder. "I don't want to let her down."

"Tell you what." Jessie brought out her coin purse and fished out a dime before placing the purse back into her pocket. "Your point is very valid regarding Ronin the escape artist here," she said, nodding toward the boy that his older sister now held. "But I'd like to treat you two. Okay?" She had no real idea why, but something about this young woman reminded her of herself at that age. Something in her eyes… a wisdom beyond her years and trying to be the good little adult before her time.

The young woman looked at her brother, eyebrows raised. "What do you think, Ronin?" she asked. "Should we get some candy to take home with us?"

"Candy!"

Jessie laughed and nodded. "Alright. I think he agrees."

Less than ten minutes later, the siblings had chosen their candy and filled one of the small paper bags with their choices. Jessie's dime in hand, the young woman took herself through the line to pay for it as Jessie kept Ronin entertained near the door.

"Okay, all ready to go."

Jessie looked up from where she'd been squatting down next to the young boy, the two watching a caterpillar inch its way to the safety of a crack in the wall. "Very good." She stood up and looked into the girl's eyes, her own penetrating. "You're sure your mom is just down the way? You're okay to get to her alone?"

"Oh yes, very okay." The young woman smiled brightly, confidence straightening her spine. "We'll be okay."

"Alright. Well," Jessie said, holding out her hand. Clearly the young woman wanted to be seen as mature enough for her own little mission so Jessie would treat her as such. "It was very nice to meet you. I'm Jessie."

The young woman took the hand and shook it firmly. "I'm Chloe."

"And you, mister," Jessie said, squatting down again and holding out her hand. "What's your name?" she asked, waiting for him to introduce himself.

"Ronin," he said, his sweet voice quiet.

"Jessie," she said, shaking his little hand. Getting to her feet, she smiled at both siblings. "You two have a good day and try not to get wet."

She laughed at the look she got from Chloe, who looked quite confused as the deluge continued outside, and pulled the door open for the pair. The awnings that ran along the face of the building did little to shield them from the rain. Chloe took her brother's hand then waved at her before the two headed on.

"Okay, Ronin," Chloe said to her brother. "Let's sing, okay?" At the little boy's vigorous nod, Chloe began to sing.

Jessie was about to head back inside when she stopped cold. She slowly turned and watched the two, a gasp falling from her lips as she heard the song.

It's a beautiful, beautiful day

The sun is shining on our way!
The road is long, so we'll sing our song
Until everything is okay.

"But it's raining, Chloe!" Ronin exclaimed. "The sun isn't shining."

The young woman laughed. "You're right. Okay, let's sing again, but we'll say the rain is falling on our way, how's that?"

"Okay!" Ronin began to skip along excitedly as they began to sing again with the new lyrics.

Jessie could hardly breathe.

❧❧❧❧

After the rain subsided a bit, though it was still coming down in a gentle wash, Jessie decided it was time to head out home. She and her father had been working in two different places today, so he was clear on the other side of town. Even walking, she'd probably make it home before he did.

Hands tucked into her pockets, she wandered. She found herself wandering in the center area of downtown. Brick buildings lined the street, the bottom level stores of one sort or other and apartments in the upper levels of many of them. Her mind wandered as much as her feet did. Her thoughts were all over the place, ping-ponging from this to that back to this and then over to those.

Her emotions were nearly as much all over the place. Damn it all, though. Things were fine! Things were calm and peaceful in her life. No bumps or bruises, overall. She got sick of the strange looks she got from people, wondering why on earth a young woman was dressed the way she was. Even a few hateful words here or there, but one of her best superpowers was becoming a wallflower. Most people didn't even really pay her much mind, which was what she wanted.

Damn it, George Russ. Why couldn't he have left well enough alone? For that matter, why couldn't have she? She hadn't needed to respond to that letter requesting her and her father's presence. She didn't owe him a damn thing. So, why had she?

"You know why, Jessie," she muttered, giving a small smile to a woman who looked at her strangely as she passed her, hearing Jessie speaking to apparently nobody. The woman moved on, and so did Jessie.

Suddenly, she realized things looked familiar. She stopped at the street corner, noting the small deli before her. Though the name and product sold inside had changed, the large plate glass windows were the same, as was the glass and wood door. She stood just outside, watching as customers stood in a neat line along the glass case, behind which a couple young men in striped aprons with paper hats pressed up into a ridge along the length of their heads hurried to make the requested sandwiches to perfection.

Last time she'd been in that building she'd been a worker bee, too, though she'd been busy either ringing up customers or stocking shelves. She could still smell Mr. Beason's cigars, a fat nub always poking out of the corner of his mouth. Looking away, she strolled on, her stomach lurching a bit as she knew what the next stop would be on her memory train.

An armful of material in her arms, darn near an entire bolt of it, Jessie hurried down the sidewalk headed to the Ford pickup she'd been allowed to drive to run the errand. More diapers needed to be made, and it had to be a very particular kind of material from a very particular store—no ifs, ands, or buts.

She glanced down at the scrap of paper on which she'd jotted down the list of other items she was to pick up, when she ran into something hard, a moment later finding herself flat on her back on the sidewalk.

"Oh my goodness!"

Jessie was pretty darn sure birdies and stars were playing peek-a-boo with each other around her head. It took her a moment to realize somebody was kneeling next to her. She only came out of her daze when cool fingers touched her face.

"Are you alright?"

Jessie blinked several times before she was able to focus on the deeply concerned face of the woman who knelt next to her. "Uh..."

"Damn, kid," a man's voice said from far above. "Need to look where you're going."

Jessie blinked up at the man looking down at her. He wore a suit with a loosened tie and a fedora set back on his crown. A cigarette dangled from his lips. In a moment of clarity, she worried the dangly bit of ash was going to land on her face.

"Be nice, Ed," the woman muttered. "It was my fault. I wasn't paying attention when I opened the car door."

Jessie's vision cleared a bit, the birdies taking flight, though she was left with a horrific headache. She studied the woman for a woman, noting she was a lovely blonde. Her hair was stylish, as was her dress. She wore makeup with red lipstick. For some reason, those scarlet lips caught Jessie's gaze. She hadn't seen red lipstick on a woman in person before.

Something her mother had once said entered her rattled brain: Only whores and fire engines wear red. A little giggle left her confused mind and out her lips as she thought, well, she's not a fire engine…

"Oh look, you're bleeding," the woman said, her dark blue gaze growing even more concerned. "Ed, help me get her up and gather the things she dropped. I need to clean her up."

Somehow, Jessie managed to walk and even mount the long, narrow set of stairs to the second-floor apartment. The man named Ed carried her bundle, dumping it on the couch once they entered the small place.

"Let's get you seated, hon," the woman said, helping Jessie to sit in a kitchen chair at a small table in the tiny area that wasn't much more than a nook with an icebox, stove, sink, and small patch of counter. "Be right back," the woman said to her once Jessie was settled.

Jessie was just barely aware of the woman and the man talking. He sounded irritated, and Jessie watched as the woman playfully snapped one of his suspenders.

"Give me just a couple minutes, Ed," she all but purred, her body mere inches from his. "I can't leave her bleeding and all fuzzy in the head." She tugged lightly on the necktie the man wore. "It'll be worth the wait, I promise," she murmured, eyeing him before turning to head back to Jessie.

Jessie looked away so as not to make the other woman think she was eavesdropping, though that was nearly impossible in the small apartment. The tiny kitchen nook stretched out into a tiny sitting room with a couch and coffee table. A slightly less tiny bedroom, which Jessie had barely made out on her way to the kitchen chair, was down the hall next to a closed door, which she assumed was a bathroom or closet.

"Alright," the woman said, resting a hand on Jessie's shoulder as she bent down to look at her face. "Oh, darlin'." She sighed. "That's gonna be an ugly shiner in the morning. Let me get you cleaned up."

Jessie nodded dumbly as she noticed Ed shrugging out of his suit jacket, which he tossed, along with his hat, to the couch near her bundle of material. He whistled softly under his breath as he began to loosen his tie and collar as he walked into the bedroom, the door slamming behind him.

"This might sting a bit," the woman said, suddenly sitting in the other kitchen chair, which she'd pulled around next to Jessie's. The woman's lovely face winced in sympathy along with Jessie's hiss of pain as the hydrogen peroxide she'd splashed onto a cloth was used to clean the cut on the bridge of Jessie's nose from the solid hit with the car door. "Sorry," she whispered.

"Sorry I interrupted your night," Jessie managed.

The woman met her gaze before returning it to her task. "Don't worry. Ed will live." She looked back into Jessie's eyes. "You have the prettiest green eyes I've ever seen," she commented absently. "Like new spring leaves."

"Thank you."

The woman sat back in her chair and reached to the table, where she'd set out a few medical supplies. She poured a bit more peroxide onto the cloth, which the woman had folded over again to form a clean spot, from the clear brown glass bottle. "What's your name, honey?"

"Um..." Jessie had to think for a second, her mind still fuzzy from the hit she'd taken. "Jessie."

"How old are you, Jessie?" she asked, again gently wiping at the cut, lightly pressing the cloth against the wound.

Jessie's eyes closed as the pressure, gentle as it was, made her head feel like it was going to explode. "Uh, nineteen."

"Oh, goodness." The woman smiled. "Just a baby." Her smile widened as she leaned in just a bit, lightly blowing on the small cut to dry the peroxide. The cooling breath felt nice against the sting. "Well, I feel just awful about this," the woman said, moving away as she began to clean up the small mess she'd made cleaning Jessie's wound. She lightly rested a hand on Jessie's trouser-clad knee. "If you need anything, you just come and tell me, okay?"

Jessie nodded, able to see the genuine concern and apology in the woman's eyes. "Okay. What's your name?"

The blonde twisted the cap back onto the brown glass bottle and wadded up the soiled cloth she'd used to clean the cut. "Name's Molly."

Thumbs hooked into the belt loops of her trousers, Jessie stared up at the building she'd called home for a short time. As images of that first day and the horrible black eye faded, she realized that it had truly been where everything ended. Where that part of her life had ended.

She let out a heavy sigh as she turned away and decided it was time to go home. Yes, that first chapter of her life had ended, but the next one, where she was now, left her feeling very lost when she didn't keep herself distracted with hard work.

Chapter Three

Denver, Colorado – 1918

Eyes wide, little Jessie Lowrey sat on her mother's lap, though her face was all but plastered to the window as the train eased up to the station with a loud sigh and hiss, steam billowing all around them. She saw lots of people standing on the platform between the huge buildings, which her father had told her was called the Denver Union Station.

"Why are they standing there, Mama?" the curious six-year-old asked her mother. She took in the women and men donned in fancy clothes as well as normal ones, like she and her family wore. Trunks were piled off to the side, as well as bags and hat boxes. So exciting! "Are they there to tell me happy birthday?"

"Well, honey," Louise responded. "They don't know you, so they don't know it's your birthday."

Jessie looked back at her mother. "Are you going to tell them?" she asked, eyebrows raised in excitement. Normally a quiet and shy girl, today was her special day and she was riled up.

"Well, sweetheart—"

"Louise, get you and Jessie together, and I'll see about our luggage," Jessie's father interrupted his wife's response. He was on his feet, holding on to the wood pole near their seat for stability as the train came to a stop.

"Yes, okay," Louise said up to him before turning

back to her daughter, running her fingers lightly through the girl's long hair. "Okay, my love, let's go."

Mother and daughter made their way off the train with the other passengers, Dobbs standing on the platform surrounded by the two large trunks the family had brought with them from Kansas City.

"Madam," a man said, holding his hand up from where he stood on the platform to help Louise and Jessie step down from the train.

"Thank you," Louise said, accepting the help.

Jessie glanced up at the man who tipped his hat at them both, then her wide gaze went to take in as much as possible. So much activity, with new sounds and smells and sights. Back in Kansas City, they'd lived on a horse ranch with the Taylor family. Her father had worked on the ranch, her mother in the house.

She didn't know why, but suddenly they'd upped and boarded a huge train and come out to this new place called Denver, Colorado. Jessie was used to lots and lots of dust and animals and the stink of horsey poo. Now, as they stepped onto the platform, with people coming and going, calling out to each other, chatting, or hugging and saying goodbyes, she was fascinated.

"Hello, Lowrey family!" a man's voice boomed.

Jessie's gaze whipped to the sound and saw a man headed their way, all smiles. He was dressed in a fine suit, a stiff-brimmed straw hat upon his head. He had a large belly, unlike her father's thinner frame. His cheeks were rosy, his dark eyes bright, and he looked to be in his forties—older than her father, at least, who was in his late twenties. He strode up to Dobbs and held out his hand.

"Harvard McGovern," he said, the two men shaking hands. "You can call me Harv."

"Nice to finally meet you in person, sir," Dobbs said. "This here is my wife, Louise." He placed a hand on her mother's lower back and gently pushed her toward the man. "And, this shy one here is our daughter, Jessica."

The big man took Louise's hand, leaving a chivalrous kiss to her knuckles before he knelt down on one knee. Jessie was stunned as, in such finery, he rested that knee on the dirty wooden platform where people walked and spat tobacco. He met her gaze.

"Hello there, Jessica," he said, holding out his large hand, which she looked at. "I'm Harv."

Jessie looked up at her mother, whom she leaned back into, to make sure it was okay to talk to this strange man. At her nod, she looked back to the man, taking his hand as she'd seen her father do. "I'm Jessie."

"Jessie!" His eyebrows shot up before they fell. "Now, your father said your name is Jessica. Are you fibbing?"

A finger went to Jessie's mouth, not sure if he was teasing her or if he was mad at her. She relaxed when she saw his smile. She returned it, shaking her head, finger still in her mouth. "No," she drawled.

His smile widened, immediately making her feel comfortable. "Well, Jessie, tell me two interesting facts about yourself," he said, remaining on that knee.

"Um, I like the color red, and it's my birthday." She gave him a shy smile, hoping she wouldn't get into trouble for telling the strange man that.

"Your birthday? This very day?" At Jessie's nod, he asked, "And, how old are you today, Jessie?"

"Six," she muttered around her finger.

"My goodness," he said. "Well, happy birthday, young miss. You and my daughter are darn near the same age." He reached inside the jacket of his suit, bringing out a chocolate bar. "Happy birthday."

Jessie's eyes grew wide at the treat before again she looked up at her mother. At the nod she got, her gaze again zeroed in on the chocolate. She took it, meeting his eyes as she did to make sure it was still okay with him.

"What do you say, Jessie?" Dobbs murmured in his deep voice.

"Thank you," Jessie said quietly.

"You're welcome," Harv McGovern said. "You were born on a world event. Did you know that?" When Jessie shook her head, he explained, "On this day six years ago, the *RMS Titanic* sank."

Jessie's eyebrows fell as her finger left her mouth. "What's that?"

"A big boat. It ran into a giant snowball!"

Jessie's mouth fell open. "Really?"

He nodded and brought up his hand, lightly tweaking her nose before he pushed to his feet. "Well, let's head out, shall we?" he said to Dobbs and Louise.

Seated in the back of what she found out was called an automobile, Jessie was wide-eyed as she took in what was called a city. So many automobiles on the streets, all different shapes and sizes: Fords and Buicks, she learned they were named, and what they were apparently in, called a Cadillac.

She spied children skipping along with their parents on the sidewalks, a little boy crying as he held his mother's hand on a street corner. A man and a woman hugging near a streetlight pole, and two men "exchanging words," as her father had once explained. She saw fancy dresses and suits, the denim overalls she was used to her father wearing, and everything in between. It was a whole new world.

Soon enough, however, they left the city and were out in wide-open country that was more familiar. But instead of ranches and farms like she was used to, there were huge, expansive houses and what Harv said were called estates. The Cadillac drove beneath a large wrought iron arch with the words *Greyson Manor* spelled out, and then along a long, winding path to the biggest house the six-year-old had ever seen.

"Wow," she whispered. She looked to her mother, who also looked surprised. "Is that a castle, Mama?"

Louise, wide eyes looking up at the huge house, slowly shook her head. "No, but it sure looks like one, doesn't it?"

Jessie nodded. Her little mind had taken in so much during their two-day journey that she just wasn't sure what to say anymore. Her attention was garnered when Harv spoke to the whole car rather than just to Dobbs, who was sitting up front with him.

"It's pretty late and I know you all have had a heck of a long journey. So," he said, sending a smile back to Louise and Jessie. "Let's get you all settled in for the evening and you can join us for breakfast up at the house tomorrow. How's that sound?"

All the excitement from the day quickly catching up with the family, Jessie simply nodded as she leaned against her mother.

⁂

Jessie had the unyielding feeling that she wasn't just not alone, but that she was being watched. Sleepy green eyes slowly opened, only to squint against the bright morning sunlight coming in through the two windows she had in her room. Blinking a few times, she became more awake and more aware.

Sure enough, she wasn't alone, and she was, in fact, being watched. "Are you a ghost?" she blurted, thinking of one of the stories her mom used to tell her about a little girl ghost who lived in the attic with her mice friends. Jessie had always enjoyed the stories Mama made up, but now, looking at the pretty little girl who sat on her bed staring at her, she wondered if maybe they weren't just stories after all.

"A ghost?" the little girl asked, her eyebrows falling. "Why on earth would you think such a thing?"

Sitting up in her bed, which was the most comfortable bed she'd ever slept in, Jessie focused more. The girl seemed to be around her age. Her midnight-black hair was long and flowed down her back, though it was pulled up on the sides and back from her face, tied with the same white ribbon that faced the skirt of her dark blue dress. Her eyes were the darkest in color Jessie had ever seen, as dark as her hair, but they were curious eyes, a great intelligence behind them.

"Who are you? Why are you in here?" Jessie asked, thinking maybe that was a better thing to say.

"I'm here because I've been waiting for you forever," the little girl said, as if it was so very obvious.

Confused, Jessie shook her head. "Waiting for me to do what?"

"To get here!" She scooted off the bed and began to wander around the small room, which Jessie herself hadn't been able to explore much. Once she'd been led to the bedroom that would be hers, she was pretty much out. "Why do you have my daddy's chocolate?" she asked, standing at the dresser and, on her tippy toes, looking at the top. She held up the chocolate bar and looked back at Jessie with accusation in those dark eyes.

"Harv gave that to me," she responded. "For my birthday."

"That's my father," the girl said, setting the candy back where she got it. She wandered over to the small trunk that held all of Jessie's clothing. Opening it, she continued. "Harvard Elliott Boise McGovern, III." There was pride in her voice as she glanced over at Jessie before returning her gaze to the contents in the trunk. "Is today your birthday?"

"No," Jessie muttered, feeling uneasy as her things were being touched and gone through. "Yesterday. What are you doing?"

"How old are you?" the girl asked, not answering her question.

"Six. What are you doing?" Jessie asked again.

"What's your name?" the girl said conversationally, placing the dress back into the trunk and wandering away, the lid left open.

Jessie was a naturally patient person by nature, so she wasn't really upset with the girl's actions, but she was confused. "Jessie."

The little girl stopped again, fingers brushing along the top of the footboard of the bed where Jessie still sat. "That's a boy's name."

"No, it's short for Jessica," Jessie argued.

"Then," the girl said, fingers falling away as she walked past the footboard, turning back to the side of the bed where she'd started. "If your name is Jessica, why don't you go by Jessica?"

Jessie shrugged, reaching up to brush her long hair out of her face. "I dunno. That's just what Mama and Dad call me." She studied this new person. "What's your name?" she asked again.

"Heaven," the girl said, hopping up on the bed and scooting backward until she was about halfway across the width. She turned to her side and lay across the foot, planting her elbow atop the quilt-covered mattress and resting her head in an upturned palm. "You're seven and a half months older than me," she announced. "I was born on Thanksgiving, so my daddy said he was so grateful that God sent him and Mommy a little girl. He said I was his little piece of Heaven sent on a day to be thankful."

Jessie considered for a moment, then nodded. "I think that's very sweet."

"My daddy says so am I." She pushed up from the bed again and hopped off, hard-soled shoes hitting the wood plank floor. She hurried to the bedroom door. Hand resting on the doorknob, she turned and looked back at Jessie. "You need to get up so you can go to work."

"Go to work? Doing what?"

Heaven gave her a sweet smile. "Go to work being my best friend." She was halfway out the door before she turned back to a baffled Jessie. "Happy day-late birthday, Jessie." With that, she was gone.

Jessie sat there, blinking several times as she tried to catch up with the little whirlwind that had just blown through her room. Shaking herself out of her sleepy confusion, she pushed the covers away to get up.

⚜ ⚜ ⚜ ⚜

Jessie had never seen so much food in her entire life. She and her parents had been brought into the formal dining room, which was a massive room with an expansive table. She recognized Harv, and of course Heaven, and an unfamiliar woman who looked like a blond version of Heaven and who she learned was her mother, Eliza.

The others sitting around the table were apparently other people hired to work at the house. Each person was introduced by name as well as what they did in the house or on the property. There were maids like her mother was, the butler, kitchen workers, and groundskeepers, like her father. There was even the chauffeur, whom they'd met the day before. His name was Tyson, and he'd driven the second car that had been filled with all their luggage.

"So," Harv said, his loud voice and pleasing smile gracing those present. "As you all know, we always have us a good and hearty how-do breakfast to welcome new staff to the house. So, today we welcome a trio all the way from Kansas City, Kansas. Dobbs there will be outside with you fellas, while Louise will be inside working on house chores. And that little one there," he added, indicating Jessie with a wide smile, "has the toughest job in the entire house. Keeping Heaven entertained."

Jessie's wide eyes met those around the table, their gazes on her as they laughed at the plump and joyous man's words. She felt herself shrink back into her chair a bit, feeling shy.

"And," Harv added. "Jessie there is our big birthday girl! Yesterday she turned the big six, but they arrived so late we weren't able to give her a proper birthday. Happy birthday, Jessie!"

Filled with a mixture of surprise, pleasure, and more shyness, Jessie gave a tentative smile to those who tossed out excited shouts of, "Happy birthday!" She felt her mother's arm wrap around her shoulders, no doubt to give her a little support with so many strangers focusing on her.

"In honor of our birthday girl," Harv continued, pushing to his feet as the door swung open that separated the large kitchen from the dining room. A woman hurried inside dressed in a white cook's uniform, a big plateful of pancakes that was decorated with fruit to make a smiling face. She set the plate in front of Jessie.

Jessie forgot all about the unsettling attention as her gaze feasted on the fragrant breakfast before her. "Oh my," she murmured, her mouth beginning to water. She looked up at the woman who'd put the plate before her. "Thank you," she managed, barely remembering her manners.

Finally, everyone began to dig in to the platters of breakfast foods lined up along the center of the table, loading their plates as Jessie began to dig in to her special pancakes. She glanced across the table to Heaven, who was busy cutting up a sausage link with fork and knife. She also had a small helping of scrambled eggs and country potatoes on her plate.

Looking back down to her plate again, she decided to share. "Um," she said, then clearing her throat as the simple sound had been barely a murmur. "Heaven?" She still thought it was weird to call a person by the name of a place.

The girl looked up from her task to meet Jessie's gaze. "Yes?"

"Um," Jessie muttered, her shyness coming back. "Want some?"

Heaven's dark gaze fell from Jessie's face to her

plate, the tip of a little pink tongue poking out at the corner of her mouth for a moment as her gaze met Jessie's again. With a smile, she nodded.

Chapter Four

Greyson Manor — 1945

Hands shoved into her trouser pockets, Jessie looked around. It was so strange, as if time had simply stopped, frozen forever the way it had been that day. That day, the day she'd packed up and made a decision she'd regretted. Hell, she'd known that day it was a stupid offer to accept. She looked at the shelves on the wall, filled with the books they'd read to each other.

The room and all its furnishings, wall hangings, and objects had changed as the girls had grown. She'd been eighteen years old when she'd left. A young person just beginning to discover what it meant to be an adult, and a woman. Her gaze went to her bed. It was larger than the one she'd had in the gardener's cottage, which was way larger than the cot she'd had at the ranch.

She walked over to the bed. It had a brass headboard and footboard, the rounded tops and bars shining brightly in the morning sun. She walked around to the side of the bed, the mattress bare, two pillows stacked at the head.

It was the only evidence in the room that nobody lived there anymore. Everything else was exactly as she'd left it, the furniture dusted, rugs swept, and brass polished. She leaned down and rested her hands on the mattress, pressing a few times experimentally. She turned and sat, hands resting on either side of her hips as she did.

Taking a deep breath, she fell backward to lay across the bed, her hands tucked behind her head. She stared at the ceiling, a ceiling she had stared up at many a night. She almost felt the weight against her shoulder and across her belly.

Startled when the door opened, Jessie raised her head. Through the dimness of the room, only a bit of moonlight shining in, she saw a silhouette step inside then close the door again. She watched as the dark figure hurried over and passed through a patch of moonlight before reaching the bed.

"What are you doing?" she whispered.

Heaven, in her white, ankle-length sleeping gown, lifted the heavy covers before she crawled under them and slid over to the eight-year-old who was lying on her back, hands tucked behind her head on the pillow. Her unexpected and uninvited companion said nothing as she got settled.

Jessie had no idea what to do. She felt the soft warmth of Heaven's body as she snuggled up against her, long, ebony hair trailing behind her on the other pillow as she rested her head on Jessie's shoulder. She could smell the floral scent of her perfume from her bath just before bed. Though surprised, her protective instinct took over and her right arm moved until it wrapped around narrow shoulders.

"The thunder woke me," Heaven finally said, her words whispered as another growl of thunder sounded over the house. A moment later, the tick, tick, tick on the windows as the rain began to fall.

"Are you okay?" Jessie whispered back, holding the other girl a little tighter. She knew Heaven hated

thunderstorms at night. At the nod she got, she smiled. "'Kay."

They were quiet as they lay there. Jessie glanced to the window and saw a bright flash of lightning and held Heaven tighter, as she knew a huge boom of thunder would follow. Sure enough, the smaller girl in her arms started as it rocked the house.

"It's okay, Heaven," Jessie whispered. "I've got you."

Jessie pushed her upper body up to rest on her elbows, taking in the room around her once more. So much the same, yet so terribly different. She sat up fully and got to her feet. Running a hand through her hair, she blew out a breath.

"What am I doing here?" she muttered.

"Miss Jessica?"

Jessie's head turned to see Pauly, the nurse on duty, standing in the open doorway of the bedroom that led to the hallway. Another door, closed now, led directly to Heaven's old bedroom—the one the two had most used.

"Mrs. Russ is ready for you now."

Jessie nodded. "Thank you."

She followed the diminutive brunette down a maze of hallways that Jessie realized she could still traverse blindfolded. The residential portion of the house was set up in two parts, which Eliza had called "wings." There was the wing where Eliza and Harvard's—and then her and George's—suite of rooms had been, and the second wing housed quarters for the servants as well as for Heaven and her brother, Tobias.

Being nine years older, Tobias hadn't been much a part of their childhood. He was sent off to an expensive boarding school and then to college. Last she'd heard, he was in London or some such place in business. Though with the war that had just ravaged Europe, maybe he'd come back Stateside.

She was thrown out of her thoughts when they rounded the corner into the final hall that led to Eliza's quarters. Whereas Heaven's bedroom had been primarily that—a huge bedroom with an attached bathroom—Eliza's room was called a suite for a reason. There was a large space with a massive four-poster bed at the center, and the room was big enough to fit about three of them.

The shrunken figure lying in that bed, however, took her breath away. Eliza McGovern-Russ had been a woman of incredible beauty. Her hair had been the color of spun gold, and her dark eyes had been filled with life, intelligence, and—she understood as she'd gotten older—a sexual intensity that nailed the onlooker to the spot.

As a young woman slowly beginning to understand her attraction to females, more than once Jessie had been hit between the eyes by that look. An innocent glance from Heaven's mother, to her growing awareness, had felt like a lightning strike. Her daughter had inherited that very same raw sexuality.

Now, the large bed was surrounded by medical equipment, a multi-shelf cart with what remained of the woman's lunch, and a pitcher filled with what looked to be water. She was reclined against a few pillows and wearing a silk sleeping gown. Her hair, once coifed perfection, was thin and streaked with far more gray than gold. It was pulled back from her face, aged long before its time.

Eliza was reading, a pair of glasses perched on her nose, as Jessie stepped into the room, hands tucked into her trouser pockets. She looked casual, but the truth was her hands were shaking and she didn't want the other woman to see. Heaven's mother had always made her a bit nervous, a woman that was hard to read, but Jessie was also now so afraid she'd say the wrong thing to Eliza, a shadow of the woman she'd once been.

As Jessie neared, Eliza glanced at her, reaching up to remove her glasses. She closed the book and set it aside with the spectacles. "Well." Her voice was the only thing similar to the woman of Jessie's youth. "The prodigal daughter returns," she said, a bit of teasing in her tone.

Reaching the bed, Jessie gave the older woman a smile. "Nice to see you again, Mrs. Russ. Been a long time."

"It has. Please," Eliza said, nodding toward the Elizabethan wingback chair that once used to sit with its twin in the little alcove of the turret windows. She'd seen Eliza sitting there reading more than once as a kid.

Jessie walked over to it, noting there was a closed Bible sitting upon the cushion. It hit her hard to see that, wondering if perhaps Eliza had the nurse, or whomever her visitor might be, read passages to her. She swallowed and pushed those thoughts away.

"Um," she said before moving the religious tome. "Before I sit, is there anything you need, Mrs. Russ? Anything I can get you?"

Eliza eyed her before glancing to the pitcher of water. "Might you freshen that in the bathroom tap, please?"

"Of course."

Thrilled to be given a task, Jessie grabbed the glass, which was less than halfway full, and dumped the contents into the pitcher before leaving the glass on the top shelf of the cart and taking the pitcher. She hurried across the expanse of the bedroom to the attached bathroom.

Using a fingertip, she pushed the light switch on, which relented with a firm click and illuminated the elegant room by the tulip-shaped sconces on either side of the pedestal sink in the octagon-shaped room. A deep, claw-foot tub in the same pastel purple as the tile that flanked the walls sat on the opposite side from the sink. She remembered there was also a cleverly hidden water closet in the room with a commode of the same color.

She walked over to the sink and dumped the contents from the pitcher, careful not to make a mess. Rinsing it out, she held her fingers beneath the water until it was cold, then eased the mouth of the pitcher under the gush until it was about halfway filled. She didn't want to fill it to the top, as the water could get to room temperature or stale if it sat there too long.

Remembering how anal the woman was with her house, Jessie used a nearby towel to dry the sink and chrome fixtures before she headed back to the bedroom. She gave Eliza a smile before she grabbed the glass and filled it with the fresh water. She held it out to the other woman, who took it.

"Thank you, Jessica."

"Yes, ma'am." Eliza was one of the few people who called her by her full name, and though Jessie wasn't thrilled about it, she respected that it was her way. Even Heaven's father, Harv, had been Harvard. "Anything else?" At the shake of Eliza's head as she took a drink, Jessie moved the Bible aside and sat down.

"Tell me about your life," Eliza said, holding her

glass out for Jessie to take, which she did, placing it on the cart next to the pitcher. "What do you do with yourself?" She eyed the younger woman. "You work outside," she said, a statement. "Your face and hands are quite sun-darkened."

Jessie looked down at her hands, which were placed on her thighs. Nodding, she met the woman's gaze. "Yes. I work with my father. We, well, he," she amended, "works for the City of Denver, and I work for him as his assistant. We take care of various locations around Denver, the grounds."

"I see. Do you like this work?"

Jessie shrugged. "It's work, Mrs. Russ. To me, that's all that matters. I'm earning a living and earning my keep." She smiled. "Don't much care what the work is. As long as I've got it."

Eliza nodded. Though her face was expressionless, her dark eyes held a bit of approval. "You always were a worker, Jessica." She studied Jessie for so long, the younger woman began to feel a bit uncomfortable. "I want you to work for me."

Crud. "Yes," Jessie said. "That's what Mr. Russ said. But, Mrs. Russ—"

"Eliza."

"Uh," Jessie stammered, thrown out of her train of thought. "Excuse me?"

"I wish for you to call me Eliza. After all, I've known you since you were a child, and I'm not a fool. I'm dying, Jessica." She smirked. "My days for formality are long behind me."

Jessie felt a stab of sadness. She looked down and cleared her throat, trying to push that emotion down so it wouldn't end up in her eyes or her voice. It brought back her own mother's final months. "Why do you want me to work for you, Eliza?" she asked gently. "You have plenty of house staff, I'm sure."

"We do, but I don't care about them," Eliza said, waving away Jessie's words. "I wish to be surrounded by family, not hired help."

Jessie sat forward in her chair, forearms resting along her thighs. "But you just said you want me to work for you. Isn't that hired help?" Her tone conveyed her confusion.

Eliza was quiet for a long moment, her gaze falling to her hands, which were clasped in her lap. She almost looked as though she were praying. Finally, she met Jessie's gaze again. "Before your mother died," she began softly. "She made me promise I'd make sure you were taken care of." Clearing her throat, she continued. "I wanted to do something before, but George refused to let me. Now..." She smirked. "Well, now it's not his money to dispute. These are my last days, and what Harvard had set aside for Tobias and Heaven..." She met and held Jessie's gaze. "And you, comes into effect."

Jessie stared at her, confused all over again. "What?"

Eliza held her hand out toward the cart. Realizing what she was wanting, Jessie quickly handed her the glass. Eliza sipped, seeming to need a moment to get her thoughts in order. Finally, she lowered the glass but held it in both hands at her waist, where the bedding was bunched up.

"He was quite fond of you, you see," she said. "You and your parents. You're in his will, which goes into effect when I die. I don't know what that entails, as I'm not privy to the details. That will be read after I go, but he told me he had provisions in there for you. All I know is what I have done."

Jessie was speechless. "I see," was all she could manage.

"So," Eliza continued, as if she hadn't spoken. "I want you here in these final days. I trust you and I care about you and I wish to have you here."

Jessie ran a hand through her hair before rubbing the back of her neck. "Okay," she drawled, her mind reeling. "And, what of my father? Mr. Russ mentioned him, too."

"Yes. I'd like him here as well, and if he has a good job he's concerned with, I understand. You, however, are the one I'm most interested in, Jessica."

"My father needs my help, though," Jessie said, shaking her head. "He can't do it on his own. It's too much work for one person."

"Then I'll see to it that another assistant is supplied to him at our expense."

"And," Jessie hedged. "You need an answer now?"

"Yes, right this very minute." Eliza's gaze turned hard. "I don't have much time to waste, you see. These days, things must happen in the immediate or not at all." She gave her a little smirk.

Looking at the woman who sat not five feet from her, Jessie could see how dire Eliza's situation was. And, with the fact that Heaven wasn't here, she had to wonder if perhaps her daughter was no longer in the area. Perhaps she was truly all Eliza had left. She thought of her mother—yes, what she'd want her to do, but also how frail she'd been at the end. Frail physically, emotionally, and, at times, mentally.

Louise Lowrey had been surrounded by those she loved most, including Eliza. How on earth, in any good conscience, could Jessie leave this woman now? Clearing her throat, she said, "I have one stipulation."

Eliza eyed her. "Alright. What is that?"

Jessie gave her a little grin. "If I'm to call you Eliza, I want you to call me Jessie. No more of this Jessica nonsense. I feel like I'm back in fifth grade with Mrs. Winslow."

Eliza's laugh was quiet and brittle, but it was there. "Alright. So be it." She reached out a hand that was nearly skeletal. The flesh was so translucent, it appeared like paper. "A deal?"

Jessie took her hand in both of her own, gently wrapping it in her touch. "Yes. A deal." She was taken aback by the relief she saw in those dark eyes, eyes that looked so terribly tired. It wasn't a tired from lack of rest, but a tired of the soul. Their owner was clearly done and ready for it all to end. "Can you give me a day so I can get everything cleared up with my father and tie up my life for the next bit, while I'm here?"

Eliza nodded. "Of course. Let Terry know what you need and what your father will need in his assistant."

Jessie nodded. "Alright."

❧ ❧ ❧ ❧

It had been a difficult discussion with her father. On one hand, she could tell Dobbs wasn't happy with her, but she also saw the understanding in his eyes. Like her, he'd been there when his beloved wife had literally been on her deathbed. He understood the need Eliza had.

Though he hadn't said a lot during their discussion, Jessie had the distinct feeling that he'd wanted to. Instead, he'd nodded and accepted that which he had no control over. Story of much of his life. Now, Jessie was in her bedroom at the small house, packing a trunk. George Russ's driver was due to pick her up in half an hour.

"Got everything you need?"

Jessie turned from folding the last pair of trousers to be packed to see her father standing at the open doorway of her bedroom. "Yeah," she blew out, looking over what she'd done. "I think so."

"How you feel 'bout all this?" he asked, crossing his arms over his chest. He looked concerned, a wrinkle of worry between his brows.

Jessie considered the question for a moment before she dropped the trousers into the trunk and eased the lid closed, securing the leather straps. "Well," she began. "Not exactly what I intended to do with my spring or summer, the busiest time of year for us." She met his gaze again. "But…I guess it's my duty." She shrugged. "She was there for Mama when she needed her most. I don't feel I can say no."

He nodded, leaning a shoulder against the doorframe. "Me neither." He let out a long, heavy sigh. "Guess I'm grateful they're sendin' me some help."

"I wouldn't have done this if they hadn't, Dad," she said. "I hope you know that."

He nodded as he pushed away from the doorframe. He walked over to her and slapped her on the shoulder before he turned and left the room.

Chapter Five

1919

The bedroom door exploded open and a giggling, running Heaven dashed inside, dragging an irritated Jessie behind her.

"Heaven, stop!"

"Spin!" Heaven ran them to the middle of her huge bedroom where there was plenty of room. Heaven took Jessie's other hand so she held both of Jessie's in hers, the two girls facing each other. She began to get them spinning, leaning her body back the faster they got.

"Heaven, stop," Jessie said, forced to spin along with her or they'd both go flying. She was angry and she was hurt, and playing was the last thing she wanted to do.

"Faster!"

"No." Jessie, bigger and stronger, used her size and strength to aim as she released the smaller girl, who went flying to her canopy bed, the "princess curtains" tied back to expose the huge, comfortable bed within.

Heaven squealed as she was launched as if from a slingshot. She landed on her stomach on the bed, her dress flying up and over her head as her legs nearly did. Jessie landed face-first into the large wardrobe, bouncing off and falling to her behind on the floor. She sat there for a moment before she shook herself out of it and got to her feet.

"Why did you do that?" Heaven demanded, rolling over to her back and sitting up. Her hair was in her face, so she blew it out of the way before her small hand came up to peel the midnight curtain away.

"I told you to stop and you wouldn't," Jessie said. She winced slightly as her ankle was sore now. "I'm mad at you." She pushed her own mane of hair out of her face.

Heaven stared at her. "What did I do?"

"You know I hate fish!" Jessie exploded, forced to hold this in all through dinner. "You know I do." Hands on hips and feet spread wide, she was ready to fight. "Yet, sitting there at the dinner table, you made me try it anyway. Try it so you could decide if you wanted to eat it or not. Even Cook knows I don't like fish and made me chicken."

Heaven stared at her, eyes wide and looking stricken. "But, you're my best friend," she said, sounding confused. "I thought—"

"What? That treating me like your pet dog is okay?" Jessie threw her hands up in exasperation. "You do it all the time, Heaven. All the time. Either I'm your pet dog or your living doll." She glared at the silent girl sitting on the bed. "I hate dolls." When Heaven said nothing, Jessie gnashed her teeth together, her jaw muscles working, and she headed for the door.

"Where are you going?" Heaven asked, hopping down from the bed, panic in her voice.

"Home."

"But…" Heaven ran after her. "You're my best friend, Jessie. I didn't say you could go."

Hand on the open door, Jessie looked back at her. "Friends don't treat real friends like that." With that, she left.

The late July night was warm. Jessie sat on the small back porch of the gardener's cottage. Her legs were pulled up to her chest and her arms wrapped around her shins. Her feet were bare, and her hair was pulled back into a long ponytail. She'd been sitting there for about an hour, thinking about her day with Heaven.

She worried that maybe she'd overreacted to the fish thing. But honestly, it was more than that. It had been building for a while. The Lowrey family had been on property now for a year and three months. And, as Jessie looked up at the moon, so bright overhead, she felt so sad. She loved Heaven. *She* saw her as her best friend, but that clearly didn't go both ways.

"Hey, kiddo."

Jessie turned to see her father standing in the open back doorway to the small two-bedroom cottage. He gave her a smile before stepping out onto the patio and closing the door behind him.

"Mind if I join you?" he asked.

Jessie shook her head and watched as he lowered himself to sit on the flagstone next to her, grunting as he did. He mirrored her position and looked up at the sky.

"Real pretty night," he said.

"Yeah," she muttered, resting her chin on her knees.

"Heard you had a little falling out with Heaven." He looked over at her, Jessie able to feel his gaze on her profile. She said nothing. He reached over and rubbed her back before giving her a pat to the shoulder. "You know," he began, hand landing atop the other that rested on his own shins. "You know how the three of us have always been a team." He glanced over at her, Jessie meeting his gaze. "You know, workin' together, me, you, and your mom."

"Yeah." Jessie nodded, no clue where he was going with this.

"We had to cooperate, right?" he asked. "Depend on each other. Be considerate of each other. Right?"

"Yeah," she said again, understanding more what he was saying. "We had to."

Dobbs nodded. "Exactly. We had no choice but to be a team. Now, Heaven," he added, eyebrows raised to emphasize his point. "She's kinda been left alone, Jes. Her parents kinda do their own thing and her brother is off at school."

She stared at him, her anger beginning to rise again, though not at him, just at the mention of the other girl's name. "So?"

"So," Dobbs drawled. "She don't know what it means to have to be a team player, Jessie. She don't know what it means to compromise."

"How can she not know that, Dad?" Jessie asked, angry at herself as she felt tears prick the backs of her eyes. She looked away from him. "I..." She swallowed. "I really care about her, Dad. I do. But she makes me feel so bad."

Again, Dobbs slapped her on the back. "Jes, Heaven is a sweet little girl, and I think she really needs your friendship, but she don't know how to be a good friend back." He lightly nudged her with his shoulder. "Bet you can teach her how."

She looked up at him. "You think so?"

"I know so." He slung his arm around her narrow shoulders. "Look at them stars," he muttered, pointing with his other hand up at the sky. "Oh look, a shooting star, Jes!" He grinned down at her. "Make a wish."

Jessie watched the falling star and whispered, "I wish Heaven would love me like I love her."

❦❦❦❦

After she'd had her talk with her father, Jessie had felt a little better. Maybe a bit more understanding of who Heaven was and why. Her whole life, all seven-plus years of it, it had been about hard work and helping her parents. As her father had said, they'd been a team. She'd never really had a friend before, not like Heaven. But it wasn't supposed to hurt more to have a friend than not to. Right?

What he'd said to her made sense, she supposed. Now, as she lay in her bed in the cottage, she thought about what she'd say to her in the morning. She was due back at the house just before breakfast, and then they'd spend the day in whatever way Heaven said they would.

Truth was, Jessie didn't mind. She loved making Heaven smile. She loved making her laugh. She loved making her gasp at the crazy things Jessie was willing to do to make those beautiful dark eyes grow wide in amazement. In fact, Heaven had her wrapped around her little finger, which was why it hurt so much.

Startled out of her thoughts by a noise, Jessie raised her head, looking to the window. All she saw was darkness beyond, so she rested her head back on the pillow again. The hamster on the hamster wheel that was her mind began to spin again, when once again she heard something.

Sitting up, Jessie saw a small hand appear in the

open window, grasping the sill. Her own small hand went to her chest as she gasped. A moment later, Heaven's face appeared, then her shoulders and her upper body as she heaved herself through the widow, nearly landing on her head as she flipped over the ledge and into the room.

"What on earth?" Jessie scrambled out of bed and over to her. She bent down and grabbed the smaller girl beneath her under arms and helped her to her feet. Both standing again, she reached up and, a small smile on her lips, brushed long hair out of Heaven's face. "What are you doing? You could've gotten hurt."

Straightening her hair and her nightgown, Heaven looked her in the eye, raising her chin slightly not only to make up their few inches difference in height, but almost as if in defiance. "Yes, but I came to talk to you." Without a word, she stomped by a bemused Jessie over to the bed. She pulled down the covers, then, with a glance to Jessie, climbed in. "Are you coming?" she asked when Jessie just stared at her.

"Uh," Jessie hedged. "I guess." She walked back to the bed and climbed in, looking at Heaven, who lay on her side facing her. "What?"

"Waiting for you to get settled so I can say what I have to say," Heaven said as though it was so obvious.

"Oh." Jessie turned to her side to face Heaven. They each lay on their own pillow, a scant six inches or so between them in the bed that was perfect for one child but a bit tight for two. "Okay, what?"

Heaven studied her face for a long time, her own eyes filled with so much that Jessie didn't understand. A lot of emotions, but she thought one of them was sadness. Finally, Heaven swallowed and said, "I'm sorry." She shook her head as much as she could where it lay against the pillow. "I've never had a friend before."

Jessie studied her and saw nothing but truth looking back at her. "Why did you climb in through my window?"

"Because," Heaven said softly. "I wanted to prove to you that I'm your friend."

Jessie smiled. "You could do that by being nice to me."

"I thought I was," Heaven said, her voice so sad. "I don't know how to do this, Jessie. I don't know how to be a friend." Tears came to her eyes, and she turned away. "I don't want you to leave."

Jessie felt everything inside her melt. She scooted up behind the crying girl and wrapped her arms around her. "I won't leave," she whispered.

"You promise?" Heaven whispered back.

"I promise."

✥ ✥ ✥

1945

She slowly lowered the trunk onto the bed after carrying it on her shoulder from her father's truck. It bounced a bit, her steadying hand on its top.

"Are you sure this is the room you want?" Tilda, one of the maids, asked. "Mrs. Russ said you could choose any you wanted."

Jessie spared the pretty young thing a glance. "I'm sure, thank you."

With a bow, the uniformed servant scurried away. Left alone in her old bedroom, Jessie unbuckled the leather straps and opened the lid. She began to unload it, placing her folded clothing into the dresser. It was a bit surreal, she had to admit.

The last time she'd loaded those drawers, her mother had helped her. After all, at only eight years old, she hadn't a clue how to prepare her own bedroom outside of her parents' house.

"You be respectful," Louise said as they worked side by side to refold Jessie's clothing to fit in the drawers. They were a different size than the ones she'd used in the cottage, so they no longer fit correctly. "You do as Miss Eliza says."

Jessie blew out a nervous breath and nodded. "Yes, Mama."

"I'll be here all day every day working, so I won't be far away if you need me, okay?"

Again, Jessie nodded. "Yes, Mama."

Louise hipped the drawer, filled with her daughter's clothing, closed before she turned to Jessie. She took her into a warm hug, resting the young girl's head against her motherly bosom. She left a kiss on the top of her head. "My little girl," she murmured into the hug. "All grown up so young."

Jessie's eyes slid closed as she allowed herself to be enveloped by the warm love and affection. "It'll be okay, Mama," she said.

She'd known her parents hadn't been happy when Heaven had asked them if Jessie could move into her "best friend room," which was connected to Heaven's by a door. Apparently, it had been originally built as a nursery for the original owner of the huge house. She'd been surprised when she'd heard that, as the bedroom for a newborn was larger than the entire house of some families she knew.

The night Heaven had asked her parents, Jessie

already in the know about her best friend's wishes, she'd watched her mother's face fall. Though, to her credit, Louise Lowrey had quickly covered her expression, turning to her husband for his decision.

Truth was, either Heaven was always at Jessie's house or Jessie was always at hers for sleepovers, so Jessie thought it kind of made sense. And, always at the back of her mind was the thought and understanding that, yes, they were best friends, but at the end of the day, she essentially worked for Heaven. Her parents obviously kept that in mind, too, as they gave permission for their eight-year-old daughter to move out of their house and into Heaven's.

"I'll take care of her, Mrs. Lowrey," a small voice said.

Jessie opened her eyes and saw Heaven standing in the open door of the bedroom. She looked uncharacteristically contrite as she stood there in one of her pretty dresses. Her hair was pulled back from her face and her hands were clasped in front of her.

With one final squeeze, Louise released her daughter and walked over to Heaven. Jessie watched as her friend was also gathered into a motherly hug. "I know you will," she said into dark hair. "I know."

Jessie smiled, thinking about it. By god, they'd been so young. She stared down at the folded shirt she held in her hands, running her fingers over the soft material, though she didn't see it. Instead, she was seeing Heaven's young face again. After Jessie's mother had left, the quiet, contrite girl had left, too, leaving behind an exuberant, squealing one instead.

The hug was painful, and Jessie was pretty sure

she felt her ribs groan. After being released, Heaven had grabbed her hand and tugged her to the door that was closed. She pulled it open with a flourish, revealing her bedroom on the other side.

"We'll never close this," Heaven whispered, as if it was a secret doorway that connected two very different worlds. "Ever."

Jessie nodded sagely. "Alright."

Jessie set the folded shirt down on the polished dresser top before walking to the closed door. She looked down at the brass doorknob, chewing on her bottom lip before, with a slowly released breath, she reached down and took hold. Turning it, she pushed the door open and was met by the dimness of the huge room beyond.

The room smelled a bit stale, as if it hadn't been aired out in some time. She walked over to one of the huge windows and, with a grunt of exertion, whipped open the heavy drapes. Light poured in, dust motes drifting through the sudden tall, rectangular spotlight. Turning away from the window, she saw everything was exactly as it had been last time she'd been in there.

"I don't want to do this," Heaven whispered, her face buried in Jessie's neck. "God, I don't want to."

Jessie held her, her hand cupping the back of the dark head, their bodies flush as they stood near the bed they'd shared the night before. "I know," she whispered. She felt Heaven's fingers grab fistfuls of her shirt in a desperate hold. She felt as though the other woman was desperately trying to ground herself by clinging to Jessie. "It'll be okay." She didn't believe a word of it, but she had to say it.

Heaven shook her head. "No, it won't!" She pulled away from Jessie, bringing her hands up to wipe at her tears. The massive stone of her engagement ring caught the incoming light through the windows. "I hate this." She looked to Jessie, eyes tortured and filling with fresh tears all over again. "I know you'll go on," she said, her voice thick with emotion. "You'll be gone."

Jessie gave her a smile, though she knew it was pitiful. Shaking her head, she said, "I told you, I won't leave. I promised."

Staring at the very spot of their final conversation in that bedroom, Jessie sighed. She brought up a hand and ran it through her hair before letting it fall back to her side. "I'm sorry, Heaven," she whispered. "I tried."

Chapter Six

1927

Books hugged to her chest, Jessie hurried through the hall of the high school she and Heaven were attending. It was the last day of the fall semester of their freshman year. Once they left that day, they'd be out of school for two whole weeks for the holiday break. She was excited to get away from classes for a while, and even more excited to get away from Chadwick Tapper.

She groaned inwardly as her steps slowed. Down the hall, in front of Heaven's locker, stood Chadwick. A handsome chap, his blond hair was just so, his expensive clothing just so, and his varsity sweater just so. He was a senior, and his dark blue eyes were pinned to Heaven no matter where she went.

They were now fifteen, and Heaven had grown into an absolute heavenly creature. Her skin was pale and creamy, lips full and naturally rosy. She was a small teenager, but her curves were all woman. Every boy in the school had been sniffing at her skirt since the very first day.

It was so hard on Jessie. Though she kept her attraction locked away far from Heaven's gaze, she was one of those sniffing at her skirt. It had been nine years since Jessie and her parents had arrived at Greyson Manor, and every single year, as her awareness had grown, so had her attraction and, honestly, love for

Heaven.

They were best friends, now far and above what Jessie's "job" was. There was deep friendship there, a relationship that she figured Heaven saw as more of a sisterly bond. Jessie went along with it. What choice did she have? She was so worried that, if Heaven had even the slightest inkling that Jessie… well, was as she was… Heaven would turn from her and push her away, even out of the house.

So, she was the dutiful little friend and protector. As she got closer, she saw that Heaven had turned away from her open locker to talk to Chadwick. She smiled and giggled, flashing those gorgeous dark eyes up at him. She was saying something, Jessie was too far away to hear, but she did hear her laughter, high-pitched and beautiful, like windchimes.

There was something about Heaven that reminded Jessie of a black panther: Beautiful yet something dangerous about her. Her gaze was intense and penetrating, and at times utterly unreadable. Those times were unsettling for Jessie, as she probably knew her constant companion better than anyone. She could so often know at a glance what she was feeling or thinking, no words required.

Then other times, that panther gaze would simply nail her to the spot, and she was not sure whether to freeze or run. In that moment, Heaven, still laughing at whatever her male admirer had said, looked past him and at Jessie, pinning her to the spot. She wasn't entirely certain that Heaven even always realized just how potent her gaze was, not certain that it was done on purpose. There just seemed to be a natural ability to tame anyone within range to her whim—no matter what that may be—with just a look.

Heaven looked away and back to Chadwick, who was gesturing animatedly in his tale. Jessie was freed from her hold and mentally shook herself out of it. She swallowed and walked up to the pair.

"Ready to go?" she asked, her tone far more cheerful than she was feeling. Honestly, she wanted to slam his head into Heaven's open locker and slam the door shut.

The football star looked down at her, annoyance in his eyes. "Can I help you?" he said, then a slow sneer crossed his handsome face. "Oh, wait, right. You're the hired help."

"Oh, Chad," Heaven purred, wrapping her hands around his arm and looking up at him with adoring eyes. "You don't mean to be a big jerk now, do you?"

Jessie nearly choked on her own spit. The beguiling smile Heaven sent his way clearly nailed his mouth closed. Instead, he gave her a goofy grin, clearly not recognizing that she'd just insulted him. She placed her hand on his chest and pushed him away with a little giggle, but her push was hard enough that he had to take a step back or fall down.

Heaven grabbed her jacket from her locker and slammed it shut before turning to Jessie. The satisfied smirk that resided in those eyes made Jessie purse her lips to keep from laughing. Heaven's hand rested in the bend of Jessie's arm as it always did as they began to walk away.

"I am so ready for break," Heaven blew out. She reached up to brush some hair out of her face. She spared a glance to Jessie. "I need one."

"Me, too." Jessie said nothing more until they managed to escape the congested hallways of their school and were finally out into the cold December air.

"Do you like him?" She hated herself for asking that, but the words had just kind of tumbled from her brain straight out of her mouth, filter be damned.

"Who?" Heaven asked, the two automatically turning down the sidewalk that would lead to where Heaven's father's driver would be waiting for them.

Jessie looked at her, wondering if she was being facetious. Nope, serious as a heart attack. But then, the poor girl was accosted every free moment of her day, so… "Chadwick Tapper."

"Lord, no!" Heaven looked over at her like she'd lost her mind. "He's nothing more than a big jock full of hot air."

Jessie nodded, agreeing. "Yes, but he likes you."

Heaven waved off her words, removing her hand from Jessie's arm as they neared the car. She used the hand to stabilize herself as she climbed into the back seat, Jessie following. "Thank you, Richard," Heaven said.

Jessie gave the middle-aged man a smile of thanks before he closed the door once the two young women were settled. She looked to her left when she felt a small touch to her skirt-draped leg.

"I don't care what he thinks, Jessie," Heaven said, continuing their conversation. She gave her a devilish grin. "I don't owe him anything. If he likes me, that's his problem."

Jessie held her gaze for a long moment before she nodded and looked away. The fancy car pulled away from the curb and into traffic. She looked back to her friend at the next words spoken, a question that surprised her.

"Does it bother you?" Heaven asked. "That the boys like me?"

It was one of those moments when Jessie couldn't read her. The words had been said simply, almost nonchalantly. But when Heaven closed her expression, Jessie had learned that there was always a reason behind it. She just had no clue what it was.

Clearing her throat, she shrugged. She could be nonchalant, too. "If they do they do," she said. "I mean, as long as they don't hurt you…" Her words trailed off as they both knew she'd punch any one of them who did. She'd done it before.

A sweet smile spread across Heaven's beautiful lips. "My protector."

Jessie rolled her eyes. "Whatever."

"No," Heaven said, her hand resting on Jessie's thigh for a moment. "I'm serious." She didn't speak again until Jessie met her gaze once more. "You've always been my protector, Jessie."

Jessie gave her an impish grin. "That's my job, right?"

Heaven answered with a saucy little grin of her own. "Something like that."

❧ ❧ ❧ ❧

To say that Jessie had been surprised that Harv had awoken them early for a full day downtown with him was an understatement. She liked Heaven's father a lot, and he had certainly stepped in to be a second father figure for her and was a wonderful father to his only daughter, even if he often referred to Jessie as his "bonus daughter."

He'd taken them for a decadent breakfast at the restaurant at the luxurious Brown Palace Hotel and then on an even more decadent tour of the McGovern

Chocolate Factory. Jessie hadn't been there since he'd taken her, Heaven, and her parents when the girls were nine. Now, five years later, she was even more impressed and wowed.

"Think you girls have enough chocolate to last you through the night?" he asked, amusement in his voice as he steered his Cadillac through Denver traffic carefully, the streets covered with packed snow over ice.

"Well," Heaven said with a grin as she leaned into Jessie in the back seat. "At least until school starts again."

Harv chuckled. "Well, we have one more stop. I want to have a proper discussion with you two about something."

Jessie looked to Heaven, who was already looking at her. She shrugged, no more of a clue than Jessie had. Finally, the car pulled into the parking lot of a tall building in downtown Denver. Jessie had no idea what it was to or for, but she followed along as they parked the car and entered the lobby. They took the stairs up several flights, Harv breathing heavily and sweating profusely, the large man not used to such physical exertion. Even Greyson Manor had an elevator.

Reaching the fourth floor, Harv pulled some keys out of his pocket and unlocked a door they came to. Jessie realized that it was an apartment complex. She'd heard of them but had never been in one. She was curious.

"Alright, ladies," Harv said, getting the door open and standing aside so his two charges could enter. "This is Tobias's apartment when he's in town," he explained.

Jessie looked around, noting that it wasn't terribly large but it was nice. It held a living room, a small kitchen off to the side, its own bathroom, and a bedroom.

"Let's all have a seat," Harv said, walking to the living room and lowering his girth with a grunt into the armchair. The couch was left for the ladies, who sat dutifully. "Now, I'm sure you're wondering why on earth I brought you two here." He reached up and removed his fedora, tossing it to the wood coffee table before standing again and shrugging out of his long winter coat, draping it over the arm on the couch nearest Heaven. He got seated again. "I've brought you two here to discuss something of a serious nature."

"Is everything okay, Daddy?" Heaven asked, uncertainty in her voice. She moved her leg to rest against Jessie's. As always, when she was worried, uncomfortable, or scared, she reached to touch Jessie in some way—hold her hand, touch her leg, cuddle up to her, whatever.

"Of course, princess," he said with a smile. He reached into the inside pocket of his suit jacket. He retrieved a kerchief and used it to wipe the sweat from his brow, his full face flushed from their four-floor jaunt. He eyed the two. "You ladies are beginning to reach a certain age. Jessie," he said, directing his words to the young woman in question. "You'll be sixteen in the spring, Heaven to follow in the fall. Boys will soon be part of the picture."

Jessie grimaced. Not so much, she thought. She assumed her thoughts marched across her expression. Harv chuckled.

"Well, that is to say, they'll be interested in the two of you, and eventually this will lead to marriage."

Heaven, who seemed uncomfortable, asked, "Daddy, why did you bring us here to talk about this?"

"Because I wanted somewhere where we could all speak freely," he explained. "No loud business of a restaurant nor input from your mother. At this point," he added. "Your mother is already beginning to scour our community for suitable beau for you, honey, and I just don't think that's fair."

Jessie glanced over at Heaven when she felt her tense. Automatically, she placed her hand on her leg to calm her. She was beginning to feel quite nauseous at the discussion. "Um," she said, troubled. "Are you going to set her up with somebody?" It absolutely killed her to say that, but she'd always known this day would come.

Harv met her gaze and shook his head. "No, Jessie, I'm not. But that time is coming, so I wanted to let you girls know that I need you to start thinking seriously on this subject. I want to make sure you're both taken care of and happy. However," he added, a finger raised to emphasize his point. "I want you to make that choice. Not someone else."

"What if I don't want to get married?" Heaven asked. Jessie was relieved by the question and was curious as to what her father would say. "What if Jessie and I just stayed best friends forever?"

He looked at her, heavy eyebrows raising. "Well, you can do that, my darling," he said, the smallest smile curling his lips. He looked from one young woman to the other. "Something tells me the two of you will always find your way to each other, no matter where life takes you. But that is the way of life, Heaven. You're a young woman now, and there are certain things that must happen. I just want to make sure you are involved in the decision of the who."

Jessie glanced over at Heaven, who looked down

at her lap. "Harv," she said softly, learning long ago that calling him "Mr. McGovern" was heavily frowned upon by the fatherly man. "I honestly have no intention of getting married," she said. "I truly don't."

He studied her, sitting back in the chair, which squeaked a bit under his weight. "What will you do, Jessie?" he asked gently. "How will you survive or take care of yourself?"

"I'll get a job," she said, a bit more defiance in her voice than was necessary, she supposed, but she felt strongly about guiding her own destiny and not some man doing it for her.

Though her parents had married young, her father treated her mother with the respect of an equal. Yes, he made most of the final decisions, that was to say, he was the one who said the words, but he and her mother discussed everything, acted as a team. And, once Jessie had been old enough to understand, she'd become the third member of that team.

"And," Harv said at length, something in his eyes that Jessie couldn't quite read. "You think you could support you and a best friend?"

Jessie blushed deeply, though had no idea why. She could feel the flush of her skin. The man's words were quite innocent, but they made her stomach flip in ways that made her nearly more nauseous. Her heart was racing, and she felt a bit faint.

"Are you okay?" Heaven asked softly, her hand on Jessie's back, fingernails running random patterns across the cotton-clad skin, which made Jessie's stomach flip in an entirely different direction. All she could do was nod.

Jessie watched the snow falling outside her bedroom window. She lay on her back, hands tucked behind her head. Her mind had returned time and time again to earlier that day, that unusual meeting in Tobias's apartment. She heard Harv's words over and over, the insinuation clear: In order for she and Heaven to have a life, a home, and all that went along with it, a man had to be involved.

Jessie meant what she'd said. She'd get a job—she'd get five of them if she had to. But who would hire her, a female? How on earth would she be able to support herself, let alone, as Harv had pointed out, anyone else? She was pulled out of her thoughts by a soft knock on the open doorway of the door that connected her bedroom to Heaven's.

"Hey."

"Hi." Heaven made her way to Jessie's bed and climbed in, as she'd done so many times over the years. For a long time, the younger girl had used her fear of nighttime thunderstorms as her reason for joining Jessie. But over time, she'd dropped any pretense and simply showed up. More than once Jessie had awoken to an unexpected bedmate.

She didn't mind. She welcomed her every time she was aware of her presence, like she did now. She held out her arm until Heaven got settled in against her, head resting on Jessie's shoulder. Immediately her arm wrapped around her shoulders.

"Thunderstorm?" she teased.

Heaven snorted. "Hey, one could strike at any moment."

Jessie was amused but said nothing for a moment. She just lay there, enjoying the feel of the warm body against her. Her abdominal muscles flinched almost uncontrollably as Heaven's nails roamed over her stomach absently. Always a touchy-feely person, Heaven's touches of late seemed to affect Jessie far differently than they had before. She was confused about why, but her body often felt like a tightly wound spring that nearly jumped to the moon at the slightest touch.

"What do you think of what my dad said today?" Heaven finally asked.

"I'm not entirely surprised," Jessie responded. "I mean, as females, isn't that kind of our lot in life? To be stuck with a man?"

Heaven raised her head from Jessie's shoulder. She looked down at her, bracing it against an open palm. Jessie looked up at her, yet again struck by her beauty. There were times, like right now, when it left her speechless. And, just barely beginning to make her way into womanhood, what on earth sort of force would Heaven be in another ten years?

"Why does it have to be that way?" Heaven asked, unwittingly pulling Jessie out of her thoughts. "I think it's ludicrous. Unfair."

Jessie nodded. "I agree. Why do you think your dad took us all the way to your brother's place to tell us the inevitable?"

"Well," Heaven drawled, the fingernail of her pointer finger running up the side of Jessie's neck and along her jaw, her gaze following its path. "I think he wanted to let us know that, yes, it is inevitable, as you said, but he also wants us to choose our own destiny, at least for the small bit that we can." Her gaze met Jessie's again. "Choose whom we spend our life with."

"A man," Jessie grumbled.

Heaven nodded. "Yeah." Her hand stopped, the nail moving away only for her fingers to lightly rest against Jessie's neck. "Jessie?"

"Hmm?" Jessie's heart was racing again. She felt the energy shift in the room and was totally confused.

"I wish..." Heaven looked away for a moment, letting out a small sigh. Finally, she met Jessie's gaze again. "I wish we could just pretend you were my boyfriend and that would be the end of it."

Jessie's heart flipped at the very thought. She smirked. "Instead of Chadwick Tapper?" Her words were surprisingly clipped.

Heaven gave her the sweetest smile, her dark eyes filled with uncharacteristic understanding. Jessie had honestly expected her to get angry at the quip. Jessie couldn't help it. Heaven was so beautiful, and though Jessie knew the other young woman didn't ask for the endless male attention she got, it was so hard to watch.

"I don't want Chadwick or Brian or Kendall or Byron or anyone else as a boyfriend." Heaven snorted. "Let alone a husband-in-training." Her fingers moved up from Jessie's neck until she cupped her cheek. "They're just simple-minded fools," she added, voice trailing off as she looked into Jessie's eyes.

For a breathless moment, Jessie thought Heaven was going to kiss her. She couldn't breathe, couldn't move. It was a heady mixture of relief and disappointment when, with an annoyed-sounding groan, Heaven moved her hand back to Jessie's stomach and rested her head on her shoulder again.

"Yup," Heaven said with finality. "We'll just pretend you're my boyfriend."

Jessie held her close. If only it were that simple, she thought. She rested her head against Heaven's and closed her eyes as her hand covered Heaven's that lay on her stomach. Her fingers lightly and absently ran over the sapphire stone ring that Heaven wore on that hand, something she did often.

Chapter Seven

1928

Jessie looked around, having never been in Harv's home office before, as she made her way to sit in the chair that Harv indicated. It was across the large desk from him, and she could see the beautiful spring day through the window behind Harv.

"Happy birthday again, kiddo," he gushed, one of his fat cigars held between his fingers as he sat back in his chair.

Jessie grinned. "Thanks. You guys didn't have to go to all this trouble today, Harv."

"Hogwash," he said, waving her words away. "You deserved a fun day for your sixteenth birthday, and I'm so pleased that Eliza and I were able to make that happen with your parents."

"Well, I really appreciate it. Truly."

"You bet." He sat forward and placed his fragrant cigar in the ashtray upon his desk. "Alright, Jessie," he said, lacing his fingers on the blotter. His eyes bored into her. "I've given a great deal of thought to what you said last Christmas at Tobias's apartment that day. I've always tried to color outside the box in pretty much every aspect of my business. Yes," he conceded. "My company is a family company, been in business for more than sixty years. But, since I took it over twenty years ago, I've tried to make more open doors for women in the company."

Jessie felt her palms become sweaty as she absorbed what he was saying to her, what she *thought* he was saying to her. She rubbed them on her skirt-covered thighs. "Yes, sir," she said more formally, as she sensed they'd left the realm of his house and had entered that of the chocolate factory.

"I've watched you over these ten years." Harv smiled, big and bright. "Why, ten years today!" He pounded the desk with his fingertips. "Gosh darn, time does fly. Anyhow, you're smart as a whip, a good worker. Even with your hands full of my precocious daughter," he said with a belly laugh. "You pitch in anywhere and everywhere you may be needed. The kitchen with Cook, helping your mother in her duties to my wife. Heck, you even helped me a time or two. Your father out on the property..." He grabbed his cigar again and took a puff of it, eyeing her the entire time.

Jessie's hands went to the padded leather arms of the chair, holding them tightly, not sure what was going to happen. She didn't feel it was going to be a bad thing, but she was still nervous.

"Were you serious when you said you wanted to work, support yourself?" Harv asked, his words coming out in fragrant smoke. "And," he added with a twinkle in his eyes and knowing smirk on his lips. "Your best friend?"

"I was," Jessie said, no hesitation. "My parents taught me to work, sir, basically since birth. I have absolutely no interest in being a kept woman for some man. A mother, chained to a role." She swallowed, hoping he wouldn't be angry at her honesty. "I know college is likely not in my future. Not many women get in, and even if they do, are they allowed to pursue the career they went to school for in the first place?"

Harv nodded. "I agree with you on the college part. Damn shame, you ask me. But, since they don't…" He grinned. "Tell you what, Jessie, I believe you and I agree with you. You should have options. Women, that is. I believe my own daughter should, but she's not shown a whole lot of interest in anything outside of being Heaven."

Jessie gave him a genuine grin at that. "I think there's a whole lot more to your daughter than meets the eye, sir. Honestly," she added with a shrug. "I don't think she feels she has the right to explore it."

He studied her from across the desk. "Interesting." He sat forward in his chair again, replacing the cigar in the ashtray. "Alright, Jessie, here's what I want to do. I want you to work your breaks at the factories. Summer break, winter break, all that. I want you to learn," he said, eyebrows raised as his intense gaze nailed her to the spot. "Understand?"

Jessie could hardly breathe. "Yes, sir!"

"Now," he added, a note of warning in his voice. "That will mean long days, lots of new things to learn, absorb, and conquer. Are you up to this challenge, Jessie? There will be those who don't want you there."

Jessie snickered. "Harv, I deal with that every day at school."

Harv grinned as he got to his feet. He extended a hand across the desk. Jessie also stood, taking his hand in a firm grasp. "Alright, then. In six weeks' time, roughly, you'll be a working woman at my business."

"Yes, sir," Jessie said again, never so proud to say two words in all her life.

Feeling like she was floating on a cloud, Jessie made her way to the wing where her and Heaven's rooms were, as well as the servants' quarters. She had always suspected it had been laid out that way by the original builder so the staff could more easily spy on whoever lived in that wing.

Her steps slowed as she heard music coming from Heaven's bedroom through the closed door in the hallway. She listened, recognizing Paul Whiteman and His Orchestra. She smiled, noting it was one of Heaven's favorites, "My Angel." Not wanting to disturb her, she walked on to the hallway door that led to her own bedroom.

The gifts she'd received from her parents, Heaven's parents, and the staff had already been delivered. She smiled, never having had such a large and elaborate birthday party before. She'd been stunned! Typically, birthdays in her family were simple affairs. Whoever had the birthday, the other two made them breakfast and offered small, usually homemade gifts.

Now, her bed was covered with new clothing, shoes, a new bag for her school books, books to read, and a lovely merry-go-round music box, given to her by her parents. She stood there looking at everything, just shaking her head. How was she so lucky?

"Birthday girl," was purred into Jessie's ear, making her start.

Turning, she saw a grinning Heaven. "Hey there. I didn't want to interrupt you."

"Interrupt me from what?" Heaven teased with a little grin as she took Jessie's hands in her own and backed up toward the open connecting door to their rooms.

Jessie grinned, allowing herself to be led, as usual.

"I don't know," she said, returning the grin. "Enjoying your music. I know you love that song."

"I do," Heaven agreed, releasing one of Jessie's hands but keeping hold of the other as she turned around and headed to the Victrola to start the song over, as it was about to end. "But," she said, turning to face Jessie again once the song started. "This isn't about me, it's about you." She released Jessie's hand and snaked her arms up around her neck. "Dance with me, birthday girl." She smiled sweetly. "It's not every day one's best friend turns sixteen."

Jessie's arms slid around Heaven's waist, their bodies just barely brushing as they began to move together. "So," she said as the two lightly spun around in the large space of Heaven's bedroom. "Are we pretending I'm your boyfriend?"

It had become a bit of a running joke between them since the holidays, as things had begun to change and shift. In some ways, Jessie felt closer to Heaven, but in another, she felt farther away, as something unsaid between them was acting as a bit of a chasm. The "pretend I'm your boyfriend" line had become a feeble rope for them to span the growing space.

Heaven grinned, the fingers of one hand playing in the hair at the nape of Jessie's neck, sending a little thrill down her spine. "No," she said. "But it's your birthday, so you can pretend I'm your girlfriend."

"Oh," Jessie said, amused. "The one day a year I get to lead, huh?"

Heaven's smile grew. "Absolutely. Best take advantage."

Jessie quirked an eyebrow. "Meaning?"

"Meaning, until midnight, your wish is my command." She looked deeply into Jessie's eyes, the softest smile on her lovely lips. "In fact," she said, her words nearly a whisper. "I'll give you three wishes. Whatever you want." She smirked. "That's within my power, that is."

"Oh, I don't know," Jessie teased, her tone bored as she quickly moved away from the other woman when the song came to an end. She played coy, but the truth was, she needed to put some space between them because her body was on fire, and she had no idea what to do about it. Looking into the dark pools of Heaven's eyes, she had found herself getting lost, and it scared the hell out of her. She playfully waved off her friend. "Such limitations…"

Heaven giggled. "Oh, come now," she said, grabbing Jessie's hand again and tugging her toward her. "I'm capable of quite a lot, you know."

Jessie allowed herself to be taken into Heaven's arms again, reprising their former position even though the music had stopped. Heaven ran her fingers through Jessie's long hair, looking into her eyes. Once again, Jessie found herself getting lost.

"You have the most beautiful eyes," Heaven said, her voice soft, almost as if in a trance. "Like looking into spring. So green." She used the backs of her fingers to lightly caress the side of Jessie's face before saying, "I have a gift for you."

"Didn't I get enough gifts?" Jessie asked. "I've got an entire bed full of them."

Heaven smiled. "And you deserve every single one." She reached up and left a soft kiss on Jessie's cheek, her fingertips caressing the opposite one. "I'll get it for you," she whispered against Jessie's skin.

It took Jessie the entire time that Heaven moved away until she returned to catch her breath. Heaven's closeness, her perfume, all had Jessie's head spinning. She'd never had a single sip of alcohol in her entire life, but how she felt in that moment must be how it felt to be, as her father called it, tipsy.

"Okay," Heaven said, walking back over to her. She held a small box wrapped in red paper. "I know you like red," she said, holding the small package out to Jessie.

Touched, Jessie smiled. "Thank you."

She carefully removed the paper, not wanting to tear it. Inside was a small jeweler's ring box. She spared a glance at Heaven, noting the excitement in her eyes before her own gaze fell to the box in her hand. She opened the box, the tiny hinges squeaking slightly. Inside, tucked into a pillow of satin, was a gold band with a small inlaid ruby.

"I know you don't really like jewelry," Heaven explained. "And you definitely don't like anything ostentatious. But," she said softly. "I wanted to give you something that you could always keep. Always wear and know what you mean to me."

Jessie was stunned. She met Heaven's gaze and shook her head. "I don't know what to say." She was so deeply touched.

"Well," Heaven said, giving her a smile. She gently took the box from Jessie and carefully wiggled the ring out of its little pocket. "I know rubies aren't your birthstone, but again, I know how much you love red." She set the ring box down on a nearby table. Turning back to Jessie, she took her right hand in her own and eased the ring onto Jessie's ring finger. Her smile was big and bright. "Perfect fit. I was a little worried."

Jessie stared down at it as she held her hand up, fingers spread. "It's so beautiful, Heaven." She met her friend's gaze. "I don't deserve anything like this."

"Of course you do, silly." Heaven took her into a tight hug.

Jessie's eyes closed as she held the smaller young woman to her. She felt Heaven's head rest on her shoulder, her hot breath against her neck. She felt the warmth of her body against her own, the softness of her curves pressing against her own. She felt gentle fingers in her hair, and she felt the pull.

"So," Jessie whispered. "You said I get three wishes."

Heaven nodded against Jessie's neck. "Yes."

Jessie had no clue where the words came from, where the courage came from, but she whispered, "I want to kiss you."

Heaven didn't respond in words. Instead, her head rose from Jessie's shoulder, her eyes downcast as her face moved into Jessie's personal space, their lips mere inches apart. One of Heaven's hands cupped the side of Jessie's face as their eyes met. Jessie, honestly terrified, had never kissed anyone and had no idea what had possessed her to ask for such a thing. Best friends didn't do this.

But girlfriends and boyfriends did. Wasn't that their safe word, after all?

The first touch of Heaven's lips was just that—heaven. They were so soft, so pliant. They pressed together for several moments, lingering until Heaven moved away, just a bit. She looked up into Jessie's eyes.

"What's your second wish?" she asked, her voice barely a whisper.

It was a strange feeling, Jessie thought. Though they stood in a huge room surrounded by a giant house, it felt like their world had shrunk down to a tiny bubble. Their world was just that—the two of them.

"Actually," Heaven said, a sweet little smile on her beautiful face. "Can I steal one?"

Jessie rolled her eyes and sighed dramatically. She grinned at the playful swat she took to the shoulder. "Yes."

"Will you stay in here tonight?" Heaven asked, nodding toward her princess bed. It was a huge canopy bed with curtains that could be loosed to create an entire cocoon of slumber.

"Well, considering my bed is completely covered with gifts, I guess." She sighed in contentment, her lips still buzzing from the kiss. Her body swarmed with a feeling she couldn't define, but the tipsy analogy returned to mind. "You didn't need to use a wish on that one, though."

"Okay, then you get your wish back. What's your second one?" Heaven asked.

"I wish for you to never leave my life. To always be here, no matter what."

"Granted." Heaven gave her a big smile.

"Promise?" Jessie asked, using Heaven's own word.

"Of course," Heaven said. "And your third?"

Jessie considered for a long moment then said, "Can I save it?" She shrugged sheepishly. "Right now, I have everything I need or want."

"Yes, you can save it," Heaven hedged.

"What?" Jessie laughed, feeling absolutely on top of the world with such a birthday. "Is there a 'but' in there?"

"Yes, there is." Heaven moved away from her and walked over to her bed. She tugged down the covers and walked around to the four posts of the canopy, untying the holds that kept the draperies in place. They fell, creating a wall to shield those inside. "When it's my birthday in November, I get three wishes, too." She turned to face Jessie and began to unbutton her dress. "Deal?"

Jessie forced herself to look away. They'd seen each other in every state of undress, even naked, over the last decade, but somehow tonight it hit her harder than usual. "Yes, of course," she managed. "I'll be back. Going to get ready for bed."

Jessie hurried back to her room, her chest heaving. *What is wrong with me?* She leaned back against a wall and closed her eyes. She placed her hand to her stomach, which was nauseous again. What had she been thinking? To share a bed with Heaven that night was foolish. But then, she thought, forcing herself away from the wall, no doubt Heaven would have ended up in her bed anyway.

She was in trouble, though she had no idea what to do about it. She had no real understanding of what the "trouble" was. "Yes you do," she murmured to her own reflection in the mirror above the dresser.

She removed her dress and satin slip, leaving her standing there in only panties and a bra. They were quickly shed, too, and her nightgown pulled on. It felt good to have the full gown on, which reached nearly to her ankles. She grabbed her brush and brushed her long, light brown hair until it flowed in waves around her shoulders and upper back.

Looking at herself once more in the mirror, she blew out a breath before she closed her bedroom door to the hallway. No reason to let any of the servants see that she wasn't sleeping there tonight. She made a quick trip to Heaven's bathroom, her friend already finished in there. Afterward, she made her way to Heaven's bed.

"Knock, knock," she said teasingly.

"Enter," Heaven said dramatically, making Jessie smile.

Jessie pushed the curtains apart just enough to climb through and onto the massive bed. They fell shut behind her leaving them in total darkness. "My goodness," she said, using her hands to feel her way as she crawled farther onto the bed. "It's pitch black in here."

"I'll help you."

A hand grabbed Jessie's and yanked, tugging her roughly with a *whoop* of surprise. She landed on her stomach, Heaven's warmth partially beneath her, and her hand landed on a very soft object. No, a very soft body part. She gasped when realization hit her of what her hand cupped. She whipped her hand away as if it had been burned.

"I'm sorry," she gasped.

Heaven giggled. "You don't need to apologize, Jessie. Isn't that what you'd do if I were your girlfriend?"

"Um, uh, well, I, uh," she stammered. She knew her face was flushed a deep shade of embarrassed, even if nobody could see it.

"It's not a big deal," Heaven assured her. Her hand reached blindly until it found Jessie's hand and placed it back on her cotton-covered right breast. "See?"

But it was a big deal, as Jessie could hardly breathe. Her hand felt like it had been placed inside a raging flame that quickly spread up her arm and into her body. She took a moment and, once her hand was released, removed it. She had to sit there for a moment and try to gather herself. Oh, this had been a super bad idea.

"Jessie?" Heaven said, her voice sounding concerned. "Are you okay?"

Jessie squeezed her eyes shut and took a few long, quiet breaths. Finally, she nodded, even though Heaven couldn't see it. "Yes. I'm okay."

"Lay down," Heaven said, lightly tugging on the sleeve of Jessie's nightgown.

Jessie did as bade, lying on her back. She felt Heaven scoot over to her, though she didn't snuggle into her as she usually did. She couldn't see her, but she could feel her looming. She felt a hand caress the side of her face before resting against her jaw.

"If I was your girlfriend," Heaven whispered, the breath of her words brushing against Jessie's lips. "I'd want to kiss you good night."

Jessie's eyes closed as the softness of Heaven's lips touched her own again. This time, it was more than just a lingering kiss. She brushed their lips together, almost as if trying to see how Jessie's lips would feel caressing her own. Jessie's hand found its way to rest at Heaven's waist as Heaven's forearm rested on the other side of Jessie, leaving her partially lying atop her.

She could feel Heaven's soft right breast pressed against her own in that position. She tried to push that out of her mind. She'd felt her breasts in any number of phases of development, like her own, over the years. No big deal, right? Focus on the kiss, she told herself. That's what mattered.

Finally, Heaven left one final kiss on her lips before lifting her own head. "Happy birthday, Jessie," she whispered. "Thank you for being my best friend." With that, she settled in with her head resting on Jessie's shoulder.

Chapter Eight

1945

Jessie said nothing as she allowed the flavors and spices to roll around on her tongue. The sauce was fantastic, but she was pretty sure it was a bit too much. Looking at the expectant cook, she shook her head. "John, this is amazing, but I don't think she'll be able to keep it down. I think it's too spicy."

"Well," the elderly man said, his smile bright white against his dark skin. "I was afeared of that, so..." He walked them over to another pot on the huge stovetop, eight burners strong. He lifted the lid to reveal a much smaller serving simmering.

A bark of laughter escaped Jessie's lips as she accepted the clean spoon filled with the second pot's sauce. She again tasted the master cook's offering, nodding. "Yes," she said, pairing the second spoon with the first and placing both into the sink to be washed later with the dishes used to cook the meal. "Perfect."

The older man smiled brightly, his hazel eyes twinkling. "I'll have her up a dish in a jiff, Miss Jessie."

She patted him on his shoulder. "I appreciate you, John. Thank you." She was about to leave the kitchen when she stopped. She turned and looked back at the man, who sang softly to himself. She'd often heard his wonderful voice singing some of the old songs from his ancestors' past on Southern plantations. He'd shared with her long ago that he was the first generation born after the Civil War. "John?"

He stopped singing and looked over at her. "Yes, Miss Jessie?"

"Do you know if Tobias or Heaven have been called in?" she asked. She'd yet to get a straight answer to that question in the two weeks she'd been back at the house.

"Well, now, let's see." He tugged the ever-present white dish towel from his shoulder and wiped his hands on it. "I know Mr. Tobias is still in London on business for Mr. Russ. As for Miss Heaven," he said, a hint of sadness in his voice. "I ain't seen her 'round here since the big fallin' out she had with Miss Eliza." He whistled through his teeth. "Been a long time now since that day." He met and held Jessie's gaze. "You was there."

Jessie nodded and looked down at her clasped hands. "Yes. I was." She swallowed and took a deep breath. "Alright, thanks, John." She gave him a smile, then turned and headed back upstairs.

Eliza had good days, and she had horrible days. Some days it was a little of both. It was hard to watch, and the doctors just had no real concrete answers. At the moment, Eliza was sleeping peacefully, but Jessie could see just how frail she really was. Dobbs was coming for dinner that night, and to see Eliza, so while he was there, Jessie decided to borrow his truck.

❧ ❧ ❧ ❧

Jessie was surprised by how clearly she remembered the way, considering how many years it had been since she'd last been there. That awful, awful morning. She pulled the old Ford into the circular drive and pulled the brake. Looking up at the sandstone structure, Jessie was awed all over again.

Though the house wasn't nearly the beast that Greyson Manor was, it was still very impressive. It was located in what was known as Millionaire's Row in the Capitol Hill neighborhood of Denver, a place filled with huge, impressive houses built by the titans of industry in the latter part of the nineteenth century.

Kingston Rawlins was not one of those titans, but his daddy had been. And, as a young senator—one of the youngest in the country when he was elected in 1928—he fit in just fine. A family property, she figured. It was quiet at the moment. She sat there, unable to make herself open the door and leave the safety of her father's truck. She felt like a bit of a coward but couldn't help it.

Raking the leaves on the massive property was a huge task, but one she did with relish. It had been almost a year since the crash of '29, which had decimated so many families across the country and, from what she heard and read in the papers, around the world. Lord knew it had decimated the happiness and lives of those in Greyson Manor. It had decimated Jessie's soul.

She'd been kept on, though she was relegated to her father's grounds team. She'd been forced out of the house and back into the gardener's cottage several months ago. Then again, her "charge" no longer lived there, so she supposed it was only right that neither did she.

She was grateful to work for her father, as grown men were in dire circumstances across the country, taking any work they could find. Grateful for what she had, she worked her butt off to keep it.

"There you are."

Jessie looked up from her rake. The dashing man

she'd only seen a few times was walking over to her. He was dressed to the nines, as he had been every time she'd seen him. His suit was fine and fit his frame perfectly. His fedora was tilted just so on his slicked-back dark brown hair.

"Yes," she said. "You found me, I suppose. What can I do for you, Senator?"

He reached her and looked around at the piles of autumn leaves, the fruit of her hours of hard labor. "My goodness," he said, grinning at her. "Looks like a lot of work."

She said nothing. She just wanted him to leave and let her get back to work. She didn't need to give George Russ any reason to be cross with her.

"So, listen," he said, getting down to business. "As you know, my business is back in Washington, DC, where I must spend most of my time. Heaven will of course be staying here at the house." His grin widened. "Our house."

She gripped the handle of the tool she leaned against with near-white-knuckle ferocity. "Yeah," she managed.

"Well, I wouldn't be one bit worried about my new bride being there alone. Plenty of staff. But we've gotten great news. She's expecting our first child. Seems our wedding night did the trick," he added almost conspiratorially.

Jessie swallowed. Hard. "Well, congratulations, Senator."

"Thank you. Now, she tells me that you were her personal assistant here up until we got married. Though," he said, placing his hands on his hips. "I must say, for the two of you to have been so close, I don't recall seeing you at our wedding back in June. But I guess that's

neither here nor there. My wife wants you to come be her personal assistant once again," he said, finally getting to the point of his visit. "At least until the birth of the baby. After that, she'll have the finest nannies money can buy." He grinned. "As it were."

Jessie honestly wasn't sure if she wanted to cry or vomit. Both bodily functions were getting dangerously close to the surface. "Um," she said, looking down at the rake handle and where her hands gripped it. "Senator—"

"Kingston," he said. "Come now, Jessie. You were so close to my wife, I think we're past formalities, hmm?"

She nodded, sparing a glance at him. "Um, I have a job here, Kingston."

"I understand that," he said. "You'll be paid, of course, and once the baby is born in the spring, you can return here if you wish." He indicated the grounds and all her piles of colorful leaves. "So," he said, looking at her with expectant eyes. "Will you come?"

Jessie blew out a heavy breath and ran her hand through her hair. That had been the stupidest decision of her life, she thought. She gathered her courage, pulled the keys out of the ignition, and climbed out of the truck. The heavy metal door squeaked in protest as she slammed it shut. She walked around the front of the truck to the stairs that led up to the impressive wood and glass front door.

Noting the doorbell, Jessie pressed it with her finger. She immediately heard bells chime within the house, announcing her presence. She waited but heard nothing. She pushed the brass-ringed button again, releasing more chimes inside. Finally, she heard harried footsteps across a hard surface, wood or marble, she assumed.

Through the beveled glass, she could see movement, though not enough to discern the identity of the person who was unlocking the door. A moment later, it was pulled open, and Jessie found herself looking into the face of Chloe Rawlins. The lovely young woman looked at her with wide eyes, recognition in their green depths.

Jessie smiled. "Good evening, Chloe," she said, fighting so many emotions that were swirling inside her. Oh, how she wanted to take the young girl in her arms and sing to her just like she used to. "I'm sorry to just drop by, but I need to speak to your mother."

Her hands wringing in uncertainty, the girl nodded. "Um, okay." She stared at her. "You're the lady from the store."

Jessie nodded. "I am." She extended a hand to her. "Jessie Lowrey," she introduced herself, though she'd told Chloe and her brother her name that day.

Chloe took the hand and returned the smile. The wide, surprised eyes turned more friendly and accepting. "Come in," she said after they shook hands. She stepped aside. "I'll see if Mama's ready to accept company."

Jessie nodded, stepping inside the foyer just enough so Chloe could close the front door. "I'll wait here," she said, with no desire to wander through the house that Heaven shared with her husband.

"Okay. I'll be right back." Chloe scurried away and up the stairs.

Jessie stood there dutifully, looking around. The home was beautiful, to be sure. Lots of dark wood wainscoting, coffered ceilings, and brass sconces. It was clearly a family home, as it hadn't been updated in some time. From her years at Greyson Manor, she understood that wealthy families seemed to have a strange fetish for keeping the family home exactly as it was the day the first family member set foot inside it.

She rocked on her heels as she waited, hands clasped in front of her. A few minutes later, she heard footfalls and glanced up. Chloe made her way down the stairs again, though she looked troubled. She spared a glance at Jessie before looking down at her feet.

"Um," she said, stepping up to Jessie. "She said…" The girl swallowed. "She said she wants you to leave."

The words were a dagger in Jessie's heart, and they took her breath away for a moment. She did her level best to keep her reaction neutral as she shoved her hands into the pockets of her trousers. Nodding, she gave the upset-looking girl a small smile.

"Okay." With that, she turned and let herself out. She trotted down the stairs as she pulled the truck keys from her pocket.

"Wait!"

Turning, she saw Chloe running out of the house, down the stairs, and over to her. Jessie waited until the girl reached her. "Are you okay?" she asked gently. This young woman, even thirteen years later, still brought out her maternal side, something she honestly didn't even think existed until March 13, 1931, at 4:16 in the morning.

"Push, Heaven!" the doctor demanded from where he knelt at the end of the bed between his patient's spread legs.

Heaven used the body behind her for leverage as she growled deep in her throat, eyes squeezed shut and veins standing out in her neck as she pushed with everything in her. Jessie nearly felt like she was being crushed by the sheer power of Heaven's body pressing back into her own.

"Almost there," she encouraged. "Almost there!" She grabbed Heaven's discarded nightgown and wiped the sweat off her face and brow. A moment later, a very angry and shrill cry rent the air in the bedroom. "You did it! Oh my god, you did it."

Heaven laughed through her tears. She collapsed back into Jessie, spent. The doctor handed the crying newborn to his nurse, who quickly went about her business to prepare the baby before the tiny, flailing creature was placed upon Heaven's chest.

"Congratulations, Mommy," the nurse said sweetly.

"Oh, Chloe," Heaven cried, Jessie's own tears falling down her cheeks as she watched over Heaven's shoulder. "Oh, Jessie," she whispered, turning her head to meet Jessie's gaze. "We did it." Her words were quiet, for Jessie's ears only. "Our Chloe."

Jessie nodded, unable to speak as she was so moved by the entire situation. Finally, she said, "I love you. And Chloe."

"I love you, too."

Jessie swallowed that beautiful memory, still stunned to see the lovely young woman standing before her now. She so badly wanted, despite everything, to hug her, to tell her, *Chloe, I'll always be here for you.*

"I'm really sorry," Chloe gushed, inadvertently pulling Jessie out of her memory and thoughts. "When I told her who you were and that you wanted to talk to her, she looked so upset, like she'd seen a ghost. I was really surprised, and when she said to send you away, I was even more surprised. It's not like her at all!"

The young woman looked as though she were about to start crying. "Hey," Jessie said gently, reaching out a hand and resting it on her arm. "It's okay. Really." She gave her the most reassuring smile she could.

Chloe nodded but looked down at her feet, the toe of one of her saddle shoes nervously kicking at a small rock. "She's been so upset lately," she said quietly. "Issues with my father. I don't really know what's going on." She looked up into Jessie's concerned gaze. "Sorry. I'm not sure why I just said that."

Jessie opened her arms. "Can I… Can I give you a hug?" Chloe simply nodded, stepping into her embrace. Jessie's eyes fell closed as she held the young woman. Though fourteen now and headed toward adulthood in just a few short years, to Jessie, she may as well have been holding that baby again.

"I hate seeing my mom so unhappy," Chloe murmured. "She's such an amazing person."

Jessie nodded but said nothing. Clearly, Chloe had no idea who she was, and it was absolutely not her place to fill in the blanks. "I'm so sorry," she said instead.

After a few moments, Chloe loosened her hold and stepped out of the hug. "I'm sorry," she said shyly. "You must think I'm a real weirdo."

Jessie smiled and shook her head. "Not at all." She reached up and brushed some dark strands out of the lovely young face, so much like her mother's. "Sometimes we just need a hug, right?"

Chloe nodded. "Yeah." She blew out a breath and said, "Well, I guess I'd better get back inside. You're a really nice person, Jessie."

"I have my moments," Jessie said with a small laugh, which Chloe returned. "You try and have a good evening, okay? And," she added, remembering why she'd come in the first place. "Please tell your mother that her mother is gravely ill. That's what I came to talk to her about."

"Oh, no," Chloe said, a hand coming up to cover her mouth for a moment. So much like her mother. Finally, she nodded. "Alright, I'll tell her." She gave her a sheepish smile. "You, too, have a good evening." With a little wave, she trotted back up the stairs and into the house.

Jessie watched her go before selecting the correct key from the key ring and walking around to the driver's side door. As she pulled it open, she glanced up, sudden movement catching her eye. In a second-floor window, one side of the curtains fell back into place.

Chapter Nine

October 26, 1929

According to Heaven's words and the look she'd given her, Jessie looked good. It was the first time she'd ever been in an evening gown, provided by Harv and Eliza, of course. Her hair had been done up to perfection, as well as her makeup. She never wore makeup and certainly didn't wander around in high heels with diamonds dangling from her ears. But, since Halloween was during the week, the McGoverns had decided to have their annual masquerade ball the weekend before.

This was the first year Heaven had been invited as the daughter of the McGoverns, let alone Jessie. Now seventeen, and with Heaven turning seventeen in just about a month, they were finally old enough, Harv had announced. Jessie had also been working at Harv's chocolate company for nearly a year and a half.

He rotated her regularly among all the departments so she could get a good handle on all aspects of the business. Once she and Heaven graduated the following June, he promised her a permanent position, though she had no idea where. It was a wonderful time for Jessie.

She was certainly hurtling toward being an adult, but most importantly, she felt like one. She was treated with the respect of a woman and as the daughter of the hired help. Well, by most people, anyway. There were definitely plenty of men at the company who had a lot to say, but overall, they kept it to themselves. Harv, for his part, never allowed any back talk regarding his decision to teach Jessie anything and everything about the business.

Now, everyone was in the ballroom of the manor, with a small orchestra playing at one end. As a black-tie affair, the guests were dressed in their fanciest duds. Fun masquerade masks had been handed out at the door as guests arrived—feathered, glittery, you name it. Jessie's mask was black, with a slightly pointy nose making the glittery mask amusing and fun.

She knew she looked good, even though she was uncomfortable. Her dress was a deep emerald green, picked out by Heaven, of course, because it would "set off her eyes." It was fitted but very appropriate, with just the tiniest bit of cleavage. She wore a simple yet elegant necklace, borrowed from Heaven, just like her earrings.

And then there was Heaven.

In a gown of deep red with a halter-style top that revealed the creamy skin of her décolletage and shoulders, her black hair was pulled up to reveal the elegance of her neck. The dress was tasteful, but it certainly made quite clear the woman she was becoming. Her mask was white, feathered, and trimmed in silver.

Though the two socialized, they largely stuck together. Never once was Heaven not at least within earshot or a simple glance from Jessie. Jessie had been bounced from person to person, group to group by Harv. He'd made it clear he wanted her known to his executives and supervisors.

"Come, Jessie," he said this latest time, a guiding hand on her lower back. "Let me introduce you to one of our best investors." They walked up to a tall man, his dark brown hair slicked back from his face which, like everyone else, was partially covered by a mask. She noted his blue eyes, intense in their gaze. "George, this is Jessie Lowrey that I told you about. Jessie," he said, indicating the man who stood in their little trio. "George Russ."

Jessie nodded in acknowledgment, taking the hand that was offered. He brought her hand up to lightly be touched by his lips. "Nice to meet you, Mr. Russ."

"You as well, Jessie." His voice was deep. "Yes, Harv here has told me much about you." He slapped the large man on the back. "Told me you're smart, driven, dedicated, and honest with no need to dissemble."

Jessie blushed at the gushing praise from her mentor. "Well," she said shyly. "I'm surprised, as it's not really like Harv to obfuscate on his opinions so much."

Both men broke out into laughter, Harv patting her on the shoulder with a look of approval. She gave him a sheepish grin. "Well, George here is on the board, of course, as our largest investor. He's quite interested in the goings-on."

"Understandable, Mr. Russ."

"Good evening, gentlemen, Jessie."

Jessie looked to her right to see that Eliza had stepped up to their little group. She gave each a smile in turn.

"Darling," she said to Harv. "Some of our guests are leaving and wanted to say good night."

"Ah, yes. Thank you, my love. You remember George?"

"Of course I do," Eliza said, giving the tall man a smile. "Nice to see you again."

"You as well, Eliza," George said, returning the smile.

The couple excused themselves, and George gave Jessie a curt nod before he, too, wandered off. Jessie watched him go, wondering how much interaction she'd have with him once she got back to work. Being late October, Christmas break was coming up soon, so perhaps she'd get to know him a little better. From what Harv had said about him, he seemed quite important.

"That man has had a crush on my mother for years."

Jessie turned to see that Heaven had stepped up beside her. Her gaze was on the retreating man's back before she met Jessie's eyes. "Really?"

"Yup." Heaven hooked her arm into the bend of Jessie's. She led them in another direction. "The party will be over soon," she said, her tone softening from the hard edge she'd had when mentioning George Russ to the sweetness she so often used with Jessie, especially as they'd gotten older.

"It is," Jessie agreed, noticing the dance floor beginning to clear and people not just chatting, but saying goodbyes and wishing each other a Happy Halloween for the upcoming Thursday.

"So," Heaven said, leaning into her a bit. "I was thinking that maybe, if you wanted to, Saturday night and all… we could go swimming."

The house offered an inside pool, which Jessie had never seen before she saw the one at Greyson Manor. She and Heaven had spent endless hours playing in it throughout their childhood. A huge space to swim, wrapped in its own little glass building-type structure that jutted off the back of the main house. Jessie considered for a moment, then nodded. "Yeah. I think that would be fun."

Heaven grinned and tugged on Jessie's arm with playful excitement. "Excellent."

❧ ❧ ❧

Fancy dresses gone, makeup removed, and jewels stowed, Jessie and Heaven enjoyed a leisurely swim. It was so wonderfully warm in the water, the windows fogged from the steam inside, contrasting with the cold late-October night outside. It felt like they were in an amazing cocoon, just the two of them.

In the year and a half since their first kiss on Jessie's sixteenth birthday, there had been a massive shift between them. They had kissed again since then, but it wasn't a nightly or daily thing. There was still that chasm between them—one that, in some ways, had grown. For Jessie, that chasm was born from her incredibly intense want for Heaven, but she was terrified that she'd push the other woman away.

Now, the question was: what did she want from or with Heaven? Yes, her heart wanted her love, but her body burned for her. She had no clue what that even consisted of, considering they weren't a man and a woman but two females. What did that mean? If one of them was missing the pertinent body part for a physical relationship, was it even possible?

The terrifying notion had crossed her mind more than once. In their years together, so often Heaven looked to Jessie to go first. Jessie, the braver of the two so often, teaching the other. Was that what was happening? Inadvertently, was Heaven learning how to be a woman through her friendship with Jessie?

"Amazing, isn't it?" Heaven said, pulling Jessie

from her morose thoughts.

Jessie glanced over at her, Heaven treading water fifteen feet or so away. Her hair was slicked back from her beautiful face, and a contented smile was on her full lips. Her bathing suit was of the period, consisting of a fitted body suit that ended at the upper thighs with straps over the shoulders. Heaven's was black, while Jessie's, dark blue.

"It is," Jessie agreed, moving toward the wall to lean against it. She watched as Heaven swam over to her. To her shock, she didn't move beside her but straight at her. With a devilish grin, Heaven wrapped her legs around Jessie's waist, holding onto the tiled edge of the pool on either side of Jessie's shoulders. "Well, hello there." Jessie's hands instinctively went to Heaven's hips to help keep her stable in the buoyant water.

"Hi," Heaven responded, a sexy little grin on her lips. She brushed some of Jessie's drying hair out of her face. "You looked so absolutely beautiful tonight."

"Thank you. Not exactly my thing, but I guess now and then I'll survive. But you, Heaven, were stunning. In your element."

"Well, believe it or not, I don't enjoy it, either." Heaven tilted her head slightly as she studied Jessie's face, her fingers lightly tucking more hair behind Jessie's ear. Her touch was so gentle. "Guess I've just had to deal with it longer. Then you have my mother," she added, with a little snort. "She lives for that stuff."

"I think Mama would enjoy getting all dolled up just for the sake of making my father swoon, but that would be the end of it." Jessie grinned at Heaven's laugh.

"I'm sure we could make that happen." Heaven leaned in and gave Jessie a small kiss on the lips. "Have I told you lately how proud I am of you?" she asked, pulling back just enough to look Jessie in the eyes.

"For what?" Jessie asked, her words a bit breathier than she'd like. With Heaven's intimate closeness against her, she was finding it harder and harder to hold a thought in her head, let alone allow said thought to drift out of her mouth.

"For how well you've done with Daddy at his business. I know he adores you. He was so upset that Tobias went into banking rather than follow in his footsteps." Her hand slid to Jessie's face. "I think he sees a bit of a second chance in you."

Jessie grinned. "The 'son' he never had in chocolate?" She readjusted her hands on Heaven's hips, accidentally holding her by the behind.

Heaven giggled at Jessie's expression, the pure *uh-oh!* she felt. "It's okay, silly," she said. "I won't break."

No doubt blushing, Jessie simply nodded. Swallowing, she said, "You're always teasing me about being your boyfriend, so I guess it makes sense if your father saw me that way, too."

Heaven grew serious and shook her head. "No. I don't have a boyfriend, Jessie, because I don't want one. There are plenty of options out there, believe me," she added, rolling her eyes.

"Then," Jessie said, confused. Yes, she knew Heaven had said she didn't want one, but she so often used that reference with Jessie. "What do you want?"

Heaven suddenly looked uncharacteristically shy. "You. I don't know what it means or if it's even possible, but that's what I want, Jessie. I need you with me."

"That's what I want, too," Jessie whispered. Despite the fact that Heaven had said it first, somehow she was terrified to say it aloud.

There was no need, as the brilliance of Heaven's

smile melted any fears of rejection. The lips that touched her own were so soft, and the kiss was different from any they'd shared before. There was a neediness to it, a passion that Jessie craved. As Heaven's fingers slid into Jessie's hair, the kiss deepened.

The first touch of Heaven's tongue against Jessie's sent a fiery jolt through her, making her entire body gasp with delight. She accepted the gentle stroke, quickly catching on and responding. A soft sigh of pleasure emanated from Heaven as they both settled into the beautiful kiss.

Using Heaven's behind as leverage, Jessie pulled her closer into her body, which garnered another sigh from the woman she kissed. She could feel Heaven's breasts against her own, and this time, she allowed herself to feel it, feel what was actually pressed against her. Before, she had forced it out of her mind, that crazy feeling that made her equal parts giddy and uncomfortable, but now, she embraced the sensation, letting it wash over her.

As the kiss deepened even more, she felt the chasm of the last couple years begin to close. What had needed to be said, at least in part, had now been said and acknowledged, and a shared need was now being addressed. The kiss ended, leaving both of them breathing hard.

Heaven's face was flushed as she met Jessie's gaze, her eyes burning with the same need that Jessie felt. Jessie's body was thrumming, and she had no idea what to do about it. Heaven looked shy for a moment as she released the edge of the pool behind Jessie and shrugged out of the straps of her bathing suit.

Jessie watched, eyes wide in shock. Of course she'd seen Heaven's breasts before, over the years. How could she not, the two of them living in such close living quarters? But this was very different. This was Heaven purposefully revealing them, and as she placed her hand on the back of Jessie's neck, gently tugging, she was offering them to her.

Jessie stared at what was before her. Her breasts were absolutely beautiful, proportionate to her small frame, the nipples that Jessie had noticed pushing against the material of the suit now on full display. Jessie's mouth watered and her fingers itched. She glanced up into Heaven's eyes, not entirely sure of what to do.

Again, Heaven gently urged her head down. Understanding, and allowing instinct to take over, Jessie closed her eyes as she brought a hand up to cup one of the bared breasts. So soft, she thought. Yet firm. She lowered her mouth to it, taking a tentative swipe with her tongue over the rigid nipple. She nearly spasmed when she heard the breathy groan above her.

As her mouth continued to explore, her hands enjoyed the feeling of Heaven's naked back, the skin slick from the water yet so soft. She could feel fingers in her hair, her head pulled to Heaven's breasts. She could feel Heaven's hips rocking lightly against her as she moved to the other breast, humming into her task. She'd found her new favorite pastime.

A thrill shot through her body when she heard her name whimpered from Heaven's lips. This spurred her on as, like a wick doused in oil, she felt like she was about to combust. Needing to taste her lips again, she reluctantly left Heaven's breasts and kissed and licked her way up to Heaven's neck. Heaven's head fell to the side, giving Jessie plenty of invited access.

When their mouths met again, the kiss was

hungry, demanding. Years of bottled-up desire, not fully understood until now, poured out. Heaven broke the kiss, again leaving both breathing hard.

"Let's go upstairs," Heaven whispered.

Jessie nodded. She was nervous, unspeakably so, but she absolutely wanted to go upstairs. Heaven unwrapped her legs and stood, tugging her suit top back into place. She gave Jessie a quick peck before moving over to the ladder. Both climbed out and quickly dried off before shrugging into the robes and shoes they'd worn to the pool.

Heart racing, they scurried from the pool area, heading toward the stairs when they heard a panicked voice behind them. Turning, Jessie saw John, Cook's main assistant. His hazel eyes were wide, and he looked downright scared.

"Miss Heaven!" he called again.

"What is it, John? Are you okay?" Heaven asked, turning toward him, followed by Jessie.

"It's your daddy, Miss Heaven," he said, nearly in tears. "He ain't breathin.'"

Chapter Ten

Still dressed in their poolside robes, Heaven and Jessie sat side by side, their thighs touching, on one of the couches in the great room. The entire household was gathered around them, Eliza sitting on another piece of furniture while most of the house staff stood. The silence was palpable, broken only by the occasional pop of the fire in the huge fireplace that Dobbs had built.

Jessie was still in shock—she knew she was. They were all waiting for the doctor to return and talk to them after his examination to try and determine the cause of death. Her body began to vibrate. Confused, she looked to her right and saw that Heaven had begun quietly sobbing. Jessie wrapped her arm around her shoulders, and Heaven's dark head fell against her shoulder.

She glanced over to Eliza to see Louise sitting with her, holding her hands. Heaven's mother looked downright shell-shocked. Everyone's attention shifted to the sound of footfalls approaching the huge space. Dr. Hale entered, the older man's wrinkled face wrinkled even more from his concerned expression.

"Obviously this is just my theory," he said. "We'll know more after the coroner does his autopsy, but from the years I've been Mr. McGovern's personal physician, my speculation is that it was a catastrophic cardiac event."

"Do you mean a heart attack?" Jessie asked.

The doctor met her gaze and nodded. "Yes, due to his poor health habits and obesity, that's my theory." He whipped his long coat around his body as he shoved his arms into the sleeves and then donned his fedora. "My deepest apologies, Mrs. McGovern," he said. "I'll be in touch. The men are here now to gather Mr. McGovern."

Eliza nodded. "Thank you," she whispered.

Jessie returned her attention to Heaven, waiting for any cue of what she might need. When none came, she decided it was best to get her upstairs. She gently grabbed Heaven's hand. "Come on."

Heaven nodded numbly, allowing herself to be pulled to her feet and led up the stairs to her bedroom. Once inside, the dam broke again. Jessie held her, fighting back her own tears so she could stay strong. She'd have plenty of time to cry later. Right now was about Heaven. She held her close, one hand buried in her hair while the other drew random patterns over her back.

"It'll be okay," she whispered. "I'm so sorry."

They both started when the bedroom door slammed open. Eliza stood on the other side, her red-rimmed eyes hard as she looked at the two young women. She walked over and grabbed Heaven's hand, tugging her away from Jessie.

"She needs her mother right now," Eliza said flatly, then pulled Heaven behind her as she left the room.

Jessie watched them go, stunned. But these weren't exactly normal times, and perhaps Eliza was right. Maybe Heaven needed her mother, too. She closed her eyes and let out a long, slow breath. She decided to take a quick bath after their swim and then head to the gardener's cottage.

❧ ❧ ❧ ❧

Tuesday, October 29, 1929

For three nights, Jessie had been relegated to her old bedroom in the cottage. Heaven had simply not been around. She hadn't seen her since the night Eliza had come to get her, literally tearing her from Jessie's arms. There was a strong sense of unease in the house. Though nobody said a word, Jessie noticed the house staff exchanging uncertain glances with each other.

For her part, Jessie had a horrible feeling of foreboding. She missed Heaven desperately and was doing her best to not fall apart. Family time at the cottage was quiet, with everyone affected by Harv's death. She suspected her parents were picking up on what she was feeling. She often overheard muffled late-night conversations through the wall that separated their bedrooms, though she couldn't make out the words.

Now, she was arriving home from school, having come and gone by herself, as Heaven still wasn't at the house, nor was Eliza. She hurried inside with her book bag clutched to her side, asking around until she was told where her mother was. She went to find her.

"Hey, Mama," she greeted, entering Eliza's suite, where her mother was stripping the huge bed to change the linens. Jessie dropped her book bag on a chaise lounge and rushed to help her mother. "Why are you doing this?" she asked. "They're not even here."

"They're coming back tonight," Louise said.

It was then that Jessie noticed her mother's voice was thick with emotion, her eyes rimmed with red.

"Are you okay?"

"You didn't hear?"

Jessie shook her head. "I guess not."

Louise let out a tired sigh and plopped down on the bed, looking down at her hands. Jessie quickly abandoned the linens and hurried over to her. She was getting scared. Louise looked up at her. "The stock market crashed today, Jessie," she said. "Now, that doesn't mean a whole lot to us"—she snorted—"not like we've got money anywhere anyway. But, according to what some are saying here at the house, we could be out on the street. People lost everything, honey."

Jessie could only stare at her, no clue what to say. She didn't know much about the stock market and Wall Street and all that, but she'd overheard Harv talk about it at the factory with his investors—especially George Russ. "Are we going to be okay, Mama?"

Louise exhaled again and looked at her daughter. "I don't know."

They both started when there was an explosion of sound downstairs. They looked at each other, then quickly finished making the bed and rushed down to see what was wrong.

"And I'm telling you, George," Tobias McGovern yelled at the taller man who stared him down in the great room. "This is *my* house now!"

"And how exactly do you intend to pay for it, Tobias?" George roared. "It's gone, all of it! What do you have left?"

Tobias's handsome face twisted into a snarl as he lunged at the older man. A chorus of male voices erupted as male servants appeared seemingly out of nowhere to separate the two men.

"What is wrong with you?" George bellowed,

glaring down at the younger man.

Tobias said nothing, his eyes on fire, still breathing hard. Clearly his ire had not died down. "You son of a bitch," he growled.

"What choice do you have, Tobias?" George said, his anger still evident but calmer now. "I'm making you a good offer."

Jessie stood back with her mother, chewing on her thumbnail, terrified of what it all meant. *What offer?*

⁂

1945

Jessie reached over and wiped away some blown leaves from the top of her mother's headstone before sitting back down on the grass. Her legs were folded, and she leaned on her knees. As she thought about how everything began to fall apart that year, she felt such sadness well up inside her—sadness she'd forced away for so long and simply hadn't dealt with.

Looking at her mother's grave made it all feel so much more vivid. She felt the sting of tears behind her eyes, and no matter how hard she tried, she couldn't stop them. She used the shoulder of her shirt to wipe at one that managed to escape.

"I miss you so much, Mom." She blew out a heavy breath. "One of the hardest days of my life was the day we had to leave you here."

The tears wouldn't stop. No matter what she did, they just wouldn't stop. She felt so alone, despite being surrounded by people. She had to hold up her father, who was utterly shattered, standing beside the casket next to him with her arm around his waist to literally keep him upright.

She could no longer hear what the minister was saying, as his Godly words held no meaning for her now. His God was the one who had taken her mother away. At just twenty-five years old, her mother was dead, not even fifty.

Something caught her eye. Jessie glanced to her left, past her father, to a grouping of trees about twenty yards away. A figure stood there. Her dress was black, as was the short veil that covered the upper part of her face. She rested a black-gloved hand against the trunk of the largest tree. The dress was simple yet elegant in its own way, just like the woman who wore it.

Jessie couldn't see her eyes, but she knew who it was. Even if she hadn't recognized the beautiful lips, painted a deep red, she would have known. She looked toward where she knew the woman's eyes were, and she was certain that her gaze was being met. A long tear slowly slid out from beneath the veil and down the woman's cheek.

A moment later, the woman in black turned away and was gone.

Jessie buried her face in her hands as the tears came. Sitting there in front of her mother's headstone, she cried. She cried for her lost mother, gone eight years now. She cried for all that had been taken from her so long ago. She cried in anger at herself for being a coward and leaving. She cried for Eliza. She cried… just because.

She quickly wiped at her eyes when she heard movement. Sniffling, she was about to stand to leave when she heard a voice that had haunted her dreams.

"Hello, Jessie."

Jessie shot to her feet and whirled around, stunned.

She stood not six feet away in high-waisted women's trousers and a silk blouse. Her hair was styled in shoulder-length midnight waves. She wore light makeup, though it wasn't hard to see the exhaustion in her dark eyes—eyes that no longer radiated a love for life and a twinkle of mischief. She looked uncomfortable as she clutched her purse in front of her.

"Hi," Jessie said. "How'd you know I was here?"

Heaven gave her a sheepish smile. "When Chloe gave me your message about my mother, gut feeling."

Jessie nodded, shoving her hands into her trousers. "I thought you didn't want to see me," she said, keeping her voice even, trying to hide her hurt.

Heaven let out a heavy sigh and looked down at her hands before meeting Jessie's gaze again. "No, I didn't want you to see me." She pulled a full bottom lip under straight, white teeth for a moment before releasing it. "I'm sorry I sent you away. I was just so stunned and wasn't quite ready to deal with that, too."

"With what?"

"You."

"Listen, I didn't go there to upset you, Heaven. Honest. From what I understand, your mother wasn't planning to call for you, and I just didn't think that was right." She shrugged, glancing over the sea of headstones before looking back to the woman who still made her palms sweat and heart race. "I just know that *I* needed that time with my mom. So, thought you had a right to that, too." She shrugged again. "If you even want it."

"How did you find out?" Heaven asked, cocking her head slightly to the side. "I didn't read it in the papers."

"No, she called for me and my father." Jessie smirked. "Ironically, I'm back at the house working for her. Until…" She looked down at her shuffling feet, unable to say the words.

"George Russ still there?"

As if by some silent agreement, the two wandered over to a stone bench not far away. They sat side by side, and Jessie felt like she was in the craziest Heaven dream she'd ever had. She pushed the thought away and nodded. "He is. Honestly, I think he's just trying to get this over with so he can move on with his life." She gave Heaven a sad look. "The feeling I get, anyway."

"A bastard then, a bastard now," Heaven muttered.

Jessie nodded. She clasped her hands between her parted thighs, almost as if in prayer. Not looking at the woman sitting quietly beside her, she asked, "Are you okay?" She didn't want to betray Chloe's confidence, but clearly something was wrong. When Heaven didn't respond, Jessie glanced over at her.

Heaven stared straight ahead, her body stiff as if she were a statue. Finally, she swallowed and looked down at her hands, resting atop her purse. "I will be," she said simply.

Jessie found herself in a strange place. She wanted to ask her what was wrong, wanted to offer her ear, her shoulder—whatever Heaven might need for whatever was happening in her world—but she felt as though she'd lost that right fourteen years ago. And frankly, Heaven had lost that right fifteen years ago.

Hadn't they both gone back on their promise?

"How's your father?" Heaven asked, unwittingly

pulling Jessie from her thoughts.

"He's good," Jessie replied, meeting Heaven's guarded gaze. "He and I work for the city." She gestured toward the cemetery. "Clean up the grounds here, public parks, buildings. Things like that."

"That's really wonderful." Heaven gave her a smile, and though Jessie believed it was genuine, it didn't reach her eyes. "Your father was always amazing with anything that grew." She gave a soft chuckle. "Remember that patch of grass by the birdbath that we swore was dead?" she said, a wistful smile on her lips. "Nope. Soon enough it was emerald green."

Jessie grinned. "Yeah. I have no clue how he does it. Even now. Even when I think he's out of his tree, I do what he tells me, and he's always right."

"I'm so glad the two of you have stuck together, Jessie. Truly. And," she added, meeting and holding Jessie's gaze. "I'm so sorry about Louise's death. I was stunned when I heard the news. I mean, I know it's been a long time, but I am. I'm sorry."

Jessie nodded. "Thanks. And now, unfortunately, it's your turn. I'm sorry for that. We're both far too young to have to deal with this sort of thing."

"My turn, then your turn, then my turn again," Heaven responded. "What a dubious honor."

"Dad's with her today," Jessie said, noting the bitterness in Heaven's tone. She didn't blame her. Losing her father had changed the woman beside her forever, let alone what it had done to their lives. She smirked. "I stole his truck."

Heaven raised an eyebrow. "Still a little rebel, huh?"

"Um, I think that's you." They shared a smile, but then Jessie felt a raindrop land on her nose. "Uh-oh." Glancing up, she saw the storm had finally caught them. They both got to their feet and, again, without a word passing between them, began to quickly walk toward the parking lot. More than once, the two giggled as Heaven's heels got caught in the grass.

"Oh, for heaven's sake! Here." Heaven shoved her purse at Jessie as she stepped out of both shoes and held them in her hands as they sprinted toward the parking lot, the rain now coming down in earnest.

Jessie noted the sleek black 1942 Chevrolet Special Deluxe Fleetline parked next to her father's Ford pickup. The big car was beautiful and luxurious. It very much looked like something Harv would have driven if he were still been alive.

They reached the car, and Jessie cradled the purse in one hand as she tugged open the driver's side door for Heaven.

"Oh, my goodness." Heaven laughed, falling into the car, more light in her eyes than Jessie had seen since she'd first turned around to see her. "I do love the rain, though." She smiled up at Jessie. "Oh, thank you." She took the purse Jessie held down to her.

"Sure." It was then that Jessie noticed the ring finger on Heaven's right hand. She saw the simple gold band with inlaid ruby. All she could do was stare, even as Heaven moved her hand out of sight to place the purse on the bench seat. Jessie shook herself out of it. "All in?" she asked, hands on the heavy door to close it.

Heaven got herself seated properly behind the wheel and nodded. "I am." She looked up at Jessie, reaching out her left hand to her.

Jessie took it, noting how soft her skin was. She also noticed the massive wedding ring. She ignored that and focused on the soft smile sent up to her.

"Thank you for letting me know about my mother."

"Of course. I really felt you deserved to know. What you do with that information is entirely up to you, but..." Jessie shrugged.

Heaven nodded and squeezed Jessie's hand before releasing it. "You're going to get drenched."

Jessie grinned as she looked up, the clouds really letting go. She stepped back and slammed the car door shut. They shared a wave through the window before Jessie turned and walked to the truck.

Chapter Eleven

Jessie was careful to make sure she wouldn't drip, her hand hovering beneath the spoon as she brought it to Eliza's lips. Dutifully, Eliza accepted the spoon with warm soup between her dry lips. Jessie watched to make sure it would be swallowed successfully and that she wouldn't need to use the towel slung over her shoulder like a bib again.

Slowly pulling the spoon away, Jessie dipped it back into the bowl she braced on her thigh with her other hand. She felt eyes on her and looked up, meeting Eliza's gaze. "What?"

Eliza studied her for a long moment, her tongue coming out to absently lick a small bit of soup from the corner of her mouth. "You really grew up to be quite lovely," she said, her voice raspy.

"Thank you," Jessie said, returning her gaze to her task, not entirely sure what to say.

"Why are you here?" Eliza asked, once again opening her mouth for the incoming spoonful of fragrant soup.

Jessie smirked. "Because you needed your lunch."

Eliza gave her a weak smile as she swallowed, Jessie gently wiping at her chin with a napkin where a bit of soup had dribbled. "Of course," Eliza said after a moment. "But, I mean here. Why are you here?"

Jessie sat back from where she was perched on the side of the bed and considered the question. She understood that she was being asked a deeper question than just why she had taken Eliza up on her offer. She stirred the soup around, small bits of chopped carrot and potato bobbing in the spoon's wake.

"If Mama were still alive, she'd be here." She met Eliza's gaze. "Regardless of what happened in the past, she'd be here." She was surprised when the eyes looking back at her began to well with tears. Jessie had no idea how to respond, as she'd never seen Eliza cry. Not even when Harv died, and she knew she'd loved him.

Eliza looked away, shaking her head subtly when Jessie held up the empty spoon in silent question. Jessie slid the spoon back into the bowl and set it aside on the top shelf of the cart, then grabbed the water glass.

"Thank you," Eliza said, accepting the drink. When she was finished, Jessie once again wiped her mouth. "Heaven called me this morning."

Jessie looked at her, surprised, as she set the glass aside next to the bowl. "She did?"

Eliza's eyes lit up, even as she reclined further back into the nest of pillows Jessie had helped the nurse arrange behind her. Today was a particularly weak day, the kind of day when Jessie and the medical staff exchanged small glances of concern.

"You did that," Eliza asked. "Didn't you?"

It had been two days since Jessie and Heaven had spoken in the cemetery, and there had been no contact between them since. She was a bit surprised, though pleased, that Heaven had reached out to her mother. "Heaven is a grown woman, Eliza. She called you because that's what she wanted to do."

"Yes, but you told her, didn't you." A statement, and not one of accusation.

"After going through this with my own mother, I felt Heaven had a right to know. She had the right to choose how to deal with this. She's the one who will be left behind, Eliza, dealing with her grief. I didn't want her to have to deal with regret, too."

Eliza held out her hand, and Jessie took it. "Thank you." She looked deeply into Jessie's eyes, her own watery and tired. "Thank you for always being so strong. Harvard saw it, all the way back then, when you were just a girl." She placed her dry palm against Jessie's cheek for a moment before her hand fell back to the bed. "I think I need a nap."

Jessie smiled and squeezed the hand she still held before releasing it. "Absolutely. I'll get this all cleared out and leave you be." She pushed to her feet. "Do you need anything, Eliza? To use the facilities or anything?"

Eliza shook her head. "No, but would you mind going into the attic? Near a set of steamer trunks, you'll find a small wooden trunk. Inside are a few photo albums." A wistful smile spread across her lips as her eyelids grew heavy. "Pictures of my parents and brothers and sisters."

"Sure, I'll go on up and try to find it."

"Thank you, dear." With that, Eliza's eyes closed.

Jessie grabbed the handle of the cart and was about to push it away from the bed. but she glanced down at the frail woman sleeping peacefully. So sad, she thought. But she was glad Heaven had called. Perhaps amends could be made.

With a sad sigh, she pushed the cart out of the room to the elevator.

"Hey there, Miss Jessie," John said from behind the butcher-block cooking island, his strong hand kneading a large chunk of dough.

"How do, sir?" she said, pushing the cart into the large kitchen. She unloaded Eliza's dishes onto the counter near the sink before pushing the cart out of the way and returning to wash the lunch dishes.

"I doin'," he said with a wide smile. "I doin'. How'd Miss Eliza do?"

"She ate about a fourth, I guess," Jessie said, dumping the remaining bit of soup into the trash. "She's pretty weak today, but I was happy she got down as much as she did."

He nodded. "Just a cryin' shame," he said, lifting the large ball of dough and flipping it over before slamming it back down on the flour-covered workspace. He slapped at it with his large hands to begin the flattening process all over again.

Jessie's mouth watered. knowing he was making the most incredible bread she'd ever tasted. She met his gaze and made a show of smacking her lips together in anticipation. He chuckled deep in his throat.

"I've got a task to do for Eliza in the attic this afternoon," she said, pointing a finger at him. "But when I'm done, I expect a slice right out of the oven, mister."

He grinned and nodded. "Can do."

⁂

Jessie pulled herself up from the pull-down ladder, stepping into a dim, dusty space, as expected in an attic. It was huge, spanning about half the size of the floor below. Old furniture, some covered in dusty sheets and others pieces left uncovered, filled the space. There was a huge empty bird cage sat on a tall wooden stand, several old clocks, and an endless sea of trunks, hatboxes, carpetbags, and several military-style footlockers.

She rubbed the back of her neck as she turned in a small circle, trying to spot the steamer trunks she'd been told to find. A circular vent, about five feet in diameter and placed far above the front portico of the massive house, was the only source of light. It sent a dim yellowish splash of light over the expanse, dust motes drifting upon unseen streams of air.

Finally, toward the far left corner, she thought she saw a stack of steamer trunks near a dresser. She carefully made her way over to it, moving a few things out of the path, including an armful of dresses that looked like they belonged in a museum rather than an attic. Reaching the trunks, she eyed them, wondering what they'd seen in their lifetime.

She remembered Harv once telling her that he'd lost a cousin on the *Titanic* when it sank, a story he reminded her of on every single birthday, as she'd been born at nearly the exact same moment the ship went down. One year, he'd even given her a cast iron replica of the ship which currently sat on the mantel over the fireplace in the house she shared with her father.

Looking at the steamer trunks, she thought of dragging such a thing on a voyage like that. So awkward and large. She couldn't imagine lugging that thing behind her. Glancing away from the steamer trunks, she searched for the smaller wooden one Eliza had mentioned and found it—or at least she hoped it was the right one.

Opening it, she dug beneath some fabric and found a photo album. Three of them, actually. Not sure which one Eliza was after, she grabbed all three. She was about to close the lid when something caught her attention. Setting the photo albums aside, she pulled the material out completely and saw that she was looking down at a reel-to-reel tape recorder.

What had caught her attention, however, was the label on one of the reels: *The Promise – 11-28-1929.*

She reached into the trunk and took the round reel, her eyebrows furrowing. Heaven's seventeenth birthday. She remembered that day very, very well. Confused, she noted the machine to play the recordings at the bottom of the trunk. She tapped her fingertips on the reel for a moment, trying to decide what to do.

She studied the handwriting and noted that it was bold, masculine. Something told her to gather the equipment and bring it downstairs, so she did. Stowing the machine and tape reels in her bedroom, she carried the photo albums to Eliza's room.

The older woman was still asleep, so Jessie placed the photo albums on the bed out of the way but close enough that Eliza could grab them without needing assistance. She checked to make sure Eliza was breathing okay, as she was so still that for a moment Jessie feared the worst.

Relieved when she felt the slow, even breaths against her fingers, Jessie pulled the sheet and thin blanket up a bit higher on Eliza's sleeping body then left her alone, softly closing the doors behind her.

"How is she?" Mildred, the nurse for the day, asked. She was just entering the outer room from the hallway, ready for her shift.

"She's asleep," Jessie said. "Ate a fairly decent lunch today, but she's pretty weak."

"Alright, sounds good," the elderly nurse said, shrugging out of her jacket to reveal her white nurse's dress underneath. "Her doctor will be here in the morning, around nine. If you want to let her morning nurse know."

"I absolutely can." Jessie gave her a smile and headed to leave. She paused at the door and turned to look back at the nurse, who was unpacking the bag she always brought with her. As usual, she had a book tucked inside. "Are you going to want dinner, Mildred?"

The nurse glanced at her. "No, I stopped and had supper with my daughter and her family. But I'll come down and grab a plate for Eliza when it's ready."

"Okay, sounds good." Jessie left the room.

She returned to her own room, feeling more and more uncertain as she considered the tape reel she'd discovered in the attic. She knew that it could be nothing more than business dealings or personal diary, but something inside told her that wasn't the case. Those days and weeks after Harv's death had been deeply disturbing, confusing, and upsetting.

She walked over to the bed, where she'd left the machine and reels. She ran a fingertip over the white label and writing in bold black ink. Mildred was there to look after Eliza, and John and his kitchen staff had dinner preparations under control. She had a little time to kill. Her gaze shifted to her dresser and the book she'd been reading, Ayn Rand's *The Fountainhead*.

Her stomach was in knots as she looked back to the tape reel and machine it sat upon. Shaking her head, she grabbed it and moved it to rest atop her trunk. "Leave well enough alone," she muttered. She grabbed her book and plopped down on the bed, settling in to read.

She cleared her throat as she got comfortable, opening the thick tome and removing the slip of paper she'd been using as a bookmark. She scanned the page to find her place. Locating it, she began to read but struggled to focus. She tried again, readjusting her body a bit more and the pillow she was reclining against. No good.

Her mind betrayed her and went back to two days before. Heaven. She'd not allowed herself to think about, let alone dissect, the unexpected meeting. Seeing her, being around her, had brought up so many repressed feelings and emotions.

Her hand went up to the necklace she never took off but was always tucked beneath her clothes. It wasn't worn as a jewelry accessory but as something private, something only she knew about. The ring that hung on the simple silver chain fit her ring finger, though she never wore it there. She was too afraid the beautiful sapphire stone would get lost due to her physical work with her hands in the soil.

She stared off into space as she lightly zipped the ring back and forth on the chain.

Jessie grunted as she heaved the shovel filled with heavy snow off to the side of the path, which wound its way across the property. She was sweating, even though it was a cold day in late November. November 28th, to be exact, Heaven's seventeenth birthday. Yet she hadn't seen the birthday girl that day. She'd barely seen her at all in the last month since Harv had died.

She'd done her level best to push it all away. Clearly everything had changed, and after she graduated high school in June, she planned to get the hell out. She had no idea where she'd go or what she'd do, but she just couldn't stay any longer. It hurt too much.

"There you are!"

Mid-shovel, Jessie glanced over to see a bundled-up Heaven hurrying her way. It killed her. Just a matter of weeks ago, her heart would flutter almost out of her chest at Heaven's voice or presence. Now, all she felt was confusion and deep hurt.

She stood erect from her shoveling and wrapped her gloved hands around the wooden handle of the tool as she waited for the other woman to reach her. "Where you been?" she asked, her voice flat. She wanted to come off as if she didn't care, but damn it, she did.

As Heaven got closer, Jessie realized that her eyes were red-rimmed and swollen. She looked around once she reached Jessie then grabbed her hand, tugging her toward the old carriage house. "Come on."

Carrying her shovel with her, Jessie basically had no choice but to follow or have her arm pulled out of its socket. Once inside the unused building, which still held the carriages the family owned and used a couple decades before, Heaven released Jessie's hand and slammed the door shut behind them.

Jessie held on to her shovel, no clue what to think or do. She was silent, waiting for Heaven to explain, to explain anything. Heaven looked around as she walked over to Jessie, though it seemed it was more to gather her thoughts than because she was curious about her surroundings.

Finally, she took a long, tired-sounding breath. "I'm sorry I haven't been around much." She met Jessie's guarded gaze. "Things are..." Heaven chewed on her bottom lip, her gaze flitting away from Jessie's. "I don't know. I don't know what to say, Jessie. But, what are you doing shoveling snow? And why is your stuff gone from your bedroom?"

"Ask your mother that," Jessie said, angry at herself for the bitterness that had entered her tone.

Heaven stared at her, looking dumbstruck. She said nothing but looked away, and not before Jessie saw tears welling in her eyes. She walked away from Jessie, running her gloved fingers along the top of one of the wood wheels of the closest carriage before she released a long, slow breath.

Turning, she looked at Jessie but kept her distance. "George has bought the house and the business," she explained. "There's no way my mom can do it on her own, and Tobias certainly isn't in any position to." She shrugged, hugging herself almost protectively. She looked away, seeming to refuse to meet Jessie's demanding gaze. "He has no interest in the business, anyway."

Jessie nodded, leaning the shovel against the wall before mirroring Heaven's position. She felt the need to guard herself, insulate, for what may be coming. "So, now what? What does any of that have to do with you not being around?" She looked away. "Not that it matters. I don't own you. You're free to do whatever you want," she muttered.

"Don't." Heaven hurried over to her, her eyes pleading as she grabbed Jessie by the shoulders. "Do you think I like this? Do you think I want my entire life turned upside down? Do you think I don't miss you, too?" That was it. The dam had broken, and Heaven was all-out sobbing.

Despite herself, Jessie's heart melted. She gathered Heaven in her arms and held her. Heaven clung to her, burying her face in Jessie's neck. Jessie's eyes fell closed as she cupped the dark head against her. Her own tears managed to slip down her cheeks. She had the most horrible feeling in her gut.

"Are my parents' jobs in danger here?" she managed.

After several moments, Heaven finally calmed herself and lifted her head. She wouldn't look at Jessie, but she shook her head. "No. They're safe." She cupped

Jessie's face with her hand. "And you're safe to finish school."

Jessie was a bit confused by that comment. She knew the school she attended with Heaven was not the regular school she'd go to if she wasn't living there, but she didn't understand what any of this had to do with that. Before she could ask, Heaven was kissing her.

Jessie returned the kiss, which had begun as lingering but soon deepened. She allowed herself to get lost in the warmth and softness of Heaven's lips and tongue against her own. She held the smaller woman closer, Heaven sighing softly as their bodies pressed together.

Finally, after several moments that left them both breathless, Heaven broke the kiss and hugged Jessica close again. "I love you, Jessie," she whispered forcefully into her ear. "No matter what, never forget that."

Chapter Twelve

Jessie was knocked out of the memory when she had the distinct feeling she was being watched. Her hand stilled from playing with the ring on the chain, and she glanced to her right and nearly had a heart attack when she saw Ronin standing there staring at her.

"My goodness, bud!" she said, hand to her chest. "You startled me. Where'd you come from?"

Without a word, the little boy pointed to the wall that was shared with Heaven's old room. It was then that Jessie heard voices—two females. It took a moment before she realized those two muffled voices were Heaven and Chloe. From what she could hear, Heaven was showing Chloe around, the teenager asking questions.

"You wanna come up here?" Jessie asked, returning her attention to the adorable little boy who stared at her. At his vigorous nod, she patted the bed beside her.

Heaven's son climbed up onto the bed, his little tongue sticking out of the side of his mouth in concentration as he did. She was so charmed by him. Finally, he succeeded in his ascent, dark eyes bright, clearly proud of himself.

"Good job, bud!" She grinned at him. Once he got settled, sitting not far away, she asked, "Do you remember me?"

He nodded. "Candy lady."

Jessie grinned and returned the nod. "Yup. Remember my name?" Again, she was charmed when he just stuck a finger in his mouth and looked shyly at her. "I'm Jessie," she said and held out her hand to him as she'd done the first day they'd met. "And what's your name?" she asked, not wanting him to feel bad about not remembering her name.

He took her hand in his smaller one, which was a little wet from the finger being in his mouth. "Ronin."

Jessie didn't mind about the slobber. Her hand was washable. She gave him a winning smile. "It is my pleasure to meet you again, Ronin." She squeezed his little hand in a firm, yet gentle, shake.

"Why do you have short hair?" he asked once his hand was released, his steady gaze studying her face and hair.

"Well," she explained gently. "You see, I work outside a lot, and it can get mighty hot out there. So, long hair like your mommy and your sister have is really pretty, but it just gets in the way."

"Like when I play in the sandbox with Samuel," he said, eyebrows raised in his excitement of adding his own little analogy.

"Exactly!"

His smile was big and bright. Jessie was quickly losing her heart to this little guy, who was clearly feeling more comfortable with her as he scooted a bit closer. His curious gaze fell to her ring on the chain, which she hadn't tucked under her shirt in her surprise at his sudden appearance.

He reached out and lightly fingered the ring. "Why is this on a necklace and not your finger?" His eyebrows bunched in bafflement.

"Well, remember I told you I work outside?" He

nodded. "I work with my hands in the dirt. So, again, like when you're playing in the sandbox with your friends, you might lose something like this, or get it dirty." The universal look for *ohhhh!* crossed his little face, making her smile. Jessie glanced up from him when she heard Heaven's voice, a bit frantic, calling for her son. "In here!"

The connecting door opened, and a harried Heaven appeared just as Chloe ran in from the open door in the hall where Ronin had entered. So used to being the only person in the hallway of rooms, Jessie often left the door open, except while sleeping. The little guy had been able to sneak up on her.

Hand to heart, Heaven slumped against the doorframe. Her eyes closed for a moment, and she took a deep breath. She looked at the pair on the bed before her gaze landed on Jessie.

"I'm so sorry," she said. "My little Houdini over there."

"No apologies necessary," Jessie assured her. "We're just chewin' the fat, right, Ronin?" She chuckled when he looked at her, confused.

"We're not eating anything."

"Nope, we're not. But," she added, tapping his nose with a fingertip. "That means we're just chatting."

She smiled when she saw those intelligent eyes rolling over what he'd just been told. She looked up at Heaven, who walked over to the bed. Jessie watched her. Obviously, Heaven felt her child was safe, and Jessie saw her peruse the contents of the room a bit from where she stood. Jessie found it curious when Heaven spotted the tape reel and machine.

A small gasp left the standing woman's lips, and she looked stunned. A fidgeting hand found the pearls she wore, fingers absently playing with the semiprecious stones. She looked away from the tape reel and back to Jessie, her gaze falling to the necklace and ring that still hung outside of Jessie's shirt.

Lips parted in surprise, she met Jessie's gaze for just a moment before looking away. "Honey," she said to Ronin, holding her hand out to him. "Let's leave Jessie alone, okay? We need to go see Grandma Eliza."

Without complaint or question, Ronin took her hand and scooted off the bed. Jessie glanced over to Chloe, who had stepped into the room but only stood quietly by the door. "Hey, Chloe," she said with a wide, welcoming smile. "So nice to see you again."

The young woman smiled shyly. "You, too, Jessie."

Compelled, Jessie climbed off the bed and walked over to her, giving her a quick but meaningful hug, which was returned. She felt a gaze on her and turned to see Heaven watching them. She was worried she'd see disapproval on her beautiful face, but instead there was a softness in her dark eyes that was reflected in the smile on her lips.

Their gazes met and held for the briefest of moments before Heaven looked away.

⚜ ⚜ ⚜ ⚜

"Okay, Heaven, pull down her nightgown while I've got her." Jessie grunted, holding the frail body in her arms.

Heaven, who was kneeling on the bed, did just that, quickly but gently tugging on the fresh nightgown that they'd placed on Eliza's body. Together, they'd given her a sponge bath after dinner. She'd requested them to do it, as opposed to her nurse, Jessie and Heaven working side by side.

Focused solely on the business at hand, they'd worked together seamlessly to get Eliza cleaned up and changed into a fresh sleeping gown. Once Heaven had the gown pulled into place, Jessie gently lowered the older woman back to her bed, also changed with fresh linens.

"Are you okay, Mother?" Heaven asked softly as she adjusted the front of the gown as Jessie pulled up the sheet and blanket to cover Eliza's form to just above her breasts.

Eliza nodded, looking over at Heaven. She reached up a slender hand and rested the palm against Heaven's cheek. Jessie was about to leave to give the two some privacy when Eliza looked over at her, raising her other hand to rest a scratchy palm on her cheek. Jessie met her gaze before flicking it to Heaven to see that she was already looking at her.

Glancing back to Eliza, she saw that her energy was spent, as her eyes started to close. Both her hands fell away, and she fell into a deep sleep. Jessie tucked her in a bit more, then stood erect from the bed as Heaven climbed off.

"Is that it?" Heaven asked. "Anything else we need to do?"

Jessie shook her head. "Nope." She looked back at the still form on the bed. "She should be okay until morning."

Together, they left the room, Jessie closing the door softly behind them. Heaven leaned back against the wall, hugging herself. She looked off into space for a moment, then said, "How do you do this? How do you do this every day?"

Jessie shrugged, her hands shoved into her

pockets. "Honestly, because it needs to be done. She has a wonderful nursing staff, but..." She shrugged again. "I want her to see a friendly face every day, someone she knows, someone she knows that cares."

Heaven nodded and looked away. Her face seemed as if it were about to crumble, but then she tucked her lips in, obviously trying to hold back the emotions that were making her eyes a little too shiny. She hugged herself tighter.

Jessie wasn't sure what to do. The child and young woman she'd known was extremely expressive in her emotions and had no problem grabbing Jessie for a hug—whether Jessie was ready or not. This woman, a mother, was so foreign to her. She was closed off, seemingly even from her own needs.

She had no idea how to handle this Heaven. The bright life spark was gone, leaving behind eyes that were dull and very guarded. She'd known a woman who had been exuberant, beautiful, and sexy, using her body in every way to tell the story of her endless curiosity and mischief. This woman was stiff, her shoulders even slightly bent, as if the weight of the unknown burden she carried had the strong branch bowing.

Now, looking at her, Jessie worried that Heaven would break. She walked over to her and, without a word, took her into a gentle hug. She made sure to make it obvious that she could push her away or refuse. Heaven did neither of those things. Instead, she leaned into Jessie, wrapping her arms around her and allowing herself to be held.

Jessie rested her cheek against Heaven's head as the smaller woman began to cry. It wasn't loud, body-shaking sobs, but the continuous kind of tears that you just can't stop until they're done. As she cried, Jessie had the feeling that it went beyond the imminent death of her mother. There was so much that Jessie didn't understand, didn't have answers for, but she felt it was safe to say that Heaven's life hadn't gone how she'd wanted, either.

Maybe someday she'd get the answers she so badly needed, but for now, this wasn't about her. It was about Heaven. It was about comforting the person she'd loved since she was six years old. And, whether they ever saw each other again, Jessie knew she'd love her until her dying day.

⁂

It was a gorgeous day in May, the sun warm overhead as Jessie worked in the flowerbeds along the pathways on the property. It felt so good to get outside in the fresh, late-spring air. For the past month, she'd been largely cloistered inside helping to care for Eliza or, as she'd realized was needed, running the house.

There were still some maids, John and his small kitchen staff, and a single part-time gardener, but nobody to oversee things. This had been Eliza's realm, but she was no longer able to perform that task. So, Jessie had spoken to each and every member of the staff, inside and out, to find out what they needed from a leader. There was no way in hell she was going to George Russ for that.

So far, things had gone smoothly. The staff had been open to her and very solicitous to point her in the right direction whenever she wasn't sure whom to contact for one thing or another. She braced herself on her left hand as she stretched to grab a weed with her right when she heard footfalls coming up behind her.

Glancing over her shoulder, she scrambled to her feet when she saw a bemused George Russ looking down at her. He was in trousers, short sleeves, a tie, and suspenders, only lacking the jacket to his summer suit. He took a drag off the cigarette that was pinched between first and middle fingers.

Looking her up and down, he quirked an eyebrow. "What are those?" he asked, words carried off on the released smoke from his drag. He used the two fingers holding the cigarette to indicate her outfit.

Jessie looked down at herself, then back to him. "They're trousers that I cut off and rolled the cuffs on, George." She indicated the sun above. "A little too hot to work out here in full pants."

"So, perhaps a dress?" he suggested.

"Or, you could mind your own business." She smiled at him sweetly. "I'm here for Eliza, not you."

He cleared his throat, taking another drag as he eyed her. "How's Eliza doing?" he finally asked.

Jessie shrugged. "As well as can be expected, I suppose. I think at this point, they're just trying to keep her comfortable." She turned her hand over and brushed some dirt off her palm. "She's past the point of getting any better, so..."

He nodded. "I've seen Heaven around here." His tone was conversational, but something in his eyes caught Jessie's attention. "Why?"

She raised an eyebrow. "Perhaps because her mother is dying?"

"Yes, and how did she find that out?"

Jessie hooked her thumbs into the belt loops of her short pants, cocking her head to the side as she studied him. "Was it a secret?" she drawled.

"Of course not," he barked. "But I was fulfilling

Eliza's wishes."

"That may be so, George, but I was there to see her absolute delight when Heaven called on her. I was there to see her absolute delight when she got to meet her grandson for the first time and see her granddaughter for the first time in more than ten years. I was there to see her delight when—"

"I got it, Jessica," he growled. "You don't need to make more of something than need be." He smirked. "As usual."

"I'm not the one who started the conversation, George." She placed a hand to her hip. "Heaven being here make you nervous?" she asked, partly to ruffle his feathers a bit more, and partly to try and get to the bottom of what his issue was.

"Don't be silly," he said dismissively. He took a final drag off his cigarette before dropping it to the pathway at their feet, using the toe of his wingtip to smoosh it into the pavestone. "Don't let her brats make messes in my house," he said before sauntering casually away.

She watched him go, disgusted. When she'd first arrived that day back in April to answer his call, she'd been polite. After all, it had been so many years and there was a whole flood of water under the bridge. But since she'd been there, his apathetic, almost callous attitude toward his dying wife had been hard to stomach. But stomach it she had. As she'd said to him many times, she wasn't there for him, she was there for Eliza.

Now, as horrible as it sounded, part of her wished Eliza would finally find her peace so Jessie could walk away from Greyson Manor for good. She honestly didn't know if Heaven would stay in her life in any real meaningful way after that happened. Right now, they were in visual and verbal communication simply because of Eliza.

What about after? She lowered herself back to the flowerbed and her weeding, her mind continuing to ruminate. Did she even want Heaven in her life? She was still married to Kingston Rawlins, and there were reasons why she'd walked away in the first place. No doubt, those reasons still existed.

As unhappy as Heaven looked, and as much of a shell as she had become, Jessie couldn't put her own life on hold to help. Not again.

Chapter Thirteen

1930

"You got it?" Cook asked, eyeing Jessie and the silver tray she was holding. "Want me to take a few off?"

"No," the teenager said. "I can handle it." She gave the older woman a small smile, then turned and left the kitchen with her very breakable load.

What she didn't say was that she wanted to throw the whole lot against the nearest wall and watch with satisfaction as the crystal stemware filled with golden bubbly crashed into a billion pieces.

On her third tour of the ballroom, Jessie was offering glasses of champagne as the clock would soon strike midnight. The year would be 1930, and for God's sake, she hoped it would be a better one! The final few months of '29 had been the worst of Jessie's life, which wasn't always easy to start with, as the child of the servant class.

"Champagne, sir?" she asked the first man she came to who wasn't already holding a glass, desperately trying to stay out of the way of careless and inebriated New Year's guests.

Two more glasses unloaded, she continued. The evening had been a shocker, those gathered—guests and staff—met with the announcement of a double engagement. The coming spring and summer would introduce the world to Mrs. Eliza Russ and Mrs. Heaven

Rawlins, George and Kingston their respective beaux.

Jessie still hadn't caught her breath from that bombshell. She'd seen the thirty-year-old senator around the house over the past month or so, but she hadn't been sure who he was or why he was there. She figured he was just a business associate of George Russ, as she often saw them together.

Nope. He was simply the knight in shining armor from her nightmare, come to take Heaven away. She couldn't even look at the happy couples as she finished unloading her current tray of champagne. She headed back to the kitchen as the leader of the small orchestra announced that it was almost midnight.

And another thing, Jessie thought as she headed back toward the kitchen. During a time when men were literally standing in long lines down the street for a measly bit of bread and soup and there was no work to be found, Greyson Manor was holding this huge, expensive, wasteful gala. Dressed in a black maid's uniform with white apron and cuffs, Jessie felt garish and wrong.

The arrogance. The entitlement. The audacity! Jessie was furious as she reached the kitchen, placing the empty silver tray on the butcher block a bit harder than necessary. The entire kitchen started at the gong-like sound it made. She gave them a sheepish smile and entered the huge walk-in pantry just to get a moment to breathe.

The pantry was the size of a medium-sized bedroom, the walls covered in product-filled shelves. There were bags of flour, jars of vegetables canned the previous summer and fall, sugar, and other such provisions. At the center of the space was a small table where a bowl could be set and filled with small portions to save the servants from dragging a forty-pound bag of flour to the kitchen down the hall each time Cook needed it.

Jessie braced her hands on the table and let her head fall. Her eyes closed as she heard the distant countdown for the incoming new year. For so many desperate people, it was a time of hope that things would get better. For Jessie, her entire life was imploding and she'd never felt more lost. The first tear fell on her left thumb, the second on the countertop between her hands.

She registered the clicking sound of high heels growing louder, but she didn't care. Another rich guest was probably lost on her way to the facilities. Let her stay lost, Jessie thought, sniffling. She started when she felt a hand on her back. Expecting to see an irritated Cook glaring at her for wasting time, she was stunned to see Heaven.

She looked absolutely stunning, a vision of feminine perfection in plum, but it was a diamond-encrusted dagger to the heart for Jessie. It was all for her soon-to-be husband. She turned away, pushing from the table only to be whipped back to face the determined young woman who stood before her.

Her face was cupped by gentle hands, and she was brought in until soft lips pressed against her own. She could hear the distant sounds of the orchestra playing "Auld Lang Syne" and the revelers singing along. She responded to the kiss even as her tears continued to fall. Her heart broke, as it felt like a goodbye kiss.

"Why did you do that?" she whispered, her words thick with her emotion as the kiss ended, Heaven resting their foreheads together. Her fingers lightly caressed Jessie's cheek. "Doesn't that belong to him?"

"No," Heaven whispered back. "I'm not giving him that." She backed away just enough to meet Jessie's tortured gaze. "No," she said again. "For as long as I can, I'm going to give you what belongs to you." She took their hands and placed them against her flawless upper chest, bared by the dress she wore. "You already have this."

Jessie looked into Heaven's eyes, and despite the makeup, beyond the fancy clothing, hairstyle, and jewels, she saw a scared, heartbroken young woman inside. She saw herself reflected back at her in those dark eyes. For just a moment, she felt better. As terrible as it was to acknowledge, it was a relief to know that Heaven, too, was hurting.

"Don't give up on us," Heaven said softly, leaving one last kiss on Jessie's lips before pulling away and hurrying from the pantry.

❧ ❧ ❧ ❧

It was four months into the new year, and it was a very, very cold spring day. Colorado was known for getting most of her moisture—snow and rain—in March and April. For reasons not explained to Jessie, she was no longer picked up at school by a driver, though she thought she knew why. Heaven was no longer attending school. Instead, she was whisked all around to parts unknown and supposedly provided with tutors so she could graduate.

Jessie's father was just too busy to drive her to or from school, and he couldn't lose the truck for an entire day for her to drive herself. She didn't mind the two-mile walk each way. It gave her a chance to clear her head, work out some things she had for homework, and honestly, get away from Greyson Manor.

She was about halfway to the house this brisk day and considering the math test she had coming up on Monday. She knew she'd be busy all weekend, as she'd be joining her mother washing windows. Spring cleaning had officially begun at the manor. She hugged her bag of books to her side when she heard the rumble of a car engine crawling up behind her.

Not looking, Jessie made a subtle shift deeper into the sidewalk, nearly walking on the lawn of the house she was passing. Her heart began to pick up a bit when the slow rumble stayed beside her, keeping pace.

"Hey!" a man called out to her. "Wanna ride?"

She shook her head, staring straight ahead. "No, thank you."

"What, now that your buddy ain't around to protect you, you're not so brave, huh?"

Her blood went cold when she recognized Chadwick Tapper's voice. She frantically looked for an escape route. There were two more houses on the street before she would cross a huge, open field that led to the Greyson Manor property.

"Hey!" Chadwick shouted. "I'm talkin' to you!"

Her mind raced. Jessie knew she could make a run for it, but she was not sure if the driver would chance plowing into the field in the middle of the afternoon, or if the occupants would give chase on foot. She could also run back farther into the residential area or knock on the door of one of the houses that were close by.

Her decision was made for her when she was suddenly grabbed from behind, a large hand covering her mouth right after she let out a scream for help. She was pressed back against a solid body, a strong arm wrapping around her waist as she was nearly lifted off her feet.

"Move, move!" Chadwick yelled, the closeness of his voice alerting Jessie to the fact that he was the one who was holding her. "Get her in!"

Jessie began to fight against him with everything in her. She was kicking her legs in the air, using Chadwick's body as leverage. She managed to kick one of his buddies in the stomach, nearly knocking him down.

"Bitch!" he growled, steadying himself by grabbing the arm of the other young man that was there. "Just for that, I get my turn, too, Chad!"

Jessie used her tongue, anything to try to get that hand off her mouth, as it was partially covering her nose, too. She could barely breathe.

"Ow!" The hand was whipped away as she managed to bite a bit of the meaty part of his middle finger. "Damn it! Bitch bit me."

"Help me!" Jessie screeched

"Grab her, goddamn it!" Chadwick growled. "Get her into the fucking car!"

Jessie was grabbed again but froze, as did everyone else, at the unmistakable sound of a shotgun being racked. She was stunned to see an old woman— even older than Cook—standing on the porch of a nearby house, holding the gun as comfortably as if it were a pair of knitting needles.

"You boys want it all to end like this?" she asked.

"Mind your own business, grandma," one of the boys said to her.

"You let her go, now," the old woman said, ignoring him. When Jessie was still held firm, the old woman aimed the shotgun and fired. The extra tire on the back of the fancy car the boys were driving exploded.

"Jesus Christ!" Chadwick exclaimed.

"How you gonna explain that one to your rich daddy?" she asked, the gun aimed back at him. "I got one more in here. Which one of you is gonna get it?"

Jessie was shoved away, and she stumbled to the ground. She hissed as her knee scraped the sidewalk. She quickly turned and watched as the three boys piled into the car. Chadwick glared at her.

"This isn't over," he said, pointing a finger at her. With that, the car zoomed away.

"You alright, honey?" the old woman asked, suddenly behind Jessie and helping her to her feet.

Jessie nodded, doing her best to keep the tears at bay until she got home. She sniffled as she began to lose her battle.

"Aw, honey," the old woman murmured. Her small, frail-looking body, proven to be much stronger than she appeared, took Jessie in a tight, comforting hug. "It's alright, now. We scared them off." After a quick squeeze, she released Jessie and smiled up at her. "Come on, now. Let's get you home."

✦✦✦✦

After getting a bone-crushing hug from her father, a crying Jessie was passed on to her mother, who took her into a tender embrace. Louise murmured words of love and reassurance as she stroked her hair and back.

Martha, the old woman, insisted on talking to Jessie's parents when she drove her home. She'd sat down with Louise and Dobbs and told them what happened. Martha's kindness had no bounds, as it turned out. She claimed she was an old woman with nothing better to do, and she promptly offered to drive Jessie back and forth to school until graduation.

"It's going to be okay, sweetheart," Louise whispered, leaving a kiss on Jessie's cheek. "I promise. Your dad will never let anything happen to you."

"Goddamn right," Dobbs grumbled, entering the living room of the cottage with his pistol in hand. "What time you leave for school, Jes?" he asked, checking the revolver to see if it was loaded.

"Dad, I'm okay, really—"

"What time?" he demanded, slapping the cylinder back into place.

"Um." She used the sleeve of her dress to wipe at her eyes and tear-streaked cheeks. "Seven."

He nodded. "Be ready to go."

The three of them were startled when someone pounded on the front door. "Jessie?"

"Your Heaven girl is here," Dobbs said. He walked over to the door and pulled it open.

The frantic young woman burst inside, wide eyes searching until they stopped on Jessie. She hurried over to her and took her into a painfully tight hug. "I'm so sorry," she breathed into it. "So sorry."

Jessie allowed herself to get lost in the embrace. She could feel the relief coming off Heaven in waves. "Not your fault."

Heaven released the hug but took Jessie's hand. She gave a smile to both her parents before tugging Jessie toward her bedroom. Once inside with the door closed, she hugged her again, even tighter.

"Who did this?" she asked, her face buried in Jessie's neck.

"It doesn't matter—"

"Who?" Heaven demanded, pulling away just

enough to see Jessie's face. Her eyes were on fire. It was clear that a nonresponse was not an option.

"Chadwick, Raymond, and the other guy they hang out with. The one with the glasses," she said.

"Okay." The calmness in Heaven's voice was almost scary. "Will you stay with me tonight?"

Jessie shrugged. "Won't your mother or George get mad?" She smirked. "I'm the help, after all."

"I don't give two cares if they do," Heaven said. "Will you?"

"Yeah. Sure." The truth was that Jessie wanted nothing more than to be in Heaven's presence all night. It had been so very long.

❧❧❧❧

Jessie had never been held before, other than by a parent. It was always she who did the holding when it came to Heaven. But there they were, in that massive bed, with the curtains closed all around them.

Her head rested on a soft, cotton-clad breast. So comforting, even as she did her level best to push any thoughts of those breasts out of her mind. They'd done nothing more since that night in the pool clear back in October. Hell, they'd barely had five minutes alone. No doubt that had been orchestrated on purpose: Keep Heaven busy and hurtling toward her new life while Jessie was forced into servitude.

"Jessie?" Heaven said, her voice quiet in the complete darkness that was their little cocoon. "Are you still awake?"

"Yes." Jessie snuggled in closer, her arm slung almost possessively across Heaven's body while soft fingers gently combed through her hair.

"I want to take you somewhere," Heaven said. "For the weekend."

Jessie's eyebrows furrowed. "What?"

"My father has another house, a much smaller one," she said with a little laugh. "It's called Granite House. It was built by my great-grandparents when they got here from Scotland."

"Nobody lives there now?" Jessie asked, intrigued.

"Nope. But staff goes there once a month to clean, make sure the chimney is cleaned out, all that sort of stuff. Keep it functional."

"Where is it?"

"About ten miles from here. Easy for us to get to." Heaven left a kiss on Jessie's head. "I want one last weekend with you," she said, pausing. "Before I have to marry Kingston."

Jessie squeezed her eyes shut, taking slow, deep breaths. It killed her every time she thought or heard about it, but she knew they had to stay realistic. She didn't understand why it was all happening or why Heaven was agreeing to it, but her heart hurt.

Finally, she managed, "Okay. I'd love that. Won't George be angry?"

"I don't care," Heaven said, her voice hard. "I absolutely do not care." She held Jessie tighter to her.

"How did you know what happened today?" Jessie asked, needing to get the subject off anything to do with George or Kingston.

Heaven snorted. "That amazing lady, Martha, came to the house after she left your parents and insisted on talking to George and my mother. She told them what happened and warned them to keep an eye on you and other young women who live here."

"I sure hope I'm that feisty when I'm her age."

Heaven chuckled. "Oh, I have no doubt you will be, my Jessie. Turn over."

Jessie moved away from Heaven and turned to her left side. Heaven snuggled up behind her, spooning her. She held her tightly against her and released a long, contented sigh. "Good night, Jessie," she murmured. "I love you."

Jessie smiled, covering the hand that rested on the mattress up by her breasts. "I love you, too. Good night." She closed her eyes, thinking her greatest wish would be to go to sleep like that every night for the rest of her life.

Chapter Fourteen

Okay, so how many do you need?" Jessie asked Cook, looking down at the list she'd been given. "There's no number next to eggs."

"Oh, sorry," the older woman said. "I'm used to Gabrielle, who knows this recipe. Three dozen."

Jessie nodded, folding the page and tucking it into the pocket of her apron. "Yes, ma'am. I'm on it."

She hurried through the kitchen door and toward the henhouses kept on the property. Her intention was cut short when she saw George Russ headed her way. She spared him a glance but kept going. She had a job to do.

"Jessica," he called out. "A word."

She stopped at her full name, which was so rarely used by anyone save Eliza, who insisted. She turned to face him but didn't take a step. If he wanted to talk to her, he could walk to where she stood. There was something about George Russ that brought out the rebel in her. It wasn't smart, she knew that, but she couldn't help it.

"I didn't appreciate that woman coming here Thursday to tell of the so-called attack on you," he said, hands on hips as he looked down at her. He was dressed impeccably, as usual, in his three-piece suit. "You made this household look bad."

She stared at him. "How did *I* make this household look bad, Mr. Russ?" she asked, nearly spitting out the words. She cursed herself. She had to be careful. She didn't like him, but he still held the purse strings for all of them. "Those boys attacked me, sir," she said, her voice calming to a more conversational tone.

"And, what did you do to provoke them?"

Jessie was stunned. Her entire life she'd been surrounded by amazing men, like her father and Harv, who had treated women with respect, and on some occasions, as equals. She certainly knew men like George Russ were around, but foolishly, perhaps naively, she believed they were the minority. She was learning that was not the case as she got older and was exposed to more men outside of the protective circle in which she'd been raised.

"Well," she drawled, "If walking home from school is provocation, then…"

He bent slightly over her, pointing a finger at her. "Don't back-talk me, girl." He stared her down, and though it took every ounce of her willpower, Jessie held his gaze. She was stunned when he looked away first. "You know," he said, straightening to his full height again, eyeing her. "You really don't need a job here. There are so many men out there that deserve your position more than you do, as a woman."

An internal alarm was going off inside her, and Jessie had the distinct feeling that she needed to be smart here. She had to play her cards well. "I'm not so sure a man would want to carry out my duties, Mr. Russ," she said. "I help my mother change beds, wash all the linens in the household, and scrub commodes." She paused a moment, allowing that to sink in. "I don't just help my father on the grounds."

His expression softened, a strange look entering his eyes that she couldn't quite read. She did know, however, that it made her incredibly uncomfortable.

"You know," he said, his voice almost wistful. "You'd make a wonderful wife."

Panic seized her guts, but she did her level best to not react. She was grossed out as he reached out and trailed his thumb and forefinger down some long strands of her hair, which had come loose from her bun during her Saturday morning chores.

"Yes," he said, as though deciding something in his own mind. "My tailor's son is looking to get married." He lightly touched her cheek with his fingers before his hand fell away. "Yes." He nodded. "I believe I'll introduce you to Joel."

She opened her mouth to rebuff the thought, but he abruptly turned and strode away, leaving her staring after him. Her fury began to rise in her like Jesus from the cross. Eggs forgotten, she stormed over to the gardener's cottage, which was empty, her parents both at work. No clue why she was there, she looked around for inspiration. Then, it hit her.

In the bathroom, she looked through cabinets until she found what she was looking for. Item set on the sink basin, she looked at her reflection in the mirror above the sink. She barely recognized herself. Her eyes were the darkest green she'd ever seen them, and she knew it was from all the rage she'd felt build up since the previous autumn.

She let loose her bun and grabbed her mother's brush, quickly brushing out the long strands until they fell around her shoulders like a shiny light brown curtain. One more look into her face, and she knew she had to do it.

Taking the large, sharp scissors in hand, she went to work. The snip-snip of the scissor blades filled the room, again and again, long strands of her hair falling into the sink and around her feet on the floor. She snipped away, watching the young woman turning eighteen in a matter of days morph into looking like a fourteen-year-old boy.

She didn't care. He didn't want to give a job to a woman? So be it. Finished, she slammed the scissors down on the basin and ran her fingers through the short and somewhat choppy locks. It felt good, lighter. Next stop on her mission—clothing. She stripped out of her dress, careful to shake off all the long strands first before she wrapped up the shorn hair into a bundle so as not to leave a trail.

Leaving the wadded-up dress on the seat of the commode, she headed to her parents' bedroom. Opening the drawers of the dresser, she kept going until she found what she was looking for. Heading back to the bathroom, she stripped off her panties and bra and did a very quick sponge bath to get rid of all the tiny hairs that had fallen down her dress collar, then donned her new duds.

Everything was huge on her, and the trousers had to be rolled up substantially as well as the sleeves on the button-up shirt, but she didn't care. This initial outfit was to make a point. Even if she lost her damn job, she wasn't going to allow George Russ—or *any* man— choose her fate. Her parents, and Harvard McGovern, had taught her better than that.

She gathered the long strands of her hair into a nice little bouquet, then headed out. She went to the house, ignoring the stunned looks she got as she passed. Nobody said a word to her, no doubt the look in her eyes and clear determination in her walk freezing any thoughts or questions on their tongues.

George was standing in the foyer of the grand

house, speaking to his personal driver. The two men stopped when she approached them. The driver looked at her with wide eyes but wisely said nothing. His boss, however, looked her up and down with obvious disgust and disdain.

She said nothing as she looked him in the eye and raised her hand, the long strands draped over her fingers like her life's blood. She opened her fist, and the hair fell to the polished floor at his feet. "Problem solved," she said coolly.

His eyes never left hers, though to her surprise, there seemed to be a touch of amusement in them. "You are so lucky I'm a man of my word," he murmured softly. He turned to his driver. "Fred, we'll leave here by nine, sharp."

"Yes, sir," the driver said, seeming to release a small sigh of relief as he hurried from the foyer and out the front door.

Without another word or look at Jessie, George left the foyer as well, his long legs carrying him swiftly toward the great room and office beyond. Standing there alone, Jessie covered her face with her hands, stunned at what she'd done.

"Oh boy," she whispered, hands sliding down until they fell from her face. She looked down at the mess at her feet. "Oh boy."

❧ ❧ ❧ ❧

1945

She hadn't slept well the night before, so Jessie was tired as she headed to Eliza's bedroom. She got her fed and ready for the morning nurse or doctor—

whoever was on the schedule. She was surprised to see that the curtains had been opened, breakfast had already been brought up and eaten, as evidenced by the dishes on the cart, and Eliza's hair had been brushed.

Eyebrows drawing, she looked to the chair to look for any indication that the morning nurse had arrived early. No sign, but her attention was grabbed by the sound of running water in the bathroom. A moment later, Heaven appeared, a damp washrag in her hand. She gave Jessie a quick smile before reaching Eliza's side.

"Let's get your face washed up, Mother," she said kindly. "You went a little nuts with your oatmeal this morning." She gently wiped at the older woman's mouth.

Jessie watched, touched. A little more of Eliza was slipping away each day. She wondered if perhaps she was beginning to let go now that Heaven was back and she'd finally been able to spend some time with her grandchildren. She stayed back to keep out of Heaven's way, but she also wanted to give mother and daughter that time together.

Eliza said nothing, simply stared up at her daughter with adoring eyes. At one point, her lips moved, but nothing came out. Eliza's doctor had told her he felt she was getting close, but only time—and Eliza, herself—would tell.

"Jessie?"

Heaven's soft voice interrupted her thoughts. She shook herself from her ruminations and met Heaven's gaze. "Yes?"

"Can you pour a little water into that glass, please? She wants a little sip before her nap."

"Of course." Jessie did as she was asked, then

passed the glass to Heaven. "I'll hold her head up if you want to focus on the glass?"

"Yes, thank you."

The two met gazes for a moment before they turned to their joint task, which wasn't an easy one. Eliza was essentially no help to them, so full attention had to be paid. When Eliza was finished with what she wanted to drink, Heaven took the glass away as Jessie gently rested Eliza's head back against the pillow.

"Comfortable?" she asked, looking into the tired eyes of the woman who, though only in her fifties, looked ninety. At Eliza's nod, Jessie gave her a smile then moved away from the bed.

The two left the room, walking to the elevator in companionable silence. Jessie pushed the cart, Heaven opening and closing doors for her, as well as pushing the button to the elevator when they reached it.

"I'm sorry I encroached on your routine this morning," Heaven said as they waited for the door to slide open. "I had to take Chloe to school and dropped Ronin off at his aunt's house, so I came here." She gave Jessie a shy smile. "Figured I'd save you the trouble."

The door opened and the two entered, Heaven again pushing the button to get them moving. "I don't mind at all, Heaven. I mean, hey," she said with a smile. "She's your mom."

"I know, but you've put so much time into her and everything." Heaven leaned back against the wood-paneled wall of the small elevator car. "I want to talk to you about something."

"Sure. What's up?" The door slid open as the elevator reached its destination.

The two walked together, once again on the way to the kitchen to take care of Eliza's dishes. Jessie realized she was craving a cup of morning coffee.

"Well," Heaven said. "Now that I know what's going on, I want to help. If it's okay with you, I'd like to take over my mother's care, as I know you're dealing with the rest of the house."

Jessie was surprised by the offer, but thought it was a wonderful idea. "Yeah?"

Heaven stopped her with a hand to Jessie's arm. She looked up into Jessie's eyes. "Yeah. So many people have told me how much better you've made things since you've been here. Gave them some real leadership."

Jessie smiled. "I'm pleased to hear that. These are good people."

"They are. So, I thought I could at least take that off your plate." She shrugged, looking down at the cart that was between them. "If that's okay with you."

Jessie was surprised by this woman before her. She seemed so unsure of herself, so concerned about upsetting the apple cart. That had never been how their relationship was in the past, so Jessie figured this was what Heaven's life had become over the past eighteen years. Who was this woman? So uncertain. So timid. The sudden need to take her in her arms and protect her from the world was almost overwhelming.

Jessie cleared her throat and rubbed the back of her neck to push those unwanted thoughts out of her mind. "Absolutely. I think it's a great idea." She rapped her knuckles on the cart. "Tell you what. Let's get this taken care of, let me get some morning coffee," she said with a lopsided grin, "and go sit in the garden and talk."

Heaven's smile was radiant. "Yes. Yes, okay."

Twenty minutes later, the two sat on one of the stone benches at the center of the garden path. It was an absolutely beautiful day, mild and pleasant. Jessie looked out over the blooming flowers around them, enjoying the new life as she sipped from her cup. She could feel the quiet presence beside her, and honestly, it was surprisingly comforting.

"So beautiful," Heaven said, as if reading Jessie's thoughts. She crossed one skirt-draped leg over the other, her hands wrapped around her coffee cup resting on her knee. "Someday," she continued. "Someday I really want to have a flower garden like this in my yard." She gave a quiet laugh. "Not sure I'll have one, though."

"Flowers, or a yard?" She remembered that Kingston was allergic to just about everything green.

Heaven gave her a small smile. "Yes."

"Well, I suppose I could clear out our backyard and give you carte blanche to make a garden away from home." She met Heaven's gaze. "With Dad and I working on other people's grounds all day, we decided not to put any real effort into a yard at home."

"I'd love to see your house," Heaven said, eyes bright.

"Come to dinner this weekend," Jessie blurted. She sat there for a moment, shocked the words had passed her lips. They hadn't even been in her brain. "With the kids," she added. In for a penny...

Heaven met her gaze. "Really?"

"Yeah." Jessie shrugged. No biggie, right? "Dad would love to meet them, no doubt." She held Heaven's gaze. "I think they're great kids and would love to spend some time with them, too." She grew serious. "If it wouldn't get you into trouble, that is."

Heaven looked away, hugging herself as she leaned forward over her crossed thighs. "He's never here much anymore, Jessie. Hasn't been for years. Quite honestly, it was only a drunken visit that brought Ronin into my life." Her words were so bitter, so flat, it chilled Jessie to the core.

Not knowing what to say, she simply said, "I'm sorry."

Heaven sipped her coffee, taking several moments before finally smiling over at Jessie again. "I'd really love to come for dinner. Heck, if you want, we can come early, and I can help you cook." She shrugged. "I've become pretty good at that."

"Yeah?" Jessie asked with interest. "Good, 'cause I suck at it." Her smile grew at Heaven's laugh. "No, I don't. But I'd love that. I really, really enjoy your kids. I know I've only seen them a couple times, but…"

"You were the Jessie who gave them money for the candy," Heaven said. "Weren't you?"

Jessie nodded. "I was. I was in the little store to get out of the rain, and in comes a wild Ronin." She chuckled at the memory. "I was standing by the candy counter, and he made it quite clear he was interested."

Heaven laughed and nodded. "That's my son." She took another sip, shaking her head with a smile on her lips. "Chloe was so excited to be my 'big girl' that day."

"That's what she said. She reminded me of me, actually," Jessie mused. "So desperate to be grown and impress."

"Oh," Heaven said softly, meeting Jessie's gaze. "She reminds me of you every single day of her life, Jessie. She's just like you." Her smile grew into that of a loving mother. "She's so smart, so loving and caring. So protective. I've seen her stand up to her father in ways that I see in you all over again…with George."

Left a bit speechless for a moment, Jessie had to look away from those penetrating eyes. She looked down into her coffee, taking a sip simply for something to do to allow her mind to clear for a moment. Lowering her cup to rest on the bench beside her thigh, she said, "She's a lovely young woman. She looks like a younger version of you."

"Except with green eyes," Heaven said softly. "It always amused me. Somehow, she got your eyes."

"Well," Jessie drawled. "I mean, there was the night before and all…" She sent a teasing smile to Heaven, who dissolved into girlish giggles. Jessie grinned.

Chapter Fifteen

1930

It was a two-story house made of brick, perhaps a bit larger than the average house, but overall, it was typical. It certainly wasn't Greyson Manor. There was a covered front portico and a small front lawn. From what Heaven had explained, the majority of the usable yard was in back, behind the detached garage.

Jessie got out of the borrowed car and scrambled to pull open the white garage door. After the Model T was pulled in, the two grabbed the bags they'd packed for their weekend at Granite House, then closed the garage door and headed inside the house.

She did, however, understand why it got its name. An entire wall in the kitchen was made of the stone, as well as a wall in the living room area, which had a fireplace built into it. She'd never seen anything like it.

"Wow," she said, taking it all in.

"Pretty neat, huh?" Heaven grinned as she set down one of the two stuffed picnic baskets Cook had put together for their weekend. Jessie placed the other one next to it on the counter. "I love this house."

"What's the history of it?" Jessie asked, hand on hip now that one of her burdens had been removed.

"My great-grandparents built it when they moved from the East Coast here after immigrating from Scotland. I think Daddy spent a lot of time here growing up, too." Heaven smiled. So lovely, Jessie thought. "I know this house meant a lot to him."

"Well," Jessie said, grinning at Heaven. "Then we'll do our level best to make sure to keep it as pretty as we found it."

Heaven returned the smile as she walked over to Jessie. She shrugged the bag off her shoulder that contained her clothing and toiletries and let it fall to the floor before removing Jessie's from her shoulder. She snaked her arms up around Jessie's neck, fingers playing lightly in the short strands at the nape of her neck.

"I can't believe you did that," Heaven said, amusement in her voice.

"Hey, I'd had enough of Russ that day," Jessie said, knowing full well that what she'd done a couple weeks before was pretty drastic. She'd been so furious with how he'd treated her after such a traumatic event, let alone him daring to believe he controlled her life or destiny. "My mom was so shocked that she couldn't speak for about thirty minutes."

"Oh, I bet!" Heaven leaned up and placed a soft kiss on Jessie's lips. "I like it." She looked at Jessie's face and hair as her fingers continued to play in the short strands. "We do need to clean it up a bit, though. A wee choppy."

"Best I could do in about fifteen seconds." Jessie's heart raced at the physical closeness, Heaven's body pressing against her own.

She'd been so busy dealing with school and things at the house and getting ready for their little getaway that she'd had little time to consider what they'd actually do once they got there. Or the fact that they'd be alone. Things were different now. Heaven was engaged to marry a man. Jessie knew that meant their future together was absolutely gone. So, she didn't know what it meant for their present.

"Well," Heaven said, breaking into Jessie's thoughts. "I can trim it up while we're here, if you want."

"Sure. You don't think it makes me look like a boy?"

Heaven gave her a sexy little grin. "Well, you *are* my boyfriend, right?" She laughed when Jessie rolled her eyes. "No," Heaven said, shaking her head as her fingertip ran along Jessie's cheek. "You absolutely do not look like a boy. You are so utterly beautiful, Jessie. Long hair, short hair, whatever." She left another quick kiss. "You're perfect."

Jessie responded to the deep kiss that Heaven initiated. As much as she was enjoying the fingers in her hair, the beautiful body pressed to her own, and certainly Heaven's amazing mouth on hers, the image of Kingston Rawlins wouldn't stop haunting her mind and her conscience.

Pulling away, she turned and ran shaky hands through her hair, her body alive with arousal but also guilt that she just didn't know what to do with, and it had her deeply troubled. She blew out a long, steadying breath.

"What's wrong?" Heaven asked, sounding rather uncertain.

Jessie turned and met her worried gaze. "Do you love him?"

"I very much hope that's not a real question," Heaven said quietly, hurt in her tone as she hugged herself.

Ignoring the comment—which wasn't much of an answer, in her mind—Jessie said, "Why are you here with me, Heaven? You're engaged to *him*." She turned away again, tears pricking the backs of her eyes. Like so much else, she'd had very little time to truly deal with the profound hurt, sadness and, on some level, betrayal this engagement had conjured. "Why?" she blurted, whirling around again. "Why? Why, damn it?" She slammed her palm down on the counter. The tears came hard and fast, her heart finally shattering into pieces, held together over the months by busywork and denial.

Heaven walked over to her, and even when Jessie tried to push her away, took the sobbing woman in her arms. She said nothing for a long moment, allowing Jessie to get the brunt of the storm out.

Finally, Jessie clung to her, desperately needing to be held by this woman. Out of all the billions of people in the world, only this one person could comfort her, even as she was the only person who could hurt her as deeply as she was hurting.

"I'm here with you," Heaven whispered into the hug at length, her fingers once again stroking Jessie's hair. "Because I love you. Because I need you, and I desperately want to share with you what I want you to have." She left a soft kiss on the head that rested against her shoulder. "I'm engaged to him because we both know that Daddy was the only person stopping this from happening. And, no," she added, pulling away just enough to look at Jessie's tear-streaked face. "I absolutely do not love him." She gave her a small smile. "I don't even much like him."

Jessie gave her a weak smile and nodded. Her heart still hurt, but she knew Heaven was right. They were both trapped. "I'm so sorry for acting like that. Here, of all places." She felt ashamed, as Heaven had done so much to make this weekend possible—defied her mother and borrowed the car of one of the servants, all so they could be together.

Heaven cupped her cheek. "Don't you dare apologize. I'm not the only one affected by this, Jessie." She stoked Jessie's cheek before dropping her hand and stepping out of the embrace. "Take off your ring."

Confused, Jessie looked down at her right hand and the gold and ruby ring Heaven had given her for her sixteenth birthday. It was a ring she never took off. "Why?"

"Take it off," Heaven said again, bringing up her own hands and tugging off the sapphire ring she wore on her right ring finger. Jessie did as asked, Heaven taking her right hand in hers. She gently eased the sapphire ring onto Jessie's right ring finger. Heaven placed Jessie's right hand over her heart, holding it there with her own hands. "With this ring," she said softly. "I give to you my heart, always and forever." She leaned up and left a kiss of promise on Jessie's lips.

Understanding, Jessie took Heaven's right hand in hers and slid her own ring onto Heaven's right ring finger. "With this ring," she said, using Heaven's words, looking deeply into her eyes. "I give to you my heart." She felt tears threatening again, and she tried to swallow them down. "Always and forever." She kissed Heaven's palm before placing it over her heart. "I love you."

"I love you, too," Heaven whispered, resting their foreheads together. "I've loved you since I was five years old." She laughed through her own tears, which had begun to fall, raining down on their joined hands. "When you looked so confused about why this random girl was in your bedroom."

Jessie smiled, remembering that day well. She cupped Heaven's face with her free hand and left a long kiss on her lips. "Come on," she said. "Let's enjoy the house."

❧❧❧❧

After a wonderful dinner prepared specially for them by Cook, the two lay cuddled up on the couch, a fire going in the fireplace. It wasn't entirely cool enough for a fire, but why not? Jessie lay on her back with her head on a pillow, Heaven squeezed in between Jessie's body and the back of the couch.

"So, what if we had a girl?" Heaven asked, continuing their discussion about a future for the two of them in this very house. "Margaret?"

Jessie's face squished up in disagreement. "I knew a Margaret once. Not a nice person."

Heaven chuckled, her fingers lightly tracing random patterns across Jessie's cotton-covered belly. "Okay, no Margaret. Your turn."

Jessie thought for a moment. Children had never been on her radar, as she knew she never wanted to get married. "You know," she said, a face popping into mind. "There was a woman on the ranch where we lived before we came to Colorado. She was so sweet to everyone, regardless of gender or age. Black, white, whatever. Just a damn good person."

"Okay," Heaven said, lifting her head to look down at Jessie, who met her gaze. "What was her name?"

"Chloe."

Heaven smiled, her fingers flirting with the hem of Jessie's shirt. "Chloe," she repeated, as though tasting the name on her tongue. "I like it." Her fingers trailed underneath the shirt, making Jessie lose her breath. "If we ever have a girl, Chloe it'll be."

Jessie could only take shallow breaths as those fingers trailed upward, barely brushing her bra-clad right breast. "You say we'll have a baby, huh?" she barely managed. "You must think I'm pretty darn talented."

Heaven's hand fully cupped her. "I really want to find out," she murmured, lowering her lips to Jessie's. As they kissed, slow and sensual, her hand lightly squeezed the breast, Jessie sighing into the kiss as she arched her back a bit, welcoming the touch. She gasped when her hardening nipple was pinched through the material.

Heaven sighed into their kiss, her hand sliding out from Jessie's shirt as she moved on top of her. Jessie's hand trailed down her back to her skirt-covered behind, pulling Heaven's hips into her own. Their kiss broke as they were both breathing entirely too heavily to continue.

"I have an idea," Jessie said, looking up into Heaven's flushed face. She glanced to her left at the quilt that was draped over the back of the couch. "Let's take that to the floor by the fire."

Heaven nodded, giving her a quick kiss before carefully climbing off her and the couch. As Jessie pulled herself up, Heaven tugged the heavy quilt free and spread it out as best she could. Once it landed, she and Jessie worked together to create a little nest for themselves, including the pillows from the couch.

Jessie was about to lower herself but stopped, frozen. Standing there, her gaze never leaving Jessie's, Heaven began to unbutton her blouse. Jessie was riveted as creamy flesh was revealed, one button at a time. Finally, the blouse was removed, leaving Heaven in her skirt and bra. Jessie's gaze immediately went to the gorgeous breasts that she'd dreamed about so many times over the years, especially after tasting them.

As she watched Heaven begin on her skirt, Jessie's fingers absently went to the men's button shirt she wore, tailored down by her mother to fit her, as she'd made it clear that she'd never go back to women's clothing. It simply wasn't practical for her many jobs in the manor. Heaven pushed her skirt down her beautiful legs and stepped out of it before kicking it aside.

Jessie's heart was racing as Heaven's undergarments were quickly discarded, too, leaving her completely naked. She was stunning, something that Jessie could only have imagined from the endless books she read. Her skin was pale against the darkness of her hair. She knew how soft it was, and she could smell what she'd come to learn was the scent of arousal.

As Heaven lowered herself to the quilt, Jessie hurried to discard the rest of her clothing. She was nervous, no idea what to do, but she'd dreamt of it for years. She realized now that all those times when Heaven would sneak into her bed, even at eight, nine, and ten years old, her closeness and her touch had sparked a need in Jessie that needed to mature, but it had always been there.

Finally naked, Heaven's gaze roaming over her body, which made her even more nervous, Jessie lowered herself to lie next to her. Like a magnet, their lips found each other again. As they kissed, her fingers found one of Heaven's breasts, her thumb brushing across the peak of the rigid nipple before she lightly tugged on it.

Her mouth watered. Leaving Heaven's mouth, Jessie kissed her way down along a soft neck and finally to the breast her hand had just been caressing. She felt those fingers return to her hair as she took her time loving the sensitive breast and nipple with her lips and tongue. The noises that Heaven made egged her on, her body burning.

"Jessie," Heaven whimpered. "Please." She took hold of Jessie's hand and placed it between her legs, and the incredible volcanic wetness there nearly made Jessie groan with her own need. "Please. I want it to be you."

Jessie lifted her head and looked into Heaven's eyes, so much need there. She nodded. "Okay."

Absolutely no clue what she was doing, she decided to let her own passion, and Heaven, guide her. Resting on her side, she held herself up on a forearm and trailed her fingers through the wetness, amazed at how soft yet slick the skin was. Her fingers were guided to Heaven's opening, Jessie's heart jumping at the realization.

Heaven's bare feet slid up the quilt as her knees raised and her legs spread. She draped one leg over Jessie's hip, opening herself even more to Jessie's fingers. Letting her touch guide her, Jessie lowered her lips to Heaven's again, initiating a slow, exploratory kiss as she eased a finger inside

She held her breath right along with Heaven. She pulled back from the kiss and watched the beautiful face carefully for any signs of pain or discomfort. She had no idea what it felt like but had heard the first time could be painful. Heaven seemed to be concentrating on what was happening.

"Are you okay?" Jessie whispered once she was fully inside, mind blown by that fact.

Heaven nodded, tucking her bottom lip beneath her teeth for a moment before releasing it. "Yes."

"Want me to pull out?"

Heaven's eyes slowly opened, though they were hooded. "No." Instead, she lightly began to rock her hips, a subtle invitation.

Jessie eased her finger out to the tip before slowly pushing back in. "So soft," she whispered, amazed as her finger was engulfed by all that made Heaven a woman in her most private place.

She started a slow, careful thrust inside of Heaven, whose hips continued to rock in the same slow rhythm, meeting every thrust with a counterthrust. Heaven's eyes fell closed again, her breathing increasing as she seemed to be feeling pleasure.

"Add another finger, Jessie," she whimpered.

Jessie eased a second finger inside, now pointer and middle fingers. She was amazed by the growing wetness. She was pulsing as she watched Heaven's pleasure grow, her hips rocking a bit faster, which Jessie took to mean she wanted her to thrust a bit faster, so she did.

Jessie was riveted. From Heaven's heaving breasts to the look of ecstasy on her beautiful face to the wonder of her fingers disappearing inside of Heaven's body only to reappear, covered in her desire. Heaven's breathing and whimpers were beginning to come faster and become higher pitched. She grabbed twin handfuls of the quilt beneath her as her head flew back and her eyes squeezed shut. Her cry of release was loud and guttural.

Jessie watched in awe, the need between her legs so great it was almost painful when a fresh wave of warmth flowed around her fingers and palm as Heaven's orgasm flowed from her. Desperate to the point of pain, Jessie gently removed her fingers and then moved so that Heaven's leg was no longer flung over her.

She moved atop her, straddling one of Heaven's thighs, and began to grind against it, her face buried in Heaven's neck. She felt arms wrap around her and, to her surprise, Heaven's hips rocked again against Jessie's own thigh, which was tucked snugly between her legs. Both breathing heavily and whimpering, they moved together.

Heaven held them tightly together as their hips thrust quickly against each other. Suddenly, Jessie's orgasm crashed over and through her with a speed and intensity she'd never experienced in her extremely limited understanding of such release. Her cry was loud, Heaven's joining her for a second time a few thrusts later. Her breathy whimpers in Jessie's ear warmed the skin of the left side of Jessie's face and neck.

Panting, Jessie lifted her head, looking down at Heaven's flushed face, an absolute look of love and wonder in her eyes. Smiling, Jessie cupped her cheek. "I love you," she breathed.

Heaven's smile was wide and beautiful. "I love you, too, my sweet Jessie."

Chapter Sixteen

1945

Jessie absently zipped the ring back and forth across the chain as she stood in her bedroom, only a towel wrapped around her body and hair slicked back from her face after her bath. She smelled good, she hoped. She'd been off from Greyson Manor today, but she'd helped her father catch up on a few things they'd fallen behind on over the previous week, so she'd smelled like a sweaty weed when they got back to the house.

She'd already bought the ingredients they'd need, based upon the meal she and Heaven had decided on. Now, as she stood in front of her wardrobe, she was trying to decide what to wear. Finally, she decided on a pair of her usual tailored-to-fit trousers and a simple short-sleeved button-up, again more tailored to fit her smaller size than the men it was designed for.

She tossed the articles of clothing to her bed and finished drying off her body. It was a little strange to be back at the house but certainly nice to be with her father. She missed him while staying at Greyson Manor. Undergarments tugged on, she rolled on her EverDry antiperspirant before getting dressed the rest of the way.

She was buttoning her shirt when she heard the engine of a car outside. Glancing out her bedroom window that faced the street, she felt her heart jump and palms begin to swat. She wiped them on the thighs of her trousers before grabbing the damp towel she'd discarded and hanging it up in the bathroom.

"Dad, can you get the door?" she called from the bathroom, hearing little feet run up the pathway to the front door.

"Will do," he replied from where he'd been sitting in his recliner, reading the evening post.

Jessie grinned when she heard excited greetings between Dobbs and Heaven and could imagine the excited hug Heaven would offer him. She knew her father was thrilled for tonight's dinner and to meet "the grandkids," even if he tried to play it off as just an ordinary dinner with a few folks over.

She stepped into the living room as her father was down on one knee to meet Ronin proper-like. "Nice to meet you, fella," he said, extending his hand just like she'd always seen him do with anyone.

Ronin took the large hand, which swallowed his. When the little guy noticed Jessie leaning against the archway that separated the living room from the kitchen, he took off, little feet scurrying until he threw himself at her legs, grinning up at her.

"Well, hey, mister!" She reached down and picked him up with a dramatic growl of exertion, setting him on her hip with his little legs straddling her side. One arm tucked under his behind to stabilize him, she tweaked his nose with her free hand. "How are you?"

"Good," he said, eyes bright.

"Yeah? Know what?" She grinned when he shook his head vigorously. "I'm pretty darn sure you've gotten cuter since I saw you last." She outright laughed when he nodded just as vigorously. She gave him a tight hug, making obnoxious noises as she whipped him around a bit before setting the giggling little boy on his feet. When she stood erect again, she found that three sets of eyes were on her. "What?"

Heaven gave her the sweetest smile as she walked over and took her into a hug. "Hey," she said.

"Hi." Jessie noticed, not for the first time, how good Heaven smelled. She closed her eyes as she quietly inhaled, smelling her perfume and shampoo. She was about to let go but was surprised that Heaven continued the hug for a moment longer than need be. Finally, they parted, sharing a shy smile.

"Hey, Jessie," Chloe said, stepping up to her.

"I'm guessing you don't want to be picked up and whipped around, too, so I hope a hug will do."

The girl grinned and nodded. "Yes. A hug is fine."

Jessie gave her a warm hug, feeling a maternal spark whenever she was near the young woman. It was strange, yet so comfortingly familiar. The young woman, for her part, seemed to feel incredibly comfortable around her, too. Her hugs were warm and tight, her smile genuine and sweet.

"How are you, sweetheart?" Jessie asked once the hug ended. Never one for random endearments, but Jessie found that Chloe and her brother brought them out of her.

"Really good!" the girl exclaimed, excitement in her eyes. "I got asked to the school dance."

Jessie eyed her. "I see," she hedged, teasing sternness in her voice. She looked past Chloe to Heaven, who was watching them. "I'm thinkin' I need to get my shotgun and meet this fella," she said, an exaggerated accent to her voice, which made Heaven smile and Chloe giggle. She smiled at Chloe. "Don't grow up too fast," she said softly. She left a kiss on the side of the girl's head. "Alright," she said, clapping her hands. "Who's ready to cook?"

꧁꧂

"And, so," Jessie exclaimed through her laughter, Heaven covering her face with her hands and Chloe laughing in delight. "Here comes your mom, just a skippin' along, no care in the world." Jessie pantomimed said action around the kitchen. "Meanwhile, about fourteen thousand buckets of water are falling from the sky every second. I mean, literally, with every skip, water is sloshing out of her socks and shoes.

"Oh no!" Chloe laughed.

"Oh yeah," Jessie assured her. "But it gets better. So, we finally make it to the house, and your grandfather Harv is standing there. Hands on hips and an eyebrow raised." She mimicked the pose. "He looks down at us and says, 'Gee, honey. I warned you about the storm.' Your mom." Jessie reached up and pretended to peel away a curtain of soggy bangs from in front of her face, then looked up as if looking into Harv's face. "'It's just a little drizzle,' she insists."

Chloe erupted in high-pitched laughter from where she stood at the stove, stirring the gravy that she'd been assigned to. "Just a little drizzle." Her laughter started all over again.

"Hey now," Heaven said, also laughing. "I was ten!" Hand to hip, she sent a playful glare to Jessie, who was working on mashed potatoes. "Now, let's tell some stories about—"

"Nope!" Jessie hurried over to her and grabbed her from behind, lightly placing a hand over her mouth. She glanced at a giggling Chloe from over Heaven's shoulder. "I was a perfect little angel, never did a thing wrong."

Heaven reached up and lifted the hand away just enough to say, "She's lying," before replacing it, which sent Chloe into even more laughter.

"We think you ladies are having way too much fun in here," Dobbs said, he and Ronin stepping in from the backyard. He looked at all three women, hands on hips. Jessie smiled as little Ronin imitated his position, looking up at the older man as if to make sure he was doing it right.

Jessie moved her hand away, but for some reason, not her body. Curiously, neither did Heaven, who rather leaned back a bit into her. As if it was the most natural thing to do, Jessie's hand rested on Heaven's waist.

"Oh," she said conversationally. "Just telling Chloe stories about growing up at the house with her mom."

"Did you tell her the story about the rain?" he said, eyebrows raised in amusement.

Again, Heaven's hands came up to cover her face as she groaned.

⁂

Jessie held her cards in the hand that rested on the table, her other one resting on the leg of her little buddy who decided he wanted to be her poker partner. She explained to him in a quiet tone so the other three players couldn't hear, what each card was and what she could or couldn't do with them at present.

"So," she murmured next to his ear. "You see those?" She brought her other hand up so Ronin was essentially in the cocoon of her embrace, using her finger to tap the three cards she held with the number two on them. "We need to get that number but with the puppies' feet," she explained. That's how she'd described the symbol of clubs to him. "Then we can lay our cards down." She looked at him. "Make sense?"

Ronin met her gaze and nodded vigorously as he slid yet another pretzel off their pile, quickly taking a bite out of it.

Jessie raised an eyebrow. "If you keep eating our winnings, we'll have nothing left to brag about!" She grinned at his *uh-oh* look, as well as the laughter around the table.

※ ※ ※ ※

"Dad," Jessie whispered, a sleeping Ronin in her arms, his little head resting on her shoulder. "Can you help Chloe carry the leftovers to their car, please?"

Dobbs instantly jumped into action as the girl gathered the containers that Jessie and Heaven had packed for the family of three. Heaven was cleaning up the poker game, gathering cards and wiping down the table from pretzel salt and crumbs.

Jessie swayed gently back and forth with her bundle to make sure he didn't wake up. It had been a long afternoon into evening, and it was past his bedtime. Having Heaven and the kids at the house had felt... She tried to think about just exactly how it had felt. It had felt like home, even as she was in her own house. It had felt right, like the family had been brought back together with all the members now, with the kids.

Now, winding the night down so that Heaven could take her children home, she felt sad. Her heart was heavy, and it felt like—as dramatic as it sounded—

her family was being torn from her again. It left her unsettled.

"Okay," Chloe said, she and Dobbs coming back into the house. "Car's loaded, Mom."

"Okay, sweetie," Heaven said from the sink, where she was rinsing out the rag she'd used on the table. She wrung it out and slapped it over the sink before turning to look around the kitchen and table. She met Jessie's gaze. "Well," she said softly. "Guess everything's cleaned up."

"You didn't have to help with dishes and everything, Heaven," Jessie said, lightly rubbing Ronin's back as she continued to sway with him. "Honestly."

"I wasn't going to leave that for you," Heaven said, walking over to her. She smiled as she looked at her son, her hand joining in the rubbing of his back. "He's out."

"Like a light." The two shared a smile. "And, I would have just made Dad do the dishes," Jessie quipped, both knowing she was teasing.

Heaven met her gaze for a long moment before looking away. "Well, I guess I better get these two home. Want me to take him?"

"Nope," Jessie said. "I'll follow you out."

Dobbs turned to Chloe as Heaven and Jessie walked toward the front door. He gave Chloe a tight hug before turning to Heaven, holding her for a long moment. Jessie was so moved, as it looked for all the world like he was hugging his own flesh-and-blood daughter. She hugged him right back, eyes closed as she seemed to relish the fatherly affection.

He kissed the top of her head before releasing her. "Don't you be a stranger no more," he chided gently, his voice a bit gruffer than usual with emotion.

Heaven gave him a winning smile. "I promise."

Dobbs simply gently ruffled Ronin's hair as Jessie followed Heaven out the door and into the late evening, which was cooling down from the pleasant day. Chloe had already opened the back door of the car and stood aside as Jessie slowly lowered her sleeping bundle to lie on the back seat.

"Good night, little man," she whispered, leaning in and leaving a kiss on the side of his head before standing upright and closing the car door as quietly as possible. Turning to Chloe, she gave her a tight hug, which was returned. "Thanks for coming, hon," she said into it. She smiled when she felt a nod.

Releasing Jessie, the teen smiled up at her before climbing into the front passenger seat. Jessie closed the door once she was safely settled inside the car. Turning, she saw Heaven standing there. For just a moment, they looked at each other.

Without a word, Heaven stepped up to her, Jessie's eyes falling closed at the embrace. She held the smaller woman to her. It was a hug that seemed to last forever yet not long enough. The warmth against her was so familiar. Though the perfume was different, the soap and shampoo different, the essence was the same.

She smiled at the small sigh she heard released near her ear and fought herself against answering in kind. Instead, she hugged Heaven a bit tighter before easing out of the hug. She smiled at her, bringing up a hand to brush hair out of Heaven's face as the light breeze had picked up a few midnight strands with it.

"Drive home safe, okay?" she said.

Heaven nodded, finally dropping her hands from where they'd rested on Jessie's shoulders. "I will." She leaned up and placed a soft kiss on Jessie's cheek.

"Good night," she whispered into it.

Jessie said nothing as she watched the other woman walk around the car to the driver's side. A quick glance over the car and Heaven was gone, climbing in behind the wheel. Jessie raised a hand in a blanket goodbye to those in the car, then headed back to the house. Reaching the front porch, she was surprised when she heard her name.

Turning, she saw the passenger door hanging open and Chloe running over to her. Concerned, she asked, "Everything okay?"

"Oh yeah," the teen said. "Yeah, I just…" She looked down at her fidgeting hands, her lower lip tucked beneath her front teeth for a moment, just like her mother. She met Jessie's gaze again. "I just wanted to let you know that I have never seen my mom like this. Ever. My brother and I try, but she's always so sad, so stressed." A beautiful smile spread across her lovely young face. "But tonight, to see her smile like that and laugh and just be silly…" She looked away, but not before Jessie saw the glisten of tears in her eyes. "It just meant everything to me."

Understanding, Jessie gathered the girl in her arms again. "I get it. Your mom is a very strong woman," she told her. "Don't count her out."

Chloe nodded into the hug. "I'm so glad you came into our lives, Jessie. Well." She snorted, looking up at her. "Back into my mom's life, I guess." Her expression turned serious for a moment, her eyebrows furrowing. "I don't know what it is, but there's something so familiar about you for me. It's weird."

Jessie grinned, not feeling it was her place to fill in any history for the girl. "I'm just amazing like that."

Chloe's smile was big and bright. She nodded,

pulling out of the hug. "I gotta go. But, just wanted to say thanks."

"Anytime, kiddo."

Chloe turned and jogged back to the car, climbing in before it slowly began to back out of the long gravel driveway. Again, Jessie raised her hand, Heaven returning the wave. A heavy sigh fell from Jessie's lips as she shoved her hands into the pockets of her trousers. She felt sad as she watched her heart, three times over, drive away.

Chapter Seventeen

1930

With an absolutely and nearly overwhelming feeling of foreboding, Jessie's eyes slid open. She was naked and in Heaven's canopy bed at Greyson Manor. And, she noted, she was alone. Rolling from her back to her side, she reached over and parted the canopy curtains to see that it was early morning, the sun just beginning to rise.

Allowing the curtain to fall back into place, she flopped back down to stare up at the underside of the canopy. Her eyes closed as her hands came up to cover her face. "How am I going to survive this?" she whispered into them.

It was the big day, as it were. She and Heaven had graduated from high school just the day before and had spent the night together not celebrating, but trying to squeeze in as much time together as they possibly could before Heaven was to marry Kingston Rawlins in the afternoon. They'd spent their last night together alternating between crying and making love, then starting all over again.

Blowing out a breath, she removed her hands and sat up. Running her hands through her hair, she squeezed her eyes shut. She could smell Heaven on her fingers. Hell, she could smell her all over her body. She could still feel Heaven's touch inside her as well as outside.

They'd begun to understand passion weeks ago at the Granite House, but last night had taken things to another level. It had been a passion born of desperation, a need for them both to possess. Now, it was inevitable. She shoved the covers back and scooted her way to the edge of the bed and pushed the curtain aside.

The huge bedroom was empty, though the bathroom door was closed and she could see light beneath it. Jessie followed the trail of her clothing, tugging on her undergarments as she came to them, followed by her trousers and then the button shirt that Heaven had nearly torn off her body.

The bathroom door opened as Jessie shrugged into the garment, not even having a chance to button it before Heaven reached her. She was in nothing more than her silky dressing gown, which flowed around her nakedness as she walked to her. They shared a slow kiss, filled with all the love they shared.

After it came to a natural end, Heaven was quiet for a long moment. "I don't want to do this," she whispered, her face buried in Jessie's neck. "God, I don't want to."

Jessie held her, her hand cupping the back of the dark head, their bodies flush as they stood near the bed they'd shared the night before. "I know," she whispered. She felt Heaven's fingers grab fistfuls of her shirt in a desperate hold. She felt as though the other woman was desperately trying to ground herself by clinging to Jessie. "It'll be okay." She didn't believe a word of it, but she had to say it.

Heaven shook her head. "No, it won't!" She pulled away from Jessie, bringing her hands up to wipe at her tears. The massive stone of her engagement ring caught the incoming light through the windows. "I hate this."

She looked to Jessie, eyes tortured and filling with fresh tears all over again. "I know you'll go on," she said, her voice thick with emotion. "You'll be gone."

Jessie gave her a smile, though she knew it was pitiful. Shaking her head, she said, "I told you, I won't leave. I promised." She left a kiss on Heaven's lips, salty from her tears. Resting their foreheads together, she caressed Heaven's cheek. "I love you. Never forget that."

The door to Heaven's bedroom opened, Eliza standing there in her dressing gown, hair already full of pins and rollers for the day's events. Her mouth fell open when she spotted the two, who slowly moved apart as, without a word, Eliza stepped inside the room, slamming the door behind her.

Her mouth closed and eyes narrowed as she took them in. It was clear that Heaven was naked beneath the thin gown, and with Jessie's shirt hanging open with only her bra beneath, something was amiss. Eliza took it all in.

"I think it's time for you to go now, Jessica," she said, her voice low and dangerous.

Jessie quickly buttoned her shirt and reached down to grab her boots when a hand shot out to cover her arm, Heaven's grip like a vise. She looked from the hand to Heaven's profile.

"And I think you need to mind your own business, Mother," Heaven all but growled.

"Excuse me?" Eliza said, taking a step forward.

"I said, I think you need to mind your own business. Haven't you done enough?"

"Don't talk to me that way," Eliza bit out. "I'm your mother! You never talk to me that way."

"What are you going to do?" Heaven raged. "Sell us both to the highest bidder? Oh wait!" Her laugh was almost manic. "Silly me. Get out!" She charged at the older woman, who fell back against the door. "I don't want you there today! I don't want you in my life. Ever!"

Jessie watched, stunned, as Eliza blindly reached behind her for the doorknob. Even as her face was hard as stone, tears were trailing down her cheeks. She took one last look at her daughter, then at Jessie, before she turned and left the room.

※ ※ ※ ※

An hour later, Jessie was bathed and changed into fresh clothing. She worked without comment, without even a basic greeting in the kitchen. A very special breakfast had to be made, after all. Jessie headed into the pantry to get the flour Cook had asked for.

Numb and essentially a walking shell, she dutifully went to the pantry with the measuring cup and bowl she'd been given. She grabbed the forty-pound bag of flour, which was new and needed to be cut open. Using the knife she'd brought with her, Jessie began to saw at the gingham bag, but the blade slipped, slicing her finger.

"Goddamn it!" she roared, looking at the blood that was beading up on the cut. Suddenly, absolute rage filled her. "Damn it!" she exclaimed, slamming the blade of the knife down on the butcher-block countertop at the center of the large room. "Damn it, damn it, damn it!"

Before she could even understand what she was doing, she began to stab at the hard surface, the tears as hot and fast as the blood on her finger, which was spreading everywhere with her frantic stabbings into the butcher block.

"Why!" she cried. "Why!"

"Stop. Jessie, Stop!"

Jessie tried to fight the person who was struggling with her to get the knife out of her hand. She was sobbing, loud and bitter, as the knife was removed from her bloody fingers and set atop the workspace. She was gathered into the soft, motherly embrace of a woman, her head guided to rest against a full bosom.

"I know, honey," the voice, which she recognized as Cook's, said. "I'm so, so sorry."

Jessie clung to her. "Why?" she asked again.

"Because that man don't know nothin' about love," she replied, gently rocking Jessie. "And," she continued, her tone quiet, for Jessie's ears only. "Miss Eliza is weak." She caressed Jessie's hair as she held her. "Anybody with eyes see the love between you and Miss Heaven. Just ain't right." She left a kiss on Jessie's head. "But," she added. "It's gonna be okay, girl. I promise."

❧ ❧ ❧ ❧

Cook had magically found a full day's worth of errands for Jessie to run and a borrowed car to run them in. She didn't return to Greyson Manor until late that night, by which time the wedding was over, the after-celebrations were over, and Heaven was gone. She was off on her new life, a life without Jessie.

Life went on, as it always does. Jessie was shocked to find that she and her family still had jobs after Heaven was gone, but she wasn't about to look a gift horse in the mouth, even if she hated the bastard. Strangely enough, George Russ left her alone about her hair and clothing choices. He made it clear he didn't like it, but in a weird way, she had the feeling he respected her for standing up to him.

Most bullies, after all, are usually cowards, sheep in wolf's clothing. In this case, a three-piece suit. She didn't care. She worked hard every day, to the point of exhaustion, then went home to the gardener's cottage and did her chores there before reading and going to bed.

The summer flew by, the leaves turning their menagerie of colors. It was normally something she loved and found so stunning, but this year, she only saw shades of gray. All color had left with Heaven.

Until that one day in the autumn that Kingston Rawlins showed up, requesting her employment in his home.

Something she found interesting after spending so many years at Greyson Manor was that any other home seemed to pale in comparison, regardless of how rich, large, or expansive it may be. The same could be said of her first glimpse of Kingston's house. It was large, certainly beautiful, if you were into the dark, moody style. But it lacked the character and grandeur of the Manor.

At first glance, to Jessie, it just seemed ostentatious. She was led through the house by a pretty little redhead named Mimi. She looked to be somewhere in her twenties, was a maid in the house, and in her soft little voice had told Jessie she'd be there to help in any way she could to help her settle in. Her flirtatious blue eyes seconded her words.

Jessie simply thanked her with a nod and was left alone. The room she'd be staying in was small, around the size of the one she'd had at the ranch as a girl before coming to Colorado. The absolute bare basics, which was fine with her. She didn't need a ton of space, as she'd only be in there to sleep, anyway.

Her bedroom was connected by a Jack-and-Jill bathroom to the room that would be the nursery. It was already set up with what the baby would need when it came in another four and a half months: crib, changing table, wardrobe, rocking chair. As far as she knew, she'd only be there throughout the rest of the pregnancy, then no doubt a proper nanny would be brought in and likely moved into the room Jessie was currently set up in.

Her luggage had been brought in by the senator's driver and was waiting in the room to be unpacked. Mimi had offered, but Jessie had declined. A knock on the bedroom door garnered Jessie's attention as she opened the first of the two trunks. "Come in."

The door opened and Heaven stepped inside. The two hadn't seen each other since the morning of her wedding day, back in June. And now, they were entering the month of Thanksgiving and Heaven's eighteenth birthday. It was the longest they'd ever gone without seeing each other since they'd first met.

Jessie stared at her, not sure what to say. This woman before her, who she loved more than her next breath, was now married and pregnant. The mere thought of what had happened in order for her to get in that condition made Jessie want to throw up. What should she say? What should she do?

Heaven was as beautiful as ever, just the tiniest indication that she was expecting visible through the dress she wore, a simple frock in dark blue. "Thank you for coming," Heaven said, her voice quiet, sounding as unsure as Jessie felt.

"Yeah. Of course." The air between them was heavy, tense. "Um," Jessie managed with a small shrug.

"How are you?"

Heaven said nothing, simply walked over to her and took Jessie's arms, pushing them out from her body before she stepped into the space made between them. A small smile quirking Jessie's lips, she enfolded the smaller woman in her arms, eyes sliding closed at the solid, familiar warmth. This wasn't one of her endless dreams that she'd had over the months, beautiful and filled with smiles and kisses, only to wake up alone as reality crashed over her yet again.

No, Heaven was in her arms. Yes, this was a borrowed hug, as she now belonged to someone else, till death do they part. Even so, she continued to wear Heaven's ring, which she'd put on a chain around her neck to keep safe. She'd noticed Heaven still wore her ring, as well as his. But things were different now. She had to be there in the capacity of her friend, nothing more.

That was made quite clear to her when a couple weeks later, Kingston had cornered her down in the basement where the wash was done. She was loading the electric washing machine with her own clothing.

"Well, there you are," he said with a little smile. "For a moment there, when I couldn't find you anywhere, I thought perhaps you'd decided to leave us."

"Nope," she said. "Still here."

"So, listen," he said, all business. "I'm sure by now you've seen that I run quite a tight ship here, lots of rowers, as it were, to keep things moving in the intermittent weeks that I'm in DC, doing the country's business."

"Yes, sir," she said, meeting his gaze, which wasn't cruel like George Russ in demeanor and words, but he certainly wasn't Harv, with his easy smile and teasing nature. His was hard, watchful, reading every movement, every tic of the person he spoke to. He reeked of opportunism and entitlement.

"I don't like problems. I don't like issues, and I don't like drama. With all the people who must work together here in a cohesive unit, it's easy for problems to flare up. I'd greatly appreciate it if you'd kind of keep an eye on things for me." He shrugged, nonchalant, no big deal. "Just make sure everyone is swimming the same way, and if not, let me know so I can fix any problems before they begin."

She studied his face, trying to read between the lines, if there were any. With men like Kingston, there was often an entire novel between the lines. But he was good—a politician, after all. Seemed so sincere. "Alright," she finally said. "I can do that."

"Wonderful." He gave her a genuine smile and slapped her on the shoulder. "I'll leave you to it. I'm heading back to DC in the morning, bright and early."

"Safe travels, sir," she said, watching him go before returning her attention to her task.

❧ ❧ ❦ ❦

1931

"My god!" Heaven gently turned Jessie's face to the side, her gaze troubled. "How hard did she hit you with her door?"

Jessie smirked from where she sat on the bed next to Heaven, who was nursing a two-month-old Chloe. "Well, hard enough to give me a hell of a shiner."

"I'm so sorry. Come here." Heaven urged Jessie to lean forward as Heaven left the softest of kisses on the bruised skin around her eye and then at the bridge of her nose, which held the cut from the smack that nearly knocked her out. "So sorry," Heaven murmured, her fingers caressing Jessie's cheek. "I guess it's a real battleground out there to get Chloe material so I can make her diapers."

Jessie grinned, able to see the teasing in dark eyes. "So it would seem."

She'd been living at the house and working as Heaven's "personal servant" for almost seven months. They hadn't had sex since she'd arrived, partly because Jessie wasn't okay with it, and partly because she had the distinct feeling that the walls had ears and maybe even eyes.

It would seem that Kingston had set up a round robin firing squad among the staff. He'd taken each person aside, told them he'd given them his "special trust," and had asked them to "keep an eye out." Jessie didn't think they were safe to do anything beyond their obvious and known bond as "best friends." As two women, they could get away with far more physical contact than if she were a man or they were both men. After all, women were known to have special affectionate bonds. But Jessie didn't see any reason to push the envelope from affection to sexual touch—not when she felt Kingston had pitted the staff against each other.

This time of night was Jessie's favorite. It was just the three of them, no servants bothering Heaven. Dinner was done, any instructions she needed to give for the night or next morning were complete, and the house was quiet. It was their time, their time to be a family.

Heaven reclined against stacked pillows in her

bed, one that Kingston rarely shared. In seven months, Jessica could literally count on one hand the number of weeks he'd actually been there. Once the baby was born, he hadn't mentioned Jessie leaving, so she didn't remind him. She'd stayed on and helped Heaven raise her daughter.

"She's so beautiful," she said softly, not wanting to disturb the newborn, her puckered little lips wrapped around Heaven's left nipple, sucking in cute little sounds as she took in nourishment. Jessie brushed her fingers over the silky soft smattering of dark hair sprinkled across Chloe's head.

"What was that little song you were singing to her the other day?" Heaven asked, glancing over at Jessie, who had cuddled up to the pair.

Jessie looked shyly at her. "You heard that, huh?"

"I did!" Her smile was beautiful. "Please sing it. I want to learn it so I can sing it to her, too."

Feeling a bit nervous, she cleared her throat and began to sing in a quiet voice:

It's a beautiful, beautiful day
The sun is shining on our way!
The road is long, so we'll sing our song
Until everything is okay.

The look on Heaven's face was so soft, so much love in her eyes once Jessie finished her little song. "Come here," she whispered.

Jessie leaned the few inches between them and accepted the kiss Heaven gave her. It was a simple kiss, not deepened or passionate but that said so much. She smiled. "I love you," she whispered back.

Heaven's smile widened. "And I love you." She looked down at the baby, who seemed to be done. "Would you mind?" she asked.

"Not at all. Baby girl is fed and ready for bed." Jessie smiled at Heaven. A quick glance to the closed bedroom door and she stole another quick kiss before easing the tiny bundle from Heaven's breast and gathering her in her arms. "I'll let you get some sleep."

"No," Heaven said, shaking her head. "Would you mind terribly grabbing me a little juice from downstairs?"

"Absolutely." Jessie carefully moved off the bed. "Be back in a jiffy."

Jessie loved putting Chloe down for sleep, though her favorite time of day was getting her up in the morning and seeing that precious face first thing. Heaven took care of her throughout the night, as only she could breastfeed her. It worked out well, Jessie making sure Heaven got enough sleep during the day, sometimes napping with her.

"Good night, my precious girl," she whispered, kissing the softness of Chloe's forehead as she lay her down in her crib after changing her britches. She'd take the soiled diaper downstairs to the pail she kept them in until morning, when she washed them. "I love you."

The house was quiet and dark as she made her way downstairs, careful to not make noise so as not to wake up any of the other sleeping staff. As she reached the first floor, balled-up diaper in hand, she slowed as she thought she heard something. She listened, trying to hear beyond the clicking of the grandfather clock that ticked away the time in the sitting room.

There it was again. As quietly as she could, she walked toward the formal dining room, entered either via an archway from the hallway or swinging door from the kitchen. She was near the archway but kept out of sight, which wasn't hard to do in the deep shadows of the house at nearly ten at night.

She was stunned to see Mimi bent over the table, the skirt of her maid's dress pushed up to reveal her shapely behind. Kingston stood behind her, trousers down around his thighs as his hips slowly thrust into her from behind. What she'd been hearing was the soft moans coming from the redhead as well as groans of pleasure from the man married to the woman she loved.

He wasn't even supposed to be home. How many times had he claimed to be in DC, when in fact he was here? Was he here simply to fuck the maid, or did he also hang out, unannounced, unobserved, to spy for himself?

Chapter Eighteen

Here's your material, miss," the man behind the counter said, giving her a smile.

Luckily, she'd bought enough from him over the months that he no longer looked strangely at her dress and hair. She took her wrapped bundle and the change and looked around. She tapped her fingers on the counter before she met the older, balding man's eyes again. "Are you hiring here, by any chance, Mr. Beason?"

He studied her for a moment. "You know I got grown men who need jobs, miss." His tone wasn't unkind. "Why should I hire you?"

"Because I may very well have a single mom with me soon who needs to eat, as does her baby." She held up the bundle. "And needs diapers."

He looked down at the bundle on the counter, as well as the chocolate bar Jessie had purchased with it. It was Heaven's favorite treat. "You been real good to me these past weeks," he said, eyeing her again. "If you need a job, you come back and we'll see what we can do. No promises."

"Yes, sir!" Jessie smiled big, gathering her purchases in her arms and nodding a thanks to him before leaving.

It was a lovely May afternoon, and Jessie had a bit of hope. It had been three days since she'd seen Kingston and Mimi in the dining room. She hadn't said anything to Heaven about it, not entirely sure what to do. But she felt that maybe she was developing a plan for them to get out.

"Well, hello there."

Jessie was snapped out of her thoughts by a female voice. She glanced over to see the blonde from just a week before. Though her bruising was beginning to fade, they were still visible. The woman sat on the stoop of the building, smoking a cigarette.

"How's the face?" she asked.

Jessie walked over to her, shrugging. "Still attached," she said, giving the seated woman a sheepish grin.

"So I see. You remember me, right?" the woman asked, her dress dark green with little white flowers all over it.

"I do, but I don't remember your name. I apologize."

The woman patted the stoop next to her. "Molly."

Jessie took a seat and nodded. "Nice to meet you again, Molly. Jessie."

"I'm really sorry about that, Jessie," Molly said, an apologetic smile on her pretty face. "I'm glad you're okay."

"It's okay. I should've been watching where I was going."

Molly nodded at the bundle in Jessie's arms. "More diapers?" At Jessie's nod she asked, "For your little one?"

"No, not exactly. My best friend's baby. Chloe." She couldn't keep the smile off her face. "The baby is Chloe."

"That's sweet," Molly said, taking another drag from the hand-rolled smoke.

"Hey," Jessie said, an idea popping into her head. She nodded at the building behind them. "Are there any apartments available in there?"

"Sure are," Molly said, eyeing Jessie. "Guy moved out just yesterday."

Jessie nodded. "Interesting."

"You lookin' for a place?" Molly asked. "Rent's reasonable. Relatively safe, I suppose." She smiled at Jessie and playfully nudged her shoulder with her own. "Be good to have a neighbor to trust won't try and attack you."

Jessie chuckled as she pushed to her feet. "Yeah, well, I can't exactly say the same thing."

Molly laughed. "True enough. Have a good day, Jessie. Give that little one a squeeze for me."

Amused, Jessie got on her way. "You, too, and will do."

As Jessie drove to the Rawlins house, she felt emboldened. She felt hopeful and like there was a way out for them. They weren't stuck under this man's thumb, and she sure as hell couldn't stand by and watch the way he treated Heaven. Yes, it was true she didn't want to see them together, but the level of neglect was pretty incredible, only for him to be having sex with a member of the house staff right under Heaven's nose.

What kind of man acted that way? She ran her hand through her hair as she drove, the window open to allow in the pleasant spring air. "An entitled one," she muttered.

She reached the house, her heart beginning to race, both with nerves and anticipation of sharing her news with Heaven. Gathering her goods for the baby and the special treat for her mother, Jessie climbed out of the truck and made her way to the house.

As always, she went in through the back entrance, which was largely used by the house staff, and the first thing she saw was Mimi. Granted, this time she was fully dressed and bent over a piece of furniture, but she blushed just the same. She'd done her level best to avoid the pretty young redhead since that night, and she'd been fairly successful.

Now, Mimi was polishing silver in a small room off the kitchen where it was all kept on shelves and in cabinets. Jessie planned to pass on by but stopped when she heard her name. Mentally groaning, she took the couple steps back until she stood in the open doorway, the smell of silver polish meeting her nose.

"Yes?" she said.

The young maid, dressed in her usual uniform, hair pulled back from her face with barrettes, met Jessie's gaze with her own sad one. "We all have to make our choices," she said, her voice quiet, for Jessie's ears alone. "Sometimes you have to do the extra to get the extras."

Jessie wasn't sure what to say. "Um," she managed, feeling very uncomfortable. "I'm not sure what you're talking about." No clue if it was the wise road to take, but perhaps if she feigned innocence…

Mimi gave her a bitter smile. "I know you saw us," she said. "And so does he. Be careful." The warning in her tone was clear but not spiteful. "He knows you love her."

Jessie's heart fell and her blood went cold, flowing through her veins until a little chill made its way down her spine. She knew that the mistrusting environment that Kingston had created in the house was meant to keep everyone divided and thus less likely to gang up in any real, meaningful way. So, she felt she had to take Mimi's warning with a grain of salt, but she also felt she needed to keep it tucked into the back of her mind.

Night had fallen once again, and her favorite time of day with Heaven had arrived. The lovely young mother was on the bed, nursing Chloe. Jessie watched, fascinated and enchanted. How on earth had this woman that she loved so very much not only develop the tiny little human within her body, but then gave birth to her, and now her body, once again, was nourishing her?

"It's an absolute miracle," she murmured, looking down at the paleness of Heaven's swollen breast that baby Chloe's hand rested on as she had her dinner. She met Heaven's contented gaze. "What a woman can do." She shook her head in wonder.

"She amazes me every day," Heaven said, using her free hand to lightly caress her daughter's chubby little cheek.

"So," Jessie began, a little nervous how Heaven would take her news and her proposal. "I have a plan and wanted to run it by you."

Heaven looked at her. "A plan? For what?"

"To get us out of here," Jessie said slowly, looking into Heaven's eyes to try to gauge her thoughts or feelings on what she was saying.

"What? What do you mean?"

"Get you out of this," Jessie said, indicating the bedroom and house beyond. "You, me, and Chloe. We can start over, as a family. Nobody telling us what to do, holding anything over our heads—"

"I can't do that, Jessie," Heaven interrupted, her voice hard.

Jessie literally moved a bit away from her as

though she'd been struck. Stunned, she stared at her. She wasn't just surprised by the words, but the tone was unusual. Gone was the warmth and love that was always there when she spoke to Jessie. In its place was a hard coldness that sounded far more like Eliza.

"Why?"

Chloe finished nursing, and Heaven didn't respond for a moment as she carefully pulled the baby away from her breast and set her on the bed beside her before she reclosed her nightgown. Other than handling the baby, her movements were jerky, as if she was irritated.

"Why, Heaven?" Jessie asked again.

"Because I can't," Heaven said, voice flat. Her entire demeanor had changed. The adoring looks and loving tone—gone. Now, she wouldn't even look Jessie in the eye.

"Look," Jessie said, deciding to give more information. Perhaps that was it—Heaven was worried. "I found a place that will hire me. I can get a job, and I know of an apartment we can rent—"

"No." Heaven's look was just as hard as that one word as she glared at Jessie before she once again took Chloe in her arms and climbed off the bed, as Jessie had done. They now stood on opposite sides of the bed.

"I don't understand," Jessie said, almost more to herself than Heaven.

"What's to understand?" Heaven murmured, bringing Chloe up to her shoulder to burp her. "I belong here, and I'm staying."

Jessie just stood there stupidly, unable to move, almost unable to breathe. She started when the bedroom door opened, the knob lightly bumping against the inside wall as it did. She turned to see Kingston enter, all smiles and greetings.

"Well, if it isn't the best friends," he said.

Heaven glanced at him over her shoulder as she continued to gently yet rhythmically pat Chloe's back. Jessie swallowed down the instant vitriol that came to mind. She was disgusted with him, plus so many more feelings and thoughts. She couldn't allow that to show in her expression, so she managed a smile, as weak as it was.

"Good evening, Mr. Rawlins."

"So, best friend," he said, ignoring her greeting. "I'd like you to do your duty and take the baby." He nodded in the general direction of Heaven and Chloe. "I'd like some time with my wife," he added with a wink. "After all, I haven't been back here in weeks."

Oh, how she wanted to claw the lying bastard's eyes out! She nodded. "Yes, sir." She walked over to Heaven and, desperately trying to hold back tears, held it together as the two women carefully exchanged the baby from one set of arms to the other. Jessie immediately continued the burping as she made her way to the bedroom door. She said nothing as she closed it behind her.

She made it to the nursery just before the tears came in earnest. She shut them safely in as her hand kept up its patting, but her head fell back against the hard, cool wood of the door. She'd been doing her level best to go along, winning and losing some of the battles with the belief that eventually she'd win the war. But now, that seemed tenuous, at best.

She walked over to the rocking chair, sitting down and gently rocking herself and Chloe. She smiled when finally a little burp escaped the baby's lips. Chloe was still and didn't fuss, so Jessie kept gently rocking, comforting them both. She rubbed the baby's back with her fingers as her mind began to drift.

Her stomach was rolling like high tide as her dread built. She heard something, her thoughts coming to an end as she focused on the sound. Her eyes squeezed shut and the tears began again when she realized it was the telltale rhythmic squeaking of the bedsprings in Heaven and Kingston's room not far down the hall.

She cupped the baby's head and brought her in to hold her close. Her own tears rained down over her own fingers and the top of Chloe's head. "It's a beautiful day, a beautiful day," she began to sing softly as the tears continued. "The sun is coming our way!" She gently held Chloe out from her to look into her sweet face. "The road is long, so we'll sing our song, baby Chloe..." She left a kiss on her forehead. "I love you, baby girl." She smiled as the two-month-old stuck her little tongue out of little lips for a moment before she settled back into sleep. "I'm sorry." She hugged Chloe to her again, one last time.

❧ ❧ ❧ ❧

Exhausted, as she'd slept little to none the night before, Jessie headed down to the kitchen in the early morning hours just before dawn. Her knapsack, packed with as much as she could stuff into it, was slung over one shoulder. She knew the man who delivered the day's meat products would arrive soon.

Her plan was to get a ride with him into town, then hitch another ride to Greyson Manor. She knew her mother would understand why she was leaving. As expected, the kitchen staff was already up and working, preparing for breakfast but also planning out the meals for the day. They all pretty much ignored her as they were focused on their work.

Jessie was, however, glad to see the woman she was looking for. "Hey," she said, the redhead turning to look at her from where she was gathering cleaning supplies to begin her own tasks. "I need to talk to you for a second."

The maid glanced at the knapsack Jessie carried, as well as the coat she wore over her clothing. "Sure."

The two went into the hallway near the dining room but away from prying ears of the kitchen. Mimi crossed her arms over her chest, looking expectantly at Jessie. "I'm leaving," Jessie said simply. "I need you to please let Mrs. Rawlins know I'll send for the rest of my things once I land."

Mimi's eyes widened in surprise. "Oh. Okay, of course."

"Thank you. And please make sure Chloe is taken care of first thing every morning if her mother doesn't get to her until later, as she often does. I usually take care of things until then. She's been taken care of this morning."

Mimi eyed her. "Does this have to do with what I said?"

"No," Jessie said, shaking her head. "No, not at all. You did nothing wrong, Mimi." She looked into the woman's eyes, wanting to make sure she understood what Jessie was really saying. "Okay?" She let out a heavy sigh and shrugged. "I think I've come to understand that we're all doing what we must to survive all this." She gave her a sad smile.

Mimi nodded. "Yes, we are." She gave her a little smile. "It's too bad, really. I'd wanted to get to know you a bit better."

Jessie held her gaze for a moment before nodding. "Well, you take care, okay? See you around."

"Good luck, Jessie," the maid said, reaching out and lightly squeezing one of her hands before turning and heading back to her work.

❧ ❧ ❧ ❧

Devastated. She was absolutely devastated. As the rain fell, Jessie thought it was so appropriate. Never had she thought her mother would act like she had. Never, ever would she think Louise would prioritize a job over her daughter's pain. Who cared if they all got fired? Clearly her mother did. So here she was, standing on the street outside of Mr. Beason's store, trying to make herself take a step inside to ask for that job.

The rain was coming down in buckets, and her hair and clothing was stuck to her head and body like a second skin. She was cold and she was tired. Turning away from the store, as she didn't think she would make much of a good impression in her current condition, she walked over to a stoop in front of one of one of the buildings and plopped down.

Head in her hands, the tears came again. Now, though, she wasn't entirely sure what was her tears and what was the rain. Suddenly, she felt a hand on her shoulder. Looking up, she saw the incredibly concerned face of Molly looking down at her, the two of them now shielded from the rain by the umbrella Molly held overhead.

"Oh, honey," Molly said softly, barely heard over the downpour. "I know that look." She grabbed one of Jessie's hands and tugged her to her feet. "Come on, you're comin' with me."

Chapter Nineteen

1945

You got it, John." Jessie took the bowl and measuring cup from the busy head cook and went to the pantry to fulfill his request.

She set the bowl and measuring cup down on the workspace, then grabbed the new bag of flour, which she'd have to cut open with the knife she'd brought with her. With a grunt, she picked up the heavy bag and set it on the butcher-block table. About to slice into the bag, she noted the small scar on her finger from all those years ago.

Jessie's eyes trailed from her finger to the scars left on the butcher block. She lightly ran her fingertips over the smattering of tiny cuts and holes from the blade that morning so long ago. So many scars, she thought, inside and out. She returned her focus to where it needed to be and gathered John's flour for him.

Once she was finished, she had nothing more to do to distract herself. Ever since she'd found that tape reel in the attic weeks before, she'd found an excuse not to listen to it. But, since her mind had traversed back to cover so much territory that she'd long tried to bury or forget, she knew she needed to listen to it.

Again, perhaps it was nothing, but perhaps it was everything. Reaching her bedroom in the huge house, she shut the door to the hall, the one to Heaven's old bedroom always closed. She looked to her trunk and saw the tape reel and the machine on which to play it. Her stomach was in knots, but she forced herself to carry it to a small table she'd brought in that sat next to the wingback chair by the window.

Plugging the machine in, she attached the reel and, releasing a very slow breath, toggled the machine on. Another deep breath, and she hit play before sitting down. The reel began to spin. She just hoped it wasn't damaged from sitting in an attic for sixteen years. She worried for naught. Though the voices were a bit tinny from the technology of its time, they were loud, clear, and very discernible.

"It is Thursday, November the twenty-eighth at... twelve-oh-four in the afternoon. I, George C. Russ, am sitting with Mrs. Eliza McGovern and Miss Heaven McGovern. They are both aware that this is a recorded agreement."

Jessie sat with her knees together, elbows resting on her thighs. She chewed on her bottom lip as one leg bounced in her nervousness. Her heart raced, and dread was flowing over her like an iron blanket.

George cleared his throat. "Alright, ladies. I'll spell out for this recording what we discussed and agreed upon. And let it be known that your agreement upon this recording is as good as your signature upon a contract." His tone was deep and filled with warning. "In return for continued residence in this house known as Greyson Manor, Eliza McGovern has agreed to marry me, a marriage which will happen spring of next year, the engagement to be kept a secret until New Year's Eve."

"Mother, no," Heaven said, her voice a bit farther

away from the recording, as though her chair wasn't as close as George's. "We can find another way."

"Heaven, quiet," Eliza said, her voice filled with the same warning as Russ's had.

As though she hadn't spoken, George continued. "Heaven McGovern, you will allow me to find you a suitable young man worthy of your bearing and my name. That engagement will also be announced upon New Year's Eve, and your marriage will take place the day after your high school graduation next June."

"I don't want to do this," Heaven exclaimed, her voice moving around as though she'd stood up. "I've changed my mind."

"Sit down!" George demanded, followed by a pounding sound, like a fist to a desktop or chair arm.

"Mother, we don't have to do this," Heaven insisted, panic in her voice. "We can figure something out! We don't have to—"

"Sit down, I said!" An eerie quiet followed, then: "You listen to me, little girl," George said, his voice sickeningly sweet. "A lot of lives depend on you. You!"

"That's not fair."

"Life isn't fair. Let me ask you this," George said. "How would you feel about seeing your beloved Jessica thrown out of school, hmm? I don't have to continue paying for her education. How about her parents thrown out onto the streets? How about that?"

"You wouldn't do that," Heaven whispered.

"Wouldn't I?" Another pregnant pause. "You and the Lowrey girl can't play house forever, Heaven. It's time for you to grow up and make your mother proud for once."

"George—"

"Quiet, Eliza," George growled. "That's the

promise, young lady. You do as I say, marry who I put before you and sit there and look pretty and shut that beautiful mouth unless your husband finds a use for it. If you don't, your beloved is out. Her parents are out. Do you understand?"

Sobbing could be heard in the background now. Finally, a barely audible, "Yes."

Jessie couldn't breathe. Her hands were covering her mouth, eyes wide as she stared at the tape reel as though she were watching the meeting that had happened so long ago. Suddenly, she felt that she wasn't alone.

Turning, she saw Heaven leaning against the doorframe of the open door between her old room and Jessie's. Her face held little expression, her arms crossed over her chest. She seemed to be waiting.

"My god," Jessie whispered behind her hands. "My god," she said again, hands falling away. "Why didn't you tell me?"

Heaven, who suddenly looked soul- tired, said, "I didn't know how." She walked over to the small table where the machine sat and clicked it off, the reel slowing and then finally stopping. She grabbed one of Jessie's hands and tugged, leading her to sit with her on the bed.

As they sat side by side, Heaven holding Jessie's hand in both of hers, Jessie wasn't sure whether to laugh, cry, scream, or all the above. She remained silent as she felt Heaven wanted to say something, though Heaven seemed to be trying to work out the words.

"I honestly thought that, since I didn't love him—I still don't," Heaven added, "that everything would be fine." She glanced over at Jessie. "It wasn't what I wanted, absolutely not. But I had no choice. And since it had to happen, I thought if I found a way to bring you into the house, too, we could still be together."

Jessie felt her heart break. "I'm sorry," she whispered. "I'm sorry I was so weak."

"No," Heaven said, her voice forceful. She cupped Jessie's cheek. "No," she said again, this time softer. "I was so young, so utterly naïve, that I thought it could work. I thought that we could continue in our little fantasy together, all the while married to someone else and the obligatory duties that entailed." She looked into Jessie's eyes. "Please forgive me," she said. "I hurt you so badly, the exact opposite of what I ever wanted to do. How absolutely cruel I was, even if I didn't mean to be. I'm so sorry."

Jessie said nothing as she gathered Heaven into her arms, holding her almost painfully tight. She buried her face in fragrant dark hair as she began to cry. It was almost as though the final puzzle piece had been laid and now, with the whole picture before her, she could finally let go. She felt Heaven's fingers running through her hair and caressing her back.

As the tears began to slow, Heaven pulled back from the hug a bit, her hands cradling Jessie's head as she left gentle kisses on both of Jessie's closed eyes, and finally, the softest of brief touch on her lips.

After a moment, Jessie's eyes opened to see Heaven looking back at her. There was so much love and understanding in her eyes, which were a bit too shiny with her own unshed tears. "I'm so sorry, Heaven," she said. "God, I'm so sorry."

Heaven let out a small sigh and gave her a weak smile. "I have my children," she said. "The absolute light at the end of this horrible tunnel. I have them, and I hope like hell I have your forgiveness."

"There's nothing to forgive on my end," Jessie said. She brought up her hand and used her thumb to wipe away a tear that had managed to escape one of Heaven's eyes. "Nothing. As you said, we were both so young and trying to navigate an impossible situation, and George Russ and Kingston Rawlins held all the cards." They held hands again, resting in Heaven's lap.

Heaven took a steadying breath before she said, "I don't want to lose you in my life again, Jessie. I can't."

Jessie's heart swelled as Heaven gave voice to Jesse's own hopes. "You won't. I mean come on, now, I'm always in this luxurious resort, aren't I?"

"I mean even after my mother dies. Yes, right now we're both here all the time, but it won't always be like that. Once she goes," she said with a shrug, "I certainly never intend to come back here, and I assume you have no reason to, either."

"No." Jessie looked around the room, taking in so many memories, wonderful and awful. "I'll never come back here again."

"Jessie," Heaven said softly. "I want you in Chloe and Ronin's life. They deserve to have someone like you."

Jessie looked down at their hands, her thumb continuing its absent caresses. "Is it crazy if I told you that I love those two?"

"No crazier than for me to tell you that I'm pretty positive they love you, too." She paused, then asked, "Where did you find that reel?" She nodded toward the table by the window where the machine still sat.

Jessie glanced at it. "Eliza sent me to the attic to find some photo albums she wanted. She told me where to look, in a small wooden trunk. They were literally sitting on top of that player, some material covering it." She shrugged, a little sheepish. "I saw the date on it, and I remembered that day. Something told me to grab it." Heaven studied her for so long it began to make her feel uncomfortable. "What?"

"I think she wanted you to find that. I know it sounds silly and like radio drama, but I think she did."

"You think she wanted me to know the truth?"

"I do." Heaven gave Jessie's fingers a squeeze before releasing them and pushing to her feet. She walked over to the window and looked out, her back to Jessie. She ran a hand through her hair before facing Jessie again. "Some of the things she's said to me since I've been here… I think it's eaten her alive, the guilt."

"So, what now?" Jessie asked from where she still sat on the bed.

"Now," Heaven responded, walking back over and reclaiming her seat. "Now we see it through to the end with my mother. Help her cross in peace, I guess. Then, walk away from this place forever. Try and pick up the pieces the best we can, I suppose." She met Jessie's gaze. "Rebuild our friendship?"

"Yes. I agree with that." Jessie smiled at her, an honest-to-goodness smile with teeth and everything. She held out her hand. Heaven looked down at it with a raised eyebrow, then took it. "Hi. Jessie."

Heaven's smile was slow as it spread across her full lips like a rising sun. "Heaven."

"You certainly are," Jessie quipped, grinning as Heaven burst into laughter. They were interrupted by the frantic knocking on Jessie's hallway door.

"Jessie?" a female voice was saying. "Are you in there?"

Jessie shared a quick glance with Heaven before

she hopped to her feet and hurried to the door. Pulling it open, she saw one of Eliza's nurses on the other side. "What is it, Tammy?"

"Have you seen Mrs. Rawlins?" she asked, brown eyes wide.

Jessie pushed the door open a bit more to reveal Heaven standing just behind her. "What is it?"

"Miss Eliza is asking for you," the nurse said, taking Heaven's hands in hers. "I think we're close."

❧ ❧ ❧ ❧

The bedroom was eerily quiet. It seemed even the wind outside had subsided in respect and anticipation. Jessie and Heaven walked up to the side of Eliza's bed, Heaven closest to the frail woman's head, Jessie next to her, their hips touching.

Eliza's head fell to the side slowly, her eyes sunken in and pale, chapped lips open a bit. She looked at them both, one at a time. "Together," she whispered, the smallest of smiles gracing her lips.

Heaven took one of her mother's hands in both of her own. "Yes, Mother," she said. "We're with you."

Eliza slowly shook her head. "My girls."

"Us, together?" Jessie asked, indicating herself and the woman standing next to her. She and Heaven exchanged a quick glance at the small nod they got.

Eliza lightly tugged on the hands that held hers. Heaven leaned toward her mother, receiving a small kiss on the cheek, then Jessie was urged to lean over. When she did, she also felt the dry lips brush her skin.

"Take care of her," was whispered to her, barely audible.

Jessie nodded. "I promise."

Standing upright once more, Jessie put her arm around Heaven's waist, as the smaller woman had begun to softly cry. They stood huddled together, watching as Eliza's head turned to look toward the foot of the bed. Her glassy eyes became very focused as the softest of smiles touched her lips.

"Harvard," she murmured. Then, with a long, slow exhalation, she was gone.

꙰ ꙰ ꙰ ꙰

She knew she wouldn't have to wait long, as she'd been told he was on his way. So, she sat on, rocking slightly in the comfy leather chair. Her feet were up on the desk and crossed at the ankles. Her fingers tapped on the arms of the chair as she waited. Soon enough, she heard the strong, steady footfalls headed her way.

The office door opened and George Russ appeared. He closed it behind him, removing his fedora and hanging it on the coat tree, whistling a happy tune. He shrugged out of his suit jacket, leaving him in short sleeves and his tie. It wasn't until he turned toward his desk that he realized he wasn't alone.

"How'd you get in here?' he asked.

"The door," Jessie said simply.

He glared at her. "What do you think you're doing?"

"I was waiting for you," she said, her booted feet falling to the floor as she sat upright in the chair.

"You have no right being in here," he said, voice loud, strong.

She smirked. "What are you gonna do?" She got to her feet and tossed the tape reel to his desk. "Fire me? Fire my parents? Leave us homeless?" She snorted, waving off the idea. "That's so sixteen years ago, George."

His gaze flicked to the reel then back to her. "You think you're real smart, don't you?"

"Don't know about that," she said, shoving her hands into her trouser pockets as she meandered around to the front of his desk to join him, not wanting to get herself trapped behind it. "But I do know you're a real son of a bitch. And I know that while you were out and about doing God only knows what today, your wife was dying." She was satisfied to see the surprise cross his eyes, but just for a moment. "She's dead, George," she yelled. "Where were you?"

"Careful, girl," he said, voice low and dangerous. "You're treading on awfully thin ice."

"Or what?" she asked. "Eliza is now dead. Heaven is gone. I'm out of here after this." She shrugged, hands flying up in a dramatic gesture. "Who's left for you to control? Who's left for you to threaten?"

He said nothing, but his eyes were growing harder by the second. She could feel his rage building.

"In the end," she said, walking toward the door, then stopped right next to him. "I can't do anything to you financially, but I can still tell you this. You lose." She met his gaze, hers filled with every ounce of hatred she'd held for him.

"What, you and Heaven?" he said, laughter in his tone. "Back together again." He snorted. "She's used goods now, Jessica. No use to anyone else. You may as well—"

With perfect form, just like John had taught her so many years before, her fist made contact with his jaw, and with a satisfying click of his teeth knocking together, he went down, taking one of the two chairs in front of his desk down with him as he tried to break his fall.

She stood over him, feet wide and hands balled into double fists. "It's over," she spat. "Now you get to rot in this house."

With that, she turned and left, not even bothering to close the office door behind her.

Chapter Twenty

1931

Finally warm and wrapped in the silkiness of the borrowed robe, Jessie opened the bathroom door and entered the main portion of the small apartment, her damp clothing hung over the towel rack as instructed. She ran her fingers through her hair to try to get it into some semblance of order as she stepped out.

She nearly choked on her tongue when she saw Molly standing at the kitchen counter in nothing more than bra, panties, and garters. "Oh, gosh, I'm sorry."

The blonde glanced over at her. "Oh, you're fine, honey. Come on out. Nothin' here you haven't seen in your own mirror." She turned her focus back to her task of pouring an inch of light brown liquid into two small glasses. She recapped the bottle on the counter before grabbing the glasses and carrying them to the table. "Sit," she said, patting one of the chairs.

Clutching the belted robe together, Jessie padded her way to the table. One sniff of the liquid in the glass sent her head jerking away. "Where'd you get this?"

"Never you mind," Molly said with a raised honey-colored eyebrow. "You take a little sippy sip while I get changed into my nightdress."

Jessie nodded as the other woman made her way into the small bedroom. She brought the glass back up to her nose before taking an experimental sip. Her eyes squeezed shut before they popped open, the liquid fire making its way down her esophagus. Coughing quickly ensued.

"Do not die, darlin'," Molly said with a chuckle, suddenly behind her and patting her firmly on the back. "Don't need the questions from the law."

Jessie chuckled through her cough as she tried to calm herself. "Holy moly."

Dressed in a silken gown that honestly wasn't much more than her very own birthday suit, Molly sat down in the other chair. She wrapped her hand around her glass. "You alright?"

Jessie nodded. "Yes. What is this?" she asked, holding up the glass.

"Whiskey," Molly said, as though it was so obvious. "Some of my boys like to leave me with a…" She grinned. "Tip."

"Oh," was all that Jessie managed. She did, however, start to notice the soft, warm feeling that the liquor was creating throughout her body. She sat back in the squeaky kitchen chair.

"So," Molly said, her tone gentle. "What happened, hmm?"

The simple question brought tears to her eyes again. She looked away, angry with herself. "Damn it," she whispered.

"Oh, sweetie," Molly murmured. She pushed back from the table and walked to Jessie, holding her hand out to her.

Jessie looked at the hand then up at the woman, unsure. Her hand was grabbed and she was tugged out of the chair and led to the bedroom. Panic filled her as she looked to the bed and the woman who wore what amounted to a sheer nightgown.

Molly snickered. "Just want to cuddle, honey," she said. "You're adorable, but you don't quite have the pieces for my puzzle." She tugged the covers back and slid under the sheet, holding it open in invitation.

Stunned by the woman's actions and confused by how she lived, she slid beneath the covers. She was gathered to cuddle with Molly, her head resting against a pale shoulder. She had to admit, it felt nice having gentle fingers run through her hair, even if she had not one clue where to put her hand.

Molly chuckled. "Sorry. Not used to having company here that isn't here for business." She grabbed Jessie's hand and tugged until her arm was draped across her warm stomach. "Now, tell me what happened."

Jessie began, intending just to tell this veritable stranger what had happened the previous night, but she found the entire story pouring out of her. Like a father confessor, Molly said nothing, simply listened to Jessie's tale. Her fingers never stopped their calming petting of Jessie's hair or shoulder. The touches were comforting, and in many ways, maternal.

Finally, she reached the end of her tale, more tears on her cheeks, but it felt good to get it all out. It was almost as if giving voice to all the events of the past twelve years had taken the heavy burden from her shoulders.

"My goodness," Molly said softly. "I'm so sorry, Jessie." She hugged her closer. "First love is the hardest, and it can cut deep. Been there, honey. And, as for your mama's reaction, I can only say that she's probably far more worried about you surviving in a pretty tough situation for work right now than your broken heart. Now," she said, her touch growing firmer as Jessie began to move away. "Not to say she doesn't care, because from what you said, your folks love Heaven, too."

Jessie considered that for a moment. This got her thinking, doubting herself. "So, you think I overreacted, then? By leaving?"

"I don't," Molly said easily. "When it comes to the heart, especially a situation that has been going on so long and has caused the devastation you two have endured over the last year, I think you did what you had to do." She gave Jessie a squeeze. "Trust me, honey, I get it."

Jessie moved away from her so she could prop her head on her hand and look at her new friend. "What happened to you?" She gave her a sheepish look. "If I can ask."

"You can ask, honey." Molly tucked her hands behind her head as she looked up at the ceiling. "Met Del in sixth grade, if you can believe it." The smile on her lips and distant look in her eyes made Jessie smile in reaction. "Families were close, and honestly, it was pretty much just expected we'd get married. We did." Her smile grew. "Damn, I loved that boy," she whispered.

"What happened?" Jessie asked when there was nothing more forthcoming. It seemed Molly was lost in memory.

"Well," she finally said. "I got pregnant pretty quick after getting married. He was so excited," she said, meeting Jessie's gaze. "Couldn't wait to be a daddy." She looked back to the ceiling, the smile falling from her lips. "I lost that baby in miscarriage, as well as the next and the next after that."

"Oh, no," Jessie murmured. "I'm so sorry."

Molly gave her an appreciative smile before continuing. "Finally, after being married for about six years, I carried the baby to term. But," she said with a tired sigh. "She only lived a few months before we lost her. Doctor said her heart wasn't wired right."

"Oh, Molly." Jessie lightly squeezed the woman's elbow. "I'm so sorry."

"Thanks, honey. Guess some women just aren't made to be mothers," Molly blew out. "Anyway, Del blamed me for it. My family blamed me for it. Eventually, Del and me grew apart, and one day he was gone. Whole damn family blamed me for that, too," she muttered. "Left and came up here to Denver to start over."

"How long have you been here?"

"Going on three years." She snorted. "Day I arrived, I celebrated my thirtieth birthday."

"Do you talk to any of them now? Your family, or Del?"

"Nah." Molly looked at her again. "What I hear, Del got remarried and has a set of twins."

Jessie winced. "Ouch. You know, Molly, you're still young, a really beautiful woman. You could find love again. A really good man that deserves you."

Molly studied her for a long moment before she lifted her head and left a small kiss on Jessie's cheek. "Thanks, honey. Same for you," she said with a pointed look. "I know you're hurtin' right now, but don't let this define you. I think you're the kind of woman who is wired to be with other women, and I know others out there exist." She smirked. "Entertained two or three myself."

Jessie's eyebrows shot up. "You have?"

Molly chuckled and nodded. "If the price is right, honey, I can make do."

❧❧❧❧

Jessie's eyes blinked open, and for a moment she was disoriented. No clue where she was, just knew that she was alone in a small bed in a bedroom darkened by a blanket covering the window, just a bit of light coming in from the top right corner where the blanket had come loose from its moorings.

She rolled over to her back, then sat up. Looking down at herself, she saw she was in a silk dressing gown, which sagged open as the sash had loosened in sleep. She heard music from beyond the closed bedroom door. As her eyes adjusted a bit, she saw her clothing folded and set upon the dresser top.

The previous day's events came back to her with a crush of emotions and dread. She covered her face with her hands for a moment before they dropped to her lap as she took a deep, steadying breath. First things first. She was relieved to tug her clothing back on, draping Molly's robe across the end of the bed after she made it with hospital-corner care.

Running a hand through her hair, which stuck up in crazy angles as she'd fallen asleep with it still damp from the rain, she pulled open the door. Molly was dressed in something simple, form-fitting, and yellow, her hair styled and makeup applied. She sat at the kitchen table reading the morning post, the fingers of one hand wrapped around the handle of her coffee cup while the other absently held a partially smoked cigarette between two fingers.

"Um," Jessie muttered, feeling shy. "Good morning, I guess it is."

Molly glanced up at her, a welcoming smile instantly crossing her painted lips. "Well, good morning, sleepy head. My goodness, you passed right out."

"Yeah," Jessie hedged, a hand coming up to rub the back of her warm neck. "Sorry. I'll get out of your hair. Thank you so much for everything, Molly. Truly." She saw her knapsack on the couch where she'd left it the night before and walked over to fish out her wallet. "Um, what do I owe you?" She glanced at the seated woman only to see a look of surprise then hurt cross Molly's features. "I, uh… Well, I took up your time, and you could've been working, and…"

"I don't charge for kindness, Jessie," she said quietly, turning to look back at her newspaper, the hurt clear in her voice.

Aw, hell. Jessie stood there for a moment, not sure what to do. She walked over to the table feeling like such an ass. "Um," she said, looking down at her shuffling feet. "Wow, I'm sorry. I wasn't, that is to say, I didn't mean to hurt you. Um." She rubbed the back of her neck again.

Molly cleared her throat before she looked up at her, blue eyes cool as she sat back in her chair. "I'm well aware what I do to pay the bills," she began. "But it's not often that I'm made to feel like a prostitute."

If Jessie could have sunk into the floor in that moment, she would happily have done so. Shoving her hands into her pockets, she nodded and looked at her boots again. "I'm sorry," she murmured. "Um, thank you for all you've done for me. You're one in a million." She spared a glance at the woman before walking back to the couch. She grabbed the strap of her knapsack and hitched it over her shoulder before she headed for the apartment door.

"Where will you go?"

Jessie paused, hand on the doorknob. "Um, I'll be okay. Really." She turned the knob and pulled the door open. "Again, Molly. I'm really sorry." With that, she stepped out into the hall and lightly closed the door behind her.

She stood there for a moment, blowing out a heavy breath before she turned and walked toward the stairs. She had no clue where she'd go. She needed to check how much money she had to see if she had enough to rent a room in a boarding house or even a motel. She also needed to eat.

The morning was a bit muggy from the evening storms before, but she knew that would burn off as the warmer May temperatures rose. She hitched her bag a bit higher on her shoulder and decided to head in the direction of Mr. Beason's. She'd see if he'd give her that job after all.

"Wait!"

She stopped and turned, surprised to see Molly rushing out of her building and toward her.

"Wait," Molly said again, reaching her. "There is no way in hell I'm gonna turn my back on you like my family did on me when I needed them most." Her eyes were hard, though her tone was kind. "I got a couch, and you're gonna use it until you figure things out. Now," she continued. "Life is about to get a whole lot different than what you've known livin' under a roof where a lot of things were provided for you. This is real life." She indicated the street and buildings around them. "And I'm gonna teach you how to do it."

And so she did.

The summer had flown by, Jessie working at the store, taking as many hours as Mr. Beason was willing to throw at her. Plus, during her off time she was helping her boss's mother, who was having issues with her hip, so Jessie did work around the two-story house since she wasn't able to climb up and down stairs as easily anymore.

Now, it was Thursday night, and that was Molly's "late night." She had a regular client who stopped by the apartment for a two-hour session, starting at five thirty in the evening. So, Jessie had to make herself scarce. They'd come up with a pretty good little arrangement. Most of Molly's clients came during the day, using their lunch hours for their entertainment, as most were married and dropping by after work wasn't an option. The rare times Molly got a drop-by, she'd leave a kerchief on the apartment doorknob to let Jessie know she needed to wander for a bit.

One time, she'd been home when that had happened, and she'd had to hide in the closet during the visit. It had been amusing, as the man had the strangest little whimper sounds as he orgasmed. Needless to say, Jessie had learned a whole lot about men and sex with men in the three months she'd been staying with the woman who had become a close and trusted friend.

She'd learned so much from her, in fact. How to budget, how to save, how to turn a dollar into two. Molly had taught her how to stretch supplies, shop and cook for one—as opposed to helping prepare meals for an entire household and small army of staff. But mostly, she'd taught her about real friendship, the kind that was built upon truly depending on one another to survive.

They'd never so much as kissed, but their bond was tight. She trusted Molly implicitly and knew she'd earned her trust in return. Though they'd come to be roommates and ultimately friends due to Jessie's total and complete heartbreak, it had turned into an invaluable time for her. She felt she was growing more now than she ever had. She was becoming an adult, and it felt good.

"Jessie?"

Knocked completely out of her thoughts, Jessie stopped, turning to look over her shoulder at the unexpected female voice. She was even more surprised to see Mimi, still dressed in her diner uniform, hurrying after her. She noted the redhead's tag that bore her name and the logo for City Diner, which was about half a block back in the opposite direction Jessie was walking.

"Hi," she said.

"Hey." Mimi gave her a wide smile. "Sorry, I was just heading out and saw you pass by."

Jessie glanced back toward the diner then at the woman before her. "Are you working a second job?"

Mimi shook her head. "No." She nodded in the direction that Jessie had been headed with a raised eyebrow in question. In silent agreement, they began walking together. "I left the Rawlins house," she explained. "Not long after you did, actually." She was silent for a moment before adding, "I'm so sorry you had to see that." She spared a glance at Jessie, who met it. "I was utterly ashamed."

"You don't need to apologize to me, Mimi," Jessie assured her, hands shoved into the pockets of her trousers as they strolled. It was early September, and the evening was pleasant. Soon enough, that would no longer be the case. "Trust me," she said with a snort. "I've learned just what men will do for sex, for control."

She gave her an understanding smile.

"You know," Mimi said with a sigh, lightly tugging on Jessie's arm to get her to take a right turn. "My uncle owns the diner," she said, hitching her thumb in the direction they'd come from. "He'd been offering me a job since high school, but I took the job with Kingston, a senator, because I thought maybe I'd meet some neat people. You know?" She gave Jessie a shy smile. "Maybe some famous people."

Jessie nodded with a chuckle. "I get that. The opportunity, the experience."

"Exactly," Mimi agreed. They walked down a street with a mixture of small houses and brick apartment buildings lining the lane. "Now I realize just how naïve I truly was."

"I'm so sorry, Mimi. Honestly, don't beat yourself up over what happened." She stopped them with a hand to the other woman's arm. "Men like Kingston are predators and opportunists. A young, beautiful woman like you didn't stand a chance." She smirked. "I'm sure that's why you were hired," she said gently.

"Is that why he married Heaven?" Mimi asked, the two turning to walk again.

It hurt to hear her name, but considering what she and Mimi had in common, it was inevitable. "I'm sure. Young, beautiful, no choice." She was angry at herself for biting out the last two words, the bitterness seeping through.

"I'm sorry, Jessie," Mimi said. "I don't know the particulars, but it was obvious that it went both ways between you two."

Jessie shrugged with a heavy sigh. "Yeah. Well, we all make our choices, Mimi. You and I chose to get out."

Mimi stopped them in front of a two-story Victorian. "I rent a room here," she explained. "Want to come up?"

Jessie looked up at the house, then nodded. "Yeah," she said. "Why not?" She gave the hopeful-looking woman a smile.

The room on the third floor was small, with a slanted ceiling near the window where the bed was tucked. The basics were there, a dresser, nightstand, and chair. It was a nice space, she thought, especially for a young woman in her early twenties trying to make a life for herself. She wandered over to the dresser and looked down at the smattering of framed pictures there.

"Is this your family?" she asked.

"It is," Mimi said, removing the name tag from her uniform dress and tossing it to the dresser top. She pointed as she named the people in the photograph. "My parents, two brothers, Joshua and Teddy, and my sister, Carla, and her husband and baby."

Jessie nodded. "Nice family. Are you close?"

"We are. Do you mind if I sit?" Mimi gave her a shy look. "Been on my feet all day."

"No, please," Jessie said, indicating the direction of the bed or chair. "It's your place, be comfortable."

Mimi plopped down on the bed and removed her saddle shoes. She groaned as the heavy footwear thudded to the floor, one at a time. "Waitressing is so hard on the feet and legs," she said.

Jessie walked over to the bed and sat down next to her. "This is okay?" she asked, indicating the bed. The chair had some books stacked on it, and she didn't feel right displacing the woman's things. At Mimi's nod, she said, "I work at Beason's Market over on Quincy, so I get it."

They sat in awkward silence for a moment before the waitress said, "You haven't asked about her."

Jessie met her gaze then looked away, shaking her head. "No, I haven't. I just can't anymore."

She felt a soft touch to her face, turning her to look at Mimi again. Her eyes fell closed at the soft touch of her lips against her own. There was that part of her that wanted to push Mimi away, tell her to never touch her again and that she loved Heaven. But the other part of her, the part that had been growing over the months, knew that she needed to move on. Heaven was lost to her—that had been made abundantly clear.

The kiss deepened quickly, both breathing heavily in the small room. Finally, Mimi pulled back a bit. "Jessie," she said, words breathy. "I want his stink off me."

Jessie nodded, very much understanding. In her own way, she needed to get Heaven's hold off of her as well. She pushed Mimi back on the bed and followed.

Chapter Twenty-One

1932

Arm-in-arm, mostly to keep Molly from sliding on the patches of ice beneath the snow, Molly and Jessie strolled down the sidewalk toward Ralph's. Molly liked the fish at the local eatery and rarely got to enjoy having it. Jessie had gotten a small raise a few days before, and the two had been wanting to celebrate since, but between the two, their schedules just hadn't been conducive for Jessie to take her to dinner—which she insisted on doing, even though Molly complained that it should be she taking Jessie to dinner.

"You seem upset tonight," Jessie commented, glancing over at her companion, who had been unusually quiet since Jessie had gotten home from work at the market. "Are you okay? Did something go wrong today?"

Molly let out a heavy sigh, which escaped painted lips in a plume of steam in the cold, February night. "Remember where I showed you I hide my money?" she asked, not taking her eyes off the night before them.

"Yeah," Jessie said, confused by the seeming non sequitur. "Of course."

"Good," Molly said, their steps slowing as they reached the door to the restaurant. She grabbed the handle in a gloved hand before pulling it open. "I just..." she said before stepping inside the warmth of the eatery.

"Is something wrong?" Jessie asked, eyebrows furrowing. "Is that creepy guy, Ed, being his creepy self again?"

"No, no," Molly said, waving off Jessie's words. "Come on, feed me."

Jessie smiled but was left feeling a bit unsettled. She was about to follow her dear friend inside but stopped, getting the distinct feeling she was being watched. She looked out over the night, seeing nothing out of the ordinary. Some people hurried down the sidewalk to their destination, a few automobiles puttered by. Nobody seemed to be paying them an ounce of attention.

She stepped inside, the door closing slowly behind her. Once they were seated and had shrugged out of their winter jackets, Molly eyed Jessie. Her demeanor seemed to have changed. She was back to her usual self.

"So," she said, opening her menu with a flourish. "You're staying at Mimi's tonight, right?"

"Yeah, she's been bugging me about it, so finally I said I would. I'm off tomorrow so I don't have to be at the store at the butt crack of dawn."

Molly eyed her for a moment, looking as lovely as ever. "I'm proud of you," she said.

Confused, Jessie looked up from her menu. "Why?"

"This relationship with the cute little redhead. I think it's healthy for you to try and find your way beyond Heaven, Jessie." Molly met her gaze and held it. "I know you love her, I imagine you always will, but you're doing the right thing."

Jessie blew out a breath. "I hope so. I just don't want to hurt Mimi. I don't think she wants anything too serious, but I absolutely don't." She sat back in the chair and met Molly's gaze. "I don't have it to give, Mol."

Molly smiled and reached across the table to cover one of Jessie's hands. "You will. Your heart knows no bounds, my sweet Jessie." She squeezed the hand. "When the time is right," she said, lowering her voice so as not to be overheard by other diners. "She'll be there. She'll give you all the love you've ever dreamed of, and you'll be ready to give it right back." Her gaze was so intense that Jessie almost felt the need to look away, but she couldn't. "Trust in that." With a loving smile, Molly squeezed her hand again before retreating to her side of the table. "Now," she said, in her normal tone. "Food!"

❧❧❧❧

Gasping, Jessie shot up in bed, eyes huge, still seeing the horrible dream images. "No!" Her naked breasts heaved with her frantic breaths.

"Jessie?"

Jessie turned toward her name and saw a startled Mimi looking back at her, also sitting up. "I gotta go," Jessie panted, pushing the covers off her as she scrambled out of the waitress's bed to get dressed.

"What's wrong?"

"I gotta go," Jessie said again, tugging on her clothing. "I have the most horrible feeling."

"Molly?" Mimi asked, getting out of bed.

Near tears, Jessie could only nod.

"I'm going with you."

Twenty minutes later, the two were running through the pre-dawn darkness, Jessie's heart feeling as though it were about to pound out of her chest. She saw her building up ahead, relieved not to see any police cars there. But, as they got closer, a dark figure burst out the front door of the building, nearly knocking Mimi over as it passed.

Jessie whipped her head around to see who it was, but the person, the size of a man, was dressed in a long jacket with the collar pulled up and his fedora pulled low. Turning back to the building, she yanked open the door and stormed inside, pounding up the stairs, Mimi behind her.

She made it to the second floor and to her horror saw that their apartment door was open. "Molly!" She sprinted to the door, nearly skidding past it on the runner that ran along the wood floors. She grabbed the doorway and pulled herself into the apartment. "No!"

Lying on the living room floor near the coffee table, which was in pieces, was Molly. She was in her sleeping gown, the portion that covered her chest a deep crimson. Jessie threw herself to the floor, tears streaming down her cheeks as she looked into Molly's face. She was still alive, though she seemed to be gasping for breath.

"Molly," Jessie sobbed, pulling her upper body into her lap and cradling her head. Blood was beginning to dribble out of her open mouth. Her eyes were wide as she looked up at Jessie.

"Oh my god," Mimi gasped.

"Call the police," Jessie said. She looked up at Mimi, who seemed to be frozen. "Call the police!"

Mimi hurried from the apartment to the communal phone out in the hall. Distantly, Jessie could hear her voice as she made her call.

"No," Jessie whimpered, looking back to Molly. It was clear she was dying. "No." She looked into wide, terrified blue eyes. The gasps were turning into a horrific gurgling sound, more blood spurting from her mouth. Finally, with a long, wheezing breath, she was gone. A loud, mournful wail left Jessie's throat, her eyes squeezing shut as she hugged Molly to her. "No, no, no!"

"Ma'am, you need to back away," a man's voice said, suddenly just across from her.

Jessie looked up to find herself looking at a uniformed police officer. "Back away, ma'am."

Jessie looked to the woman in her arms, her tears still flowing. Closing her eyes, she left a kiss on Molly's forehead. "I love you, Molly." It took two other policemen to physically pull her away from her dearest friend, one helping her to get shakily to her feet. It was then that she saw she was covered in Molly's blood.

❧ ❧ ❧ ❧

1945

"I once saw the two of you together."

Jessie looked up from Molly's headstone, fresh wildflowers placed in the bronze vase at the foot of the stone. She smiled when she saw Heaven walking over to her. She was so lovely. "You did?"

"I did." Heaven stepped up beside her and looked down at the stone. "You two were heading into Ralph's." She met Jessie's surprised gaze. "I only remember it so well because it was the next day that I read about what happened in the paper."

Jessie nodded. "Yeah, I'd gotten a raise at my job. For whatever reason, she liked the fish at that place." She gave Heaven a smirk. "We both know how much I love fish," she drawled, making Heaven smile.

"Were you two lovers?" Heaven asked, the words slow, almost hesitant.

"No. She was just a very, very dear friend, there for me when I needed it most." She leaned down and dusted off a little dirt from the top of the stone. "I miss her, even all these years later."

"I'm so sorry, Jessie." Heaven moved a bit closer, her shoulder touching Jessie's. "I really am."

Jessie appreciated the touch and the closeness. "I think you would have liked her. I know she and I would have remained friends had things gone differently."

"She was murdered, right?"

"Stabbed sixty-seven times by a man who was obsessed with her," Jessie explained. "At least they got the bastard. Fried his ass in the electric chair the next year."

"My god," Heaven murmured. "What a monster."

Jessie took a deep breath, then turned to the woman standing to her left. "Well, sorry you had to come pick me up here for the meeting." She gave her a sheepish grin. "Now that I'm back working with Dad, he needed me to do some things here since he's working over at the courthouse grounds."

"No, it's fine." Heaven gave her a smile. "I honestly have no clue why Daddy's attorney wants to meet there. I even tried to move it to your house since he requested you be there, to make it more convenient for you." She shrugged. "But, nope."

Jessie chuckled. "It's okay. Ready? I'm done here, was just killing time waiting for you."

"Yes, let's go."

Together, they walked toward the parking lot and Heaven's car. It was a full two weeks since Eliza's death, and other than the day of the funeral, the two had spent little time together. Part of the reason was that Jessie had been buried in work, as George had pulled Dobbs's helper the day Eliza had died. So now, as summer approached, it was busy, busy, busy.

Plus, if Jessie was honest with herself, she was terrified. What if it happened again? What if her heart got away from her again? Heaven was no more available to her than she'd been for the past sixteen years.

"I've missed you," Heaven said, almost as though she'd heard Jessie's thoughts. So often that seemed to happen between them.

Jessie smiled at that thought. She playfully bumped Heaven's shoulder with her own as they walked. "I've missed you, too." And, as much as she didn't want to, she meant it.

They climbed into the car, and Heaven inserted the key but didn't start the ignition. Jessie glanced over at her but said nothing. It seemed something was very wrong. She placed her hand on Heaven's arm to get her attention.

"Are you okay?" she asked when finally Heaven looked over at her.

Heaven looked like she wanted to say something, her lips even parting a bit, but she closed them again and nodded. "Yes. I'm fine." She started the car and got them going.

The drive was lovely, their destination just slightly out of town, though so much had grown up around it since Jessie had been there last. It had been many, many years. Her heart was racing a bit, not sure why they had been summoned to meet the lawyer there and not sure why she was part of it at all.

Eliza had told her that she'd been considered in

any sort of inheritance, but honestly, she hadn't taken a word of that seriously. And the only thing anyone had ever given her was the money that she got when Molly had been killed. She'd had it hidden in a mason jar under a loose floorboard in the bedroom. She'd been saving to buy a house.

A few months before she died, she'd brought Jessie into the bedroom and had shown her where it was with the explicit instructions that if the apartment were to be raided by the police, if Molly were arrested, or if anything else should happen, as she'd put it, Jessie was to take it and run.

In the end, it had been blood money. After Molly's murder, Jessie had taken the money as she'd promised. With many tears, she'd finally convinced herself that she was doing the right thing by fulfilling Molly's dream in her stead. That money had been a large part of how she and Dobbs had been able to buy their little house.

Bittersweet didn't even begin to describe it.

Now, Heaven pulled the car into the driveway of Granite House. It looked exactly as she remembered, exactly as it was in her dreams. So often she'd been transported in her mind back to that house with Heaven, the two of them making love, learning together what that meant. It was the house where they'd exchanged rings, the moment when Jessie's heart had been given to Heaven forever, it seemed.

She'd tried to love others, but she just didn't have it to give. Instead, she'd hurt Mimi and a couple other women she'd gotten briefly involved with before she decided to lock that part of herself away for good.

Heaven parked and pulled the parking brake. Turning off the ignition, she pulled out the key and glanced over at Jessie. "It's so strange to be here."

Jessie nodded. "I was just thinking that."

Heaven held her gaze for a long moment, taking Jessie's hand in her own. Something passed between them, something Jessie was so afraid of. She was deeply affected by the woman sitting next to her, just as she'd been the first time they'd pulled up to this house.

The irony was, that time, it had started the countdown to Heaven's wedding, the countdown to the day that Jessie would lose her. She gave Heaven a smile and released her hand, making herself remember that she was still lost to her.

She climbed out of the vehicle, looking as another car pulled up behind them. The man behind the wheel raised a hand in greeting before pulling his Buick to a stop. Jessie walked toward the rear of Heaven's car, where Heaven stood.

"Good afternoon, ladies," the man said as he exited his car. He was a man well into his sixties, his fedora covering his balding head, seen once the hat was removed as he let them into the house with the keys he pulled from his pocket. "After you."

Heaven and Jessie entered the house followed by the man who had introduced himself as Stanley Steinburg, Harvard McGovern's longtime attorney. He led them to the living room, his leather briefcase in hand.

Jessie's stomach flipped as she took in the room, exactly as it had been that amazing night they spent on the floor. Even the quilt was still folded in half and draped upon the back of the couch. She felt eyes on her and glanced over to see Heaven was looking at her. She could almost read her thoughts. She, too, was remembering.

"So," Mr. Steinburg said, the snaps on his briefcase

and his sudden words knocking Jessie right back into the here and now.

Clearing her throat, she sat on the granite hearth, leaving the chair for Heaven. She placed her hands between her knees to keep them from shaking. She was too damn close to their past. Too damn close to the place and the moment that had meant the most to her. Too damn close to the woman who had shared it. Too damn close.

"Alright, ladies," he said, sending a beaming smile to them both. "Here's the final will and testament of Mrs. Eliza McGovern-Russ, which," he explained, "will include your father's will, Heaven." He brought up a small packet of pages and began to read.

Jessie looked down at her bobbing knee as she tried to listen, all the legal jargon going in one ear and out the other. But then, her brain began to catch a word here and there:

... college fund ... Chloe ... Ronin ... retainer ... Mr. Stanley Steinburg ... defend Heaven Rawlins ... divorce ... all expenses paid ...

Jessie's head snapped up, not sure she'd heard correctly. The stunned look on Heaven's face told her perhaps she had. Her gaze flew to the man who continued to read, flipping another page in the packet.

... equipment ... Dobbs Lowrey ... all expenses for start-up ...

Jessie's head was spinning. She ran a hand through her hair, no idea what to say. Her father could start up his business. She popped up from the hearth, unable to contain her excitement for him.

"And, the final piece, ladies," the attorney said, again smiling at them both. "This is unusual, I must say, but this part is specific to your father's wishes, Heaven. He'd had this drawn up about six months before his death, to come into effect after your mother's death." He returned his focus to the pages in his hands. "'The house at 11 Forsythe Drive, otherwise known as Granite House, I will in a joint venture to my biological daughter, Heaven McGovern, and my bonus daughter, Jessica Lowrey, as joint recipients and owners forthwith.'"

Chapter Twenty-Two

The room was deathly quiet as both women sat in stunned silence. Mr. Steinburg had left after all the appropriate paperwork had been signed for him to file with the proper entities. Jessie had plopped down on the hearth again, her hands dangling off her knees at the wrist. Heaven sat in her wingback.

Finally, Jessie blew out a breath and glanced over at her. "Are you okay?"

Heaven nodded. "I think so." She looked down at her arms, which were wrapped around her purse, seemingly as a way to keep grounded. After a moment, she looked over at Jessie. "I'm stunned, honestly. I knew my father would always look out for his family, but he died so suddenly." She shook her head. "I never thought he'd do all this. Granted," she added, sitting back in her chair and seeming to relax a smidge. "Some of this was my mother, too."

"Where did she get the money for this?" Jessie asked. "I mean, your father lost everything after he died, no money put away."

"I was thinking the same thing. Perhaps George? I don't know." She pushed to her feet and set her purse on the chair she'd just vacated. "I want to look around here. Do you mind?"

"Not at all," Jessie said, assuming Heaven was asking since she was Jessie's ride. "I can wait here—"

"No." Heaven walked over to her and held out her hand. "Come with me. "

Jessie met her gaze for a moment then finally took the soft hand in her own. She was pulled to her feet. They stood toe to toe for a moment, Jessie unable to look away before the spell was broken and Heaven released her hand.

Together, they wandered through the house, which to Jessie's adult sensibilities was truly a beautiful home. As she'd felt as a teen, it wasn't huge like Greyson Manor or the Rawlins house, but it was very manageable. It sported a kitchen, living room, bathroom, and mud room on the first floor. Upstairs, there were two more bathrooms, surprising for the age of the house, and five bedrooms. The fifth bedroom, however, was quite small and no doubt used as a nursery for the many McGovern children.

"It's dusty up here," Jessie said, noting how stale the air felt. "No doubt, George stopped anyone from coming over here to open things up long ago."

"I agree." Heaven poked her head into the bedroom they'd reached. Next was the bathroom, then the small bedroom. The other two bedrooms were on the opposite side of the hallway, the large bedroom with the attached bathroom down at the end of the hall, set a bit away from the others. "Oh, my goodness," Heaven said, hand to her chest. Her smile was so beautiful as she looked at Jessie. "Chloe would love this!"

Jessie peeked into the room and saw the dormer window that created a little nook of space that could be used for reading. "Oh, she would." She stepped into the room, hands on hips as she looked around. There was currently furniture in the space, but it certainly didn't look like what a fourteen- or fifteen-year-old girl would want.

"In this dormer window," she said, stepping into

the little nook, which was about five feet long and three feet wide. "I could build her a desk to do homework, so it wouldn't take up space in the bedroom proper." She was already seeing it in her mind as she visually measured the space. She looked back over her shoulder at Heaven, who had also entered the room, though not the dormer. She had the softest smile on her lips. "What?"

Heaven said nothing, simply wandered farther into the room before she stopped at the center, arms crossed over her chest and right foot tilted back on her high heel. She looked around, seeming to be imagining her own additions for the bedroom, based on her appraising expression.

"Sorry," Jessie said, rubbing the back of her neck as she joined the other woman. "My mind kinda got away from me there."

"Why on earth are you apologizing?" Heaven asked, that same small smile on her lips as she looked over at her. "I love your imagination, Jessie. Always did. Your ideas are so on par for what Chloe would love in here."

Shrugging with a sheepish grin as she shoved her hands into her pockets, Jessie said, "I don't want to overstep. She's your daughter, and this is your house."

One of Heaven's eyebrows slowly slid upward. "My house, huh? Clearly you missed the part where my father left it to us both." She indicated the two of them with a finger.

Jessie nodded. "I know. But—"

"I'm sorry," Heaven said softly. "I don't want to push anything on you, Jessie. You have a house with your father. I absolutely do not want to turn your life upside down yet again." She gave her a sad smile. "Lord knows, I've done that enough."

"He knew," Jessie said, the words tumbling out of her mouth. "About us."

Heaven eyed her. "I always wondered. The stunt he pulled that night."

She didn't have to elaborate, as they both knew what she was talking about. Jessie could still feel the sting of hearing that son of a bitch have sex with the woman she loved. "I'm so sorry I left the way I did, Heaven. I know we've talked about this, but I was such a coward." She looked down at her shuffling feet, feeling so lost in that moment. "You needed me, and I left. Promised I wouldn't."

Heaven walked over to her but didn't touch her. "Please don't," she said softly. "I honestly would have done the same thing. I hated him for doing that." She used two fingers under Jessie's chin to urge her to look at her. Jessie saw so much understanding in those dark, expressive eyes. "I absolutely do not blame you for leaving. I never should have put you in that position."

"What are you going to do?"

"I'm getting out," Heaven said easily. "I'm already working as a secretary for a doctor in town, and I'll get three more damn jobs if I have to, to support my kids. I didn't have the money for a lawyer, and lord knows Kingston wasn't about to provide one. Now, I can get me and the kids out of this hell."

"I'm so glad, Heaven. I truly am. You, Chloe, and Ronin deserve to be happy. And honestly," Jessie added, nodding toward the room and house beyond. "I can't think of a better place for you to go. A place that has such wonderful memories for you."

"Well," Heaven said. "I will never, ever ask you to walk away from your life for me again. I'll say that

I want you here with us, I admit that, but I respect the fact that you already have a life." She smiled. "And I'll leave it at that."

≈≈≈≈

Jessie waited for his reaction, and she didn't have to wait long. Dobbs scrubbed at his chin with his fingers as he read over the part that pertained to him. He whistled between his teeth before he met her gaze from across the kitchen table.

"This is all legal?" he asked.

She chuckled and nodded as she sipped from her coffee. "Yep."

He sat back in his chair, which creaked beneath his weight. "Why me?" he asked. "This should be about you kids." He tapped the pages with his finger.

"Well," she responded. "You guys worked for them for years, Dad. Mama and Eliza were really close. I think since she's no longer here, she wanted to do something she knew would make Mama happy, too. For you to finally have your own business, Dad."

He eyed her from beneath heavy brows. "You still gonna go in with me?" he asked. "Like we always planned?"

"If you want me to, absolutely."

"And, what about you moving in with Heaven and the kids?" he pried, eyebrows raising as he sipped his own coffee. His gaze bored into hers.

"I can't, Dad," she said. "I can't leave you like that."

"Leave me?" he said. "Think I'm a kid?"

"No, of course not." She chuckled. "But when we bought this place, it was understood that I'd take care of you. Make sure you ate, all that good stuff."

He sat forward in his seat. "Jes, back then I was doing my level best to recover after your mom died. Though I'll never get over that fully, I've gotten myself together and will never fall back into the drink again."

Jessie nodded, knowing that was true. "I just don't want you to think I'm abandoning you."

"Jes, you're thirty-three years old. You deserve to have your own life, kid. Free of your old man, that is. If you wanna stay here, stay here. But if you wanna finally be with your Heaven girl, then go." He smiled, raising his cup. "With my blessing. But," he added. "You make sure whatever decision you make is for you. 'Kay? You've lived your whole life doin' for others, Jes. It's your turn."

❧ ❧ ❧ ❧

She tugged off her work gloves as she made her way toward the familiar spot. She was pleased to see the wildflowers were still there from three days before. She'd taken the time to really think about things after talking with her father two nights ago. A lot to think about, a huge undertaking. Regardless of whatever happened—or didn't happen—between her and Heaven, she'd be put into the role of some sort of parent, or at bare minimum, an aunt.

That was wonderful, and she relished the thought, but they'd all be under the same roof. It wasn't like picking up Chloe for a ladies' day of lunch and ice cream, or taking Ronin to the zoo then back home to his mother's house.

But, damn, she thought, a hand running through her hair, sweaty from the hard work she'd done on this warm May day. How amazing to spend all the time with them that she could possibly want. She'd ached for baby Chloe as much as she had Heaven for months after leaving the Rawlins house. More than once, Molly had awoken her from restless, tear-filled slumber on the couch.

And then there was Heaven. She was taking the money to hire a lawyer to procure a divorce from Kingston, she'd said. After all this time, was there really a chance for them? Or, more realistically, after all this time, could they live together regardless of the nature of their relationship?

She looked down at Molly's name chiseled into the simple stone. "And then there's the house," she said. "Molly, you told me you wanted that money you'd saved for so long to go toward a down payment on a house, and it did." She blew out a heavy breath. "If I leave that house, am I betraying you, somehow? Your memory?"

She lowered herself to sit cross-legged before the grave. She slapped her gloves against her leg as she glanced over at a family that was visiting a grave twenty or so yards away. She smiled as the family began to sing "Happy Birthday" to whomever belonged to the grave.

Returning her attention back to Molly, she said softly, "Give me a sign, Mol. Something. I don't know what to do."

She gasped when she felt a little tickle against the bit of skin revealed at the V where her shirt was buttoned. Stunned, she saw a butterfly sitting on her shirt, wings just barely moving, reminding her of a dog studying something, its tail just barely moving as it concentrated. A second later, the beautiful insect flew away, only to land on Molly's headstone.

Jessie brought her hand up, her fingers touching where the butterfly had landed on her. She realized that directly beneath her shirt was Heaven's ring on the chain.

❧❧❧❧

"Over there, gentlemen," Heaven said, pointing as she took the box from Chloe that the teen had carried in before scurrying back out for another load.

"Dad, I think she wants it here." Jessie grunted, her fingers wedged beneath the underside of the dining room table opposite Dobbs. They slowly lowered the heavy piece of furniture into place, Jessie blowing out a breath as she wiped her hands on her trousers.

"Only a couple more boxes, Mom!" Chloe placed the two she carried just inside the entryway before heading back outside again.

"I think we've only got the dresser and we're done," Jessie said, she and her father also heading back out. The four young men from Dobbs's work crew that he'd talked into helping were finishing up with the rest of the furniture on the flatbed outside.

Finally, an hour later, the four men had taken off, leaving Dobbs, Jessie, Heaven, and Chloe. Ronin was with his aunt so the little guy would stay out of the way. They sat at the newly placed dining room table eating the sandwiches Jessie and Heaven had put together the night before at Jessie's house. It had been a long day, and the three others looked as exhausted as Jessie felt.

"Before I head out," Dobbs said, taking a sip from his iced tea. "I'll get the beds together."

"Thanks, Dobbs," Heaven said. "I truly appreciate it. And we'll absolutely return the favor when all your equipment arrives." She gave him a winning smile. "Very, very exciting!"

Dobbs raised his glass in salute. "To new beginnings for us all."

Jessie grinned, raising her glass of water, her smile growing when she saw the excitement on Chloe's young face at being included. "To new beginnings." She looked to Heaven, who was already looking at her, glass raised.

"To new beginnings," she said quietly.

❧❧❧❧

Chewing on her bottom lip, Jessie looked from the armoire to the dresser, deciding which one she wanted to put her trousers in. Back at the house, she'd only had the dresser, so it had been easy enough to decide. At Granite House, she'd decided to keep the bedroom set that was already in the bedroom she had chosen, leaving her furniture back at the house with her father. This bedroom had more storage options as it was larger than her old one. She'd chosen the one across from the hallway bathroom, the siblings taking the two bedrooms on either side of the bathroom.

She glanced at the closed bedroom door when a knock sounded. "Come in."

The door opened and Heaven appeared. Since they'd reunited, she'd only seen Heaven dressed to the nines with perfect hair and makeup, stylish and beautiful. But now, she was even more beautiful. Makeup gone, hair pulled back into a ponytail, and dressed in her nightgown covered by a belted robe.

"Hey, there," Jessie greeted with a welcoming smile.

"Hey, yourself." Heaven stepped into the room, lightly closing the door behind her. She looked around, walking over to the bed to sit down. "I can't believe we're all here."

"Me, neither." Jessie decided on the armoire and that she would hang the trousers. She pulled open the doors, delighted to see there were already wooden hangers available. She began to hang the garments, feeling Heaven watching her from the bed. "How're the kids dealing, now that it's official?" she asked, glancing over at her companion.

"Ronin is crashed out," Heaven said, leaning on a hip as she braced her weight against the hand of an outstretched arm. "Usually the case when he spends time with his cousins. Chloe…" A beautiful smile spread across her lips. "Honestly," she said, her voice having a soft, ethereal quality. "I've never seen her happier. We've only been here a day, and she's a different kid."

"Why do you think that is?" Jessie reached for another pair, shaking them out before grabbing another hanger for them.

"I think because no matter what, Kingston there or not, his heavy presence was always felt there." Heaven's voice was somewhat bitter. "It was like you could never get away from him. I certainly felt it, and I think the kids both did, too. Particularly Chloe. You know, older, able to understand what she was feeling, articulate it."

Last pair hung, Jessie closed the doors and walked over to the bed, plopping down on it. She lay across it on her side, cradling her head in her hand. "I'm really proud of you."

"Me? Why?" Heaven mirrored Jessie's position, a foot and a half of space between them.

"Because what you've done took so much damn courage, Heaven." Jessie smiled, hoping her admiration showed in that smile. "If it was just you…" She shrugged the shoulder that wasn't against the bed. "You had the strength to take your children out of a situation that was not good for any of you. So many just stay for the sake of safety, stability, whatever."

"Well," Heaven said. "Isn't that what I did for sixteen years? Stayed for safety and stability?"

Jessie shook her head. "No. Knowing what I do now, the whole picture, no." She reached over and lightly touched Heaven's hand, which rested on the quilt in front of her reclined body. "I think you did what you thought you had to." She pulled her hand back from Heaven's but left it between them on the bed.

Heaven's gaze fell to that hand, reaching out and turning it over so Jessie's palm was facing up. She lightly traced her fingertip over the calluses on Jessie's hands. "You've worked so hard your whole life, Jessie."

Jessie watched the gentle touches, doing her level best to ignore the lightning flashes of sensation they were sending up her arm and into parts unmentioned. "The way it goes, I guess." It had been so many years since she'd been touched by a woman in any way, let alone by Heaven. The touches were completely innocent, but damn, the jolt to her system was strong.

"I have always had endless respect for you." Heaven met her gaze, her fingers still lightly tracing the strong fingers and palm. "I want my kids to learn from you. To be so well-rounded like you are, you know? Something I just don't know how to teach them." She brought the hand up and leaned down, leaving a soft kiss in the palm before closing Jessie's fingers around it. "I'm so glad you decided to move in."

"Me, too." *I hope.*

Chapter Twenty-Three

It absolutely enraged Jessie how scared Heaven was, just a few feet away. She wasn't just nervous, but outright scared. How pathetic and insecure was Kingston Rawlins that he needed to instill that sort of fear into someone to feel like the big man? Jessie said nothing, as Heaven needed that bastard's signature on the dotted line.

As the senator took his time wandering around the house, looking at this, touching that, it was clear he not only knew that, but he was going to milk the situation for every sweet little moment of angst he could. His "reasoning" for coming to the house was to make sure his children were safe and not living in "paltry conditions."

Jessie was going to go to work as usual, but Heaven had pleaded with her to stay, saying she didn't want to be alone with him. Though she felt out of place and out of her depth, she understood why Heaven had wanted her there, one last time.

Kingston Rawlins was thirteen years older than Heaven, and now a man in his mid-forties, he was still handsome but looked as though he enjoyed his life of leisure a bit too much. His hair had some gray coming in, but despite the expensive, tailored suit he wore and fine, polished shoes, it was his eyes that garnered Jessie's attention. It wasn't their color, shape, or size, but the intensity of their gaze.

As they followed him around in his tour of the

house, he took every opportunity to devour Heaven alive with that gaze. Yes, Heaven was a stunning woman, but Jessie felt this wasn't about appreciating her beauty or natural sensuality. This was about the predator within, the snake that masqueraded as Senator Kingston Rawlins.

She knew from what Mimi had told her all those years ago that he'd steadily worked his way through the house staff—not always consensually. No doubt he would have picked her number out of the hat eventually, had Jessie not left when she did. Heaven was a strong woman, Jessie knew that, had seen it and experienced it. So, for her to have such fear of him… What had he done to her? The neglect she already knew about didn't cause this reaction.

Jessie filed it away but made the protectiveness she'd carried when they were kids and teenagers roar back into play. She took a slight step closer to Heaven, subconsciously throwing that protective blanket around the smaller woman with her nearness. Just as it had always been, she felt Heaven instantly relax a bit.

"What is all this?" he asked, indicating the little play area that Jessie had created for Ronin in his own former window nook, which the boy called his "magic hallway." A toy chest had been built for him, resembling a pirate chest. He had big, comfy quilts spread out on the floor, which he curled up in to nap in the warm glow from the incoming sunlight, or sometimes simply pretend was his "ocean" to roll around in and just be a boy.

"What does it look like?" Jessie said when Heaven said nothing. "It's Ronin's play area."

Kingston glared at her. "I don't recall addressing you, *best friend.*"

"Well, considering you didn't address anyone in particular," Jessie quipped. "Open field for response."

He wandered over to Jessie, who stood near the open doorway. "You got a mouth on you for hired help, girl," he said, his voice nearly a purr.

"I'm not hired help," she said, standing to her full height, her voice clear and strong. "I'm a homeowner and hardworking constituent and voter, *Senator*."

"Is that so?" he asked.

Jessie held her ground as the politician took a step toward her. She knew he was used to people, women especially, backing down. She flat out refused. He was in *her* house now. "That's so."

He looked from her to Heaven, who stood partially behind Jessie. "I see you still have your servant girl speaking for you, Heaven." He tsked with his tongue. "So sad," he said absently, breezing by the two women as he left the bedroom.

Jessie reached behind her and found Heaven's hand, lightly squeezing it, noting how clammy it was, before releasing it and following the man who continued down the hallway to Heaven's bedroom.

"So," he said, looking around, trailing two fingers along the top of the wooden dresser with attached mirror. He looked at the fingers, rubbing imaginary dust away between them. "Do you gals still have your late-night giggle fests in bed?" He looked to Jessie, fire in his eyes. "Or has she finally let you in her pants?"

Jessie was about to attack when she felt a surprisingly firm hold on her arm. She looked over to see Heaven stepping up, glaring at her soon-to-be ex-husband. "You've seen enough, Kingston," she said. Though her voice seemed calm, Jessie knew Heaven well enough to know she was seething. "It's time for you to go."

Feeling he'd won that round, the senator smirked and walked past the women once more, this time heading down the hall with firm, confident strides to the stairs.

"I'll fucking kill him," Jessie whispered.

Heaven cupped her cheek and shook her head. "He's not worth it." Her gaze bored into Jessie's furious one. "Trust me on that." With a quick peck to Jessie's lips, Heaven hurried after the man. After a moment, Jessie followed.

When they arrived downstairs, Kingston was already sitting at the dining room table, looking over the packet of papers that had been waiting for him along with a pen. Jessie stood back toward the doorway, as she felt this part was very much not her business. Heaven took the seat across from him at the table.

"So," he said, all business, now. "I'm to believe you want nothing from me?" He glanced up at her. "Nothing?"

"All I want from you is my freedom," Heaven said, her voice cold. "And for you to leave my children be."

"*Your* children?" he said with a smirk. "Don't you think I had a little something to do with that?"

Heaven said nothing, simply sat there with fingers folded on the table before her.

His gaze fell back to the papers, continuing to read. "What of their schooling?" he asked. "I see nothing here regarding that."

"Because it's none of your concern," she said. "Let's be frank, Kingston. You didn't have any concern for their education before now, all your concern with your other family."

His head shot up. "Excuse me?"

"Debra, Connor, and the twins, Alexander and Aubry," Heaven said, her tone downright conversational.

Jessie was stunned as she stood there, shoulder resting against the archway. She wasn't only stunned that the information was being delivered with such confidence—she was also stunned at the information itself. Her gaze went to Kingston, whose profile was to her. He seemed to be staring a hole into the woman who sat before him, the mother of his firstborn.

"I see," he finally said.

"After all," Heaven continued. "You are the 'family traditions' candidate." She smirked. "Just spitballing here, but going to guess that bigamy isn't part of family traditions." She glared at him. "Nor is it legal."

"You're playing a very dangerous game, woman," he said, voice low.

"I'm not playing a game at all, Kingston. I'm trying to ensure that you leave me, those I love, and *my* children alone. I want absolutely nothing from you but your absence."

Kingston glanced over at Jessie. "Are you part of this?"

Jessie said nothing, as she had no clue just exactly what Heaven's plan was, and didn't want to say anything to add or subtract from it. She simply remained standing, leaning against the archway with her arms crossed over her chest.

Clearly very angry, Kingston reached for the pen and uncapped it. He held the cap in thick fingers before using the writing implement to scratch out his signature and initials on the document. Finished, he recapped the pen and tossed it to the table, where it nearly rolled off the edge when he pushed his chair back and stood.

Jessie watched as the politician stalked out of the house, slamming the front door behind him. She waited until she heard the car start and drive away before she was able to release the breath she hadn't realized she'd been holding.

Heaven was still seated, and she was trembling, eyes closed. Pushing away from the archway, Jessie walked over to her, noting the divorce papers sitting there, all signed and pretty, before moving on to the seated woman.

Squatting, Jessie rested her hands on the arms of Heaven's chair and looked up at the downcast face. "Are you okay?"

Heaven, too, took a long, slow breath before nodding. Her eyes opened and she met Jessie's gaze. "It's over," she whispered. "I can't believe it. It's all over."

Jessie smiled at the look of absolute wonder that began to fill Heaven's eyes. "Yes, it is. And I think it calls for one hell of a celebration. Don't you?"

Heaven nodded, studying Jessie's face. "I do." Her expression softened. "Why do you do it?"

"Why do I do what?"

"Continue to protect me, be here for me." Heaven cupped Jessie's upturned face. "Why are you so good to me?" Her head cocked to the side a bit, her gaze growing troubled. "After I put you through so much."

Jessie covered the hand on her face with her own. "Today is a new day," she said in lieu of responding directly to the question. "New start." She smiled. "Like you said, it's all over. Nothing that happened before today matters anymore."

"Nothing?" Heaven asked, sadness in her tone.

Jessie took the hand from her face and cradled it against her chest. "Nothing that we didn't choose," she amended.

A slow, tentative smile spread across Heaven's lips. "Nothing we didn't choose," she agreed quietly.

❧❧❧❧

Jessie's nose was brought into wakefulness before the rest of her. Coffee, bacon, pancakes… Her eyes popped open, and she looked around. As expected, her bedroom was empty, save for her. She propped herself up on her elbows, trying to get her bearings, when there was a little knock on her door.

"Come in," she called.

The door opened and, to her wide-eyed shock, it was Ronin, who ran in and jumped on her bed, followed by Heaven carrying a tray laden with the aforementioned breakfast goodies. Chloe followed with a second tray.

Jessie looked from the food to Heaven's face, a question in her eyes. In response, Heaven simply gave her a radiant smile. "Good morning," she said, walking over to the bed and, after Jessie quickly moved her alarm clock aside, setting her tray on the bedside table. "Chloe, go ahead and set that on the dresser, sweetheart."

"Okay, Mom."

Ronin planted himself on the bed next to Jessie, looking up at her with a huge grin. "I'm sitting here."

Jessie's eyebrows shot up. "Oh yeah?" At his vigorous nod, she grinned and wrapped her arm around his narrow shoulders. She ruffled his sleep-mussed hair and looked to see the other two ladies were unloading huge plates filled with the amazing-smelling food, obviously enough for all of them.

"Okay," Heaven said, very carefully lowering herself to the bed to sit where Jessie's legs had been moments before, as she'd drawn them up to sit cross-legged. Chloe sat across from her brother. Heaven met her gaze and held it for a moment before she placed Jessie's plate before her on the quilt and her own in her own lap, Chloe doing the same for herself and her little brother. "I know we all went out for a good dinner last night, but I wanted us all to have a good breakfast this morning, too."

"You could've asked for help, you know," Jessie teased.

"I had help," Heaven responded, nodding toward the two others on the bed. "And besides," she added playfully. "What kind of surprise would it be if you helped make it?"

Jessie chuckled as she took in a bite of bacon. "Fair enough," she muttered around the food.

It had been a week since Kingston had signed the divorce papers, which had immediately been taken to Heaven's lawyer for processing. Since that day, she'd noticed a huge change in Heaven. Every day she seemed to move toward the person she'd known. A woman who was playful, who was amusing, and at times, brash.

She'd be lying if she said it hadn't brought her great joy to see that gaudy wedding ring removed. Now, the only jewelry Heaven wore was a necklace her father had given her years ago, and Jessie's ruby ring. Her gaze fell on that ring now, as Heaven's right hand held her coffee cup. The small stone caught the morning sunlight coming in from the window.

The first time they'd been to Granite House, the night they'd lost their virginity together, they'd spoken about what life could be like for them together, as a couple. Heaven had even gone so far as to say a "married couple." No, the law and the church certainly didn't say that was possible, but the heart sure as hell did.

When they'd exchanged rings in the kitchen that first night of their special weekend, Jessie had given her heart completely to the woman who now sat before her, chatting with her daughter about her going out with friends to the picture show.

"Huh?" she asked, realizing her name had been called. "Sorry. What?"

Heaven looked amused. "I asked if you'd like to go with us to the theater." She shrugged as she sipped her coffee. "We can sit further away with Ronin and let Chloe have fun with her girlfriends."

"Yes," Jessie said immediately. "Absolutely." Though she'd planned to go do some work at City Park, she instantly felt drawn to go. She felt an insatiable need to be with her family, something she couldn't fight against and didn't really understand. She'd begun to find that she honestly didn't feel whole unless she was with them. With Heaven.

It scared the hell out of her.

❧ ❧ ❧ ❧

Jessie held Ronin in her arms as the theater was busy, and the little guy looked on with wide-nervous eyes. Heaven led the way. Chloe had split off with her group of three giggling teenaged girls, leaving her mother, brother, and Jessie to fend for themselves. Jessie had sprung for treats for the three of them, as well as for Chloe and her friends. It felt good. It felt damn good.

"This is okay?" Heaven asked, indicating a row

that was far enough away from the girls to give them some privacy and independence, yet close enough if there were any issues.

"Yes, ma'am," Jessie said, giving her a grin of approval.

The two sidestepped their way down the narrow aisle, Jessie careful Ronin didn't inadvertently kick anyone's head in the row in front of them. They got settled, Ronin in the seat between them. "Here you go, sweetheart," Heaven said, giving him the special treat he'd wanted from the concession stand. She looked to Jessie. "Licorice?"

"Thank you." Jessie took the sweet from the other woman's hand, their fingers grazing each other in the exchange. It sent a little jolt through her, and from the look in Heaven's eyes, she wasn't alone.

❧❧❧❧

Later that night, Ronin carried to bed as he'd crashed halfway through the movie, and goodnights said, Jessie was down in the kitchen making herself a lunch for the following day. She had a very long day ahead of her that would start before dawn. She'd rather not chance being tired and forgetting about her lunch while trying to get breakfast under her belt.

"Jessie?"

Turning from the sandwich she was preparing, Jessie saw Chloe entering the room, dressed in her nightgown and bathrobe. "Hey, kiddo. What's up? Want some?" she asked, indicating the block of cheddar she was cutting. At Chloe's nod, she handed the teen one of the slices she'd already cut.

Chloe nibbled on it as she stepped up to Jessie, leaning back against the counter as she watched her work. "First of all, thanks for the fun day with my friends. For letting me go."

Jessie's eyebrows furrowed as she glanced over at her. "What do you mean?"

Chloe shrugged. "Well, I know my mom asks your advice and stuff, so you obviously said yes."

"You know," Jessie began, smearing some mustard onto one of the slices of Wonder Bread. "Your mom does ask about advice and stuff a lot from me, but it's not because I hold any power in this household, hon." She spared a glance at the teen. "Meaning, I'm not the boss." She grinned. "Trust me on that one." She put the slice of bread down and rinsed off the knife before smearing mayonnaise on the other slice. "But we've known each other for so many years, I think it's just kind of natural for us both, you know?" She held her gaze. "Haven't you ever had a best friend that you just really trust? Know that, no matter what, they've got your best interests in mind? Does that make sense?"

Chloe didn't say anything for a moment as she chewed on the cheese, then finally nodded. "Yeah, it does."

"And, when it comes to your mom's place as your mom, I respect that one hundred percent. If she wants advice or my thoughts, I'll happily give them to her, but in the end, it's her word that matters." She gave her a lopsided grin. "Sorry."

Chloe chuckled. "Well, darn."

Jessie laughed. "Hey, I'll do all I can if you get in a pickle, but I'm the low woman on the totem pole, here."

"I don't know about that," Chloe said, her tone changing, becoming serious and almost thoughtful. She looked as though she were contemplating something. "Jessie," she finally said. "Are you a homosexual?"

Chapter Twenty-Four

Jessie stared at her, no clue if she'd heard the teen correctly. "Uh..."

Chloe looked away shyly, shrugging as she messed with the cheese in her hand. "My friend Edna tonight, she..." She spared a glance to a still-stunned Jessie. "She said you dress like her Aunt Tootie, and she's a homosexual."

Finally breathing again, Jessie turned back to her sandwich, not wanting to make it a big deal, as this was an incredibly important conversation. "Well, before I answer your question, and I will, do you know what that is?"

Chloe looked uncomfortable as she fidgeted with the belt of her robe, cheese eaten. "Um, from what Edna said, it's a man or a woman who loves another man or a woman. Right?"

Jessie nodded, slicing a tomato. "That's exactly right." She gave the teen a smile, letting her know that not only was she correct, but also that it was okay she asked. "How does the idea of a person like that make you feel, Chloe? As in, no big deal, uncomfortable, that sort of thing."

Chloe didn't respond right away, instead seeming to take her time to consider. One thing that Jessie was relieved about, however, was she didn't seem to be fazed by the conversation. It seemed more of a curiosity as opposed to anything that bothered or scared her. She just hoped it remained that way after she got her answer.

"Well," Chloe finally said. "We used to have a cook a long time ago, before my father made Mom get rid of all the house staff. She used to read the Bible a lot and used to talk to me about stuff God said." She met Jessie's gaze. "One thing she always used to say was that we were made exactly how God meant to make us, that he likes variety." She gave her a sheepish smile. "Which is why we have black people and white people, all that." She crossed her arms casually over her chest. "If I was made to like boys, God wanted it that way, right?"

Jessie nodded. "Sure."

"So, if Edna's aunt was made to like other girls, then God had to make that happen too, right?"

Jessie looked at her, shaking her head. "I am so proud of you, Chloe," she blurted.

Chloe gave her a winning smile, pride in her green eyes. "Thank you. But what did I do to earn that?"

"Just the heart you have," Jessie said simply. "The way you see the world. How you accept that, sometimes, it just is."

Chloe's smile brightened. "You know, Mom says I'm a lot like you." She gave Jessie a sweet smile. "We really only grew up with our mom, our father not really there, and when he was, it was just awful." Her expression closed off for a moment as she looked down at the floor at their feet.

Jessie reached out and lightly squeezed her arm in support. Chloe sent her a grateful smile, then continued.

"I hope this doesn't sound stupid, but we've only had our mom, who I love a whole lot," she rushed to say. "I have so much respect for her, all she's done for me and my brother. But is it stupid or wrong to say that it's really amazing to have another person, somebody that my mom loves and respects so much, to talk to? To look up to? I mean, obviously you're not a man or our dad, but…" She shrugged. "I don't know. It's like, a different perspective from somebody that I absolutely know loves us. Like, all of us, not just Mom."

Jessie had to blink several times to keep her emotions that threatened at bay. She was so touched. Finally, she said, "I do love you guys, Chloe." Her voice was a bit raspier than usual with the unshed emotion. She gave her a soft smile. "I hope your mom doesn't kill me for telling you this, but I was there when you were born." She met Chloe's shocked gaze. "In fact," she added, indicating the house around them. "Your mom and I were here when we talked about names for babies. We decided on Chloe that night."

Chloe's eyes welled up. She turned away for a moment, seeming to need to get herself together. This, of course, made Jessie's own emotions rise, and a tear managed to fall. She wiped at it with the shoulder of her shirt.

"You're the one who made up that song, aren't you? You used to sing that to me. Mom told me once that somebody she really loved used to sing it to me when I was a baby. That was you."

Jessie nodded. "Yup," was all she could manage.

Chloe shook her head. "Wow. Do you think that's why I feel so close to you?" she asked. "Like you're so familiar? I mean, I understand that I was a baby and have no real memories, but maybe I do, somehow. I mean, this probably sounds really stupid, but even that day in the store, with the candy. You just seemed like… like I knew you. And the fact that Ronin let you pick him up that day. Trust me, that *never* happens."

Jessie eyed her. "Guess we were all meant to be a

family, huh?" She reached over and kissed the side of Chloe's head. "And, yes. I am a homosexual."

⁂

Holy cow, she was tired. And grateful that her dad had let her shower at his house, where she'd inhaled her third sandwich of the day while they'd talked out particulars for the new business. Now, all she wanted was to see Heaven and then crash. Her work boots felt like they weighed fifty pounds each as she climbed the stairs. The house was dark, as she'd expected it to be, considering it was nearly ten.

She bypassed her own bedroom and went straight to Heaven's. She noted there was dim light beneath the door, so she decided to knock lightly. At the invitation to enter, she did. Heaven was resting against some pillows in bed, reading a book. Jessie quickly closed the door behind her.

Heaven watched her approach, a welcoming expression on her beautiful face. "Well, hello there."

"Hi." Jessie walked up to the bed and essentially did a face-plant on the unused side, her booted feet hanging off the end so as not to get the bed dirty. She groaned deep in her throat at the relief of finally getting off her feet. She nearly purred when she felt fingers running through her hair, still damp from her quick shower.

"Why is your hair wet?"

"Dad let me shower," Jessie murmured into the blanket. "I was gross." She heard a soft chuckle and turned her head to look at the woman who sat beside her. "Took an extra set of clothes this morning," she explained. "Figured I wouldn't be allowed in the house when the day was done." She grinned. "Sorry I'm so late. Dad has picked up some clients, so after our regular shift we did those houses, too."

"Oh yeah?" Heaven said, tucking some short strands behind Jessie's ear. "You need a haircut. Getting shaggy."

"Mm-hmm," Jessie agreed. She turned to her side. The gentle fingers felt so good. The next thing she knew, she was scooting and readjusting her body until her head was resting in Heaven's blanket-covered lap. She was nearly purring now, not only from the soft touches, but also the kiss that was left on the side of her head. She was in a cocoon of Heaven's touch and the smell of her shampoo and lotion.

"You don't have to work so hard," Heaven murmured, leaving another kiss. "I'm working, too. We're fine."

Jessie nodded. "I know," she slurred. "Just wanna give you a good life. Don't want you to leave." Jessie's eyes were already closed, her exhaustion leading her to be far more honest than she would have if she'd been lucid.

"Not going anywhere, baby," was whispered against her ear. "Ever again." Another kiss before Jessie was gently nudged awake. "Let's get you undressed and in bed."

Jessie nodded, forcing herself to wake up enough to walk to her own bedroom. "Sorry." She pushed herself to a sitting position, swaying for a moment before she began to scoot toward the foot of the bed to stand.

"No." Heaven climbed off the bed and moved to Jessie's boots. She removed one and then the second, gently setting the footwear on the floor at the foot of the bed. Next went Jessie's socks. "Stand."

Jessie did, and to her surprise, Heaven began to unbutton her shirt with deft fingers. As she was being undressed, she studied Heaven's face, her gaze drinking in every feature, which she had memorized decades ago.

"You're so beautiful," Jessie murmured, stunned that the words had fallen out of her mouth.

Heaven's gaze flicked up from her fingers to Jessie's eyes. Holding her gaze, she gently pushed the unbuttoned shirt off and over strong shoulders and arms. The garment fell to the floor, and Heaven's attention went to removing the undershirt Jessie wore beneath her button-ups, as she could get to sweating fiercely in her job and she didn't want her bra to become visible through the saturated material.

"Lift your arms," Heaven said softly. When Jessie did, the undershirt was pulled off, leaving her standing there so vulnerable in her bra and trousers. "You know," she said softly, gently tossing the undershirt to the bed behind Jessie. "There was this horrible fear hanging over me that you weren't coming back tonight." She gave Jessie an uncharacteristically apprehensive smile. "I know it's silly."

She moved to stand behind Jessie, between her and the bed. She unsnapped her bra, fingers lightly brushing the straps off her shoulders before it, too, was on the floor. Jessie's eyes closed as those fingers and hands smoothed over the skin of her shoulders and upper back.

"So strong," Heaven murmured. Her arms snaked around Jessie's waist, her cheek resting on Jessie's bare upper back as she hugged her from behind.

Jessie's eyes closed at the full-body hug, her hands covering those at her belly. "I'll always come back home, Heaven," she said. "Where I belong." They both knew she meant more than just a simple building or house. After a long moment, she squeezed those hands. "I need to get to my room or I'm gonna fall asleep where I stand."

Heaven left a kiss where her cheek had been and released Jessie. "No," she said, moving around to Jessie's front. She held the undershirt in her hands. Jessie noticed Heaven glanced at her naked breasts before she held the shirt open for Jessie to put on. "I want you to stay here tonight. You can sleep in this." She gave Jessie a sweet smile once her shirt was pulled down into place. "I need you close."

Jessie nodded. "Okay." She caressed Heaven's soft cheek with the backs of her fingers before her trousers were undone and she was instructed to step out of them. Then she was led back to the bed, her clothing left where it fell.

Heaven pulled the covers back, waiting for Jessie to climb in before she pulled the sheet and blanket up, tucking them in around her shoulders. She quickly moved to the other side of the bed, turned off the lamp, and climbed in on her side. She scooted over to Jessie and snuggled up to her, head resting on her shoulder after Jessie wrapped an arm around her. Within moments, they were sound asleep.

❧❧❧❧

Jessie's internal alarm clock went off and she slowly rose into a new day. Eyes still closed, she realized that she held a small body in her arms. Blinking her eyes open, she saw that she was lying on her side facing Heaven, but Ronin was curled up against her chest, between the two of them.

"He really missed you at dinner last night," Heaven whispered.

Jessie looked from her unexpected cuddle-bug to the grinning woman lying not a foot away.

"You better be sure this is what you want," Heaven continued, "because both my children are falling in love with you."

Jessie heard the teasing in her voice but saw the seriousness in her eyes. "Uh-oh," she whispered back. "That's a whole lotta Valentine's Day cards I have to make."

The smile that she received took Jessie back to the teenage girl who was filled with piss and vinegar, as her father used to say. Full of life, full of mischief, and full of hope. "I better get one, too, then."

"I think I can make that happen." Jessie grinned.

"And chocolate," Heaven quipped.

"I just so happen to know of a great candy shop."

"And roses."

"Okay, now you're just getting greedy." She was delighted by the little laugh that earned.

"Never," Heaven whispered, all smiles.

Jessie was utterly enchanted and wished she didn't have to go to work, but duty called. She surprised herself by leaning up and over Ronin's sleeping form, kissing Heaven's lips briefly. "Good morning," she whispered. "I gotta get ready for work."

Jessie gently disentangled herself from the lightly snoring Ronin, leaving a kiss to a mess of hair before she climbed out of bed, tucking him in. She moved around the room, gathering her discarded clothing from the night before. She tugged on her trousers, as she was only in her underwear and her undershirt.

Arms filled with boots and clothing, she glanced at the bed to see Heaven watching her. "What?"

Heaven shook her head, a little smirk on her lips. "Just enjoying the view."

Jessie rolled her eyes, knowing full well she looked like a mess. "Whatever," she grumbled good-naturedly before quietly leaving the room.

☙ ☙ ☙ ☙

Jessie's smile was instant. "Well, hey, pretty lady," she said, just loud enough for the intended audience to hear.

"Hey, yourself," Heaven responded, closing the driver's side door before pulling open the back passenger door.

"Can I help?" Jessie stepped up to where Heaven had parked in the cemetery parking lot.

"You can." Heaven handed her the two to-go drinks in the paper cups while she grabbed the paper bag that Jessie hoped held their lunches. "This was a great idea," she said, closing the car door as the two began to walk toward a shady spot in the mid-August afternoon. It was a warm day, but soon enough the temperatures would begin to fall as autumn approached.

"Well," Jessie said. "I figure Dr. Alton's office isn't all that far from here, and since I'd be at this locale during your lunch break… Thanks for picking this up, by the way." She shrugged and smiled as they got settled on the stone bench, Jessie straddling it to face her most welcome companion.

They were quiet for a moment as they readied their lunches and drinks. "Chloe told me about the conversation you two had a while ago."

"Which one?" Jessie asked before tossing a ketchup-drowned french fry into her mouth.

"About you being a homosexual," Heaven said quietly. Though there seemed to be nobody around, they knew they had to be careful.

Jessie nodded. It had never come up again, but to her delight—and relief—Chloe had seemed fine with everything, and the two were as close as ever. "Yeah," she said. "I hope you're not angry with me for being honest with her questions, Heaven. I just felt it would do far more harm than good to lie."

"No, not at all," Heaven said, reaching over and lightly touching Jessie's knee. "No, after the nonstop bullshit with Kingston, I won't have lying, for me or for them." She gave Jessie the most loving smile. "That's one of the things I love about you the most. I adore you for that, Jessie. But she asked me if I'm a homosexual, too."

Jessie's eyebrows shot up, both in surprise at the question and curiosity about what the answer was. Heaven had been forced into that marriage, sure, but the marriage had also put Jessie in a constant state of doubt, fear, and confusion about where Heaven stood. "And…" she hedged. "What did you say?" She felt like a shy little kid, so unsure. She focused on her food, unable to meet Heaven's gaze.

"I told her that, yes, I am."

Jessie's eyes rose to meet Heaven's unwavering gaze. She felt that touch to her knee again and looked down to where those fingers rested. She raised her eyes again at her name, so soft and beautiful on Heaven's lips.

"I was honest with my daughter, and I want to be honest with you, too," Heaven said. She took what seemed to be a steadying breath. "I am so in love with you, Jessie. I always have been. Circumstances may have stepped in the way, but how I felt never changed."

Jessie was left near speechless by the heartfelt declaration that she felt in her own heart. She could see that Heaven had more to say, so she simply listened.

"We've become a family, absolutely. And," she added with a small chuckle. "To my shock, with no real issues over these past couple months. But," she said, her fingers daring to wrap around Jessie's for a moment. "I want us to be a couple, too. I want—no, I *need* you. Your love, your touch." She sent a pleading gaze to Jessie. "I want to go to sleep with you every night and wake up with you every morning."

Jessie felt her heart rate pick up, her own need, which had been pushed down for so long, finally able to maybe, just maybe, be free.

"Do you see?" Heaven continued, so much passion in her words. "It may have taken some time, but everything we talked about that night on the couch so long ago…we did it. We dreamed it into life. After years of hating Kingston, and hating my mother and George Russ, I understand it now. All of it had to happen, Jessie." Her smile was big and bright. "In order for you and I to be able to be together, on our terms, with our Chloe, and yes, a little surprise named Ronin—all of that had to happen. We have our family. We even have the same damn house," she said with a burst of relieved laughter.

Jessie grinned, nodding. "I think your dad was listening." She felt the final chains fall from her shoulder, her heart, her very soul. As Heaven had said so many weeks ago, it was over. And yes, maybe it all had been for a reason. "Okay," she said softly.

Chapter Twenty-Five

Ahem."

Knocked out of her thoughts, Jessie looked over at the man she was working side by side with to fix the sprinkler system on Mrs. Epson's lawn. She was one of the new clients in their burgeoning business. "What?"

"You gonna help me, or sit there grinnin' like a fool?" At her blush, Dobbs chuckled, smacking her on the back. "I take it lunch went well with your angel?"

She grinned and returned her focus back to the task at hand. "Yeah," she admitted. "It did." She'd never felt more happy or more in love in all her life, and she'd yet to even really kiss her or touch her since their lunch. A quick hug and peck to the cheek had to suffice at Heaven's car in the cemetery parking lot. "It did. Which," she said, shaking herself out of her thoughts. "I was going to talk to Heaven about maybe having an end-of-summer barbecue." She shrugged as she met his gaze. "Let the kids invite a friend, have you over, that sort of thing. Interested? That is, if Heaven's on board."

"Heck yeah," Dobbs said, grinning. "Count me in. Love them kids, and lord knows I love spending time with you girls." He grew quiet for a moment and seemed to be turning something around in his head.

"Everything okay?" Jessie asked, sitting back on her heels from where they both had been on their knees leaning over the busted line.

"I, uh," the older man began. "I wanted to ask you

somethin', Jes."

"Sure. What's up?" Jessie reached into her toolbox to grab the wrench she was going to need for the stubborn bolt she was trying to remove.

"You know, watchin' you and Heaven finally get things together, and the kids and all that, it's made me awful wistful," Dobbs said.

Jessie looked at him, instantly feeling guilty. "Aw, hell, Dad. I'm sorry. Look, we have an extra bedroom, or—"

"Nah, nah," Dobbs interrupted, holding up a large hand to forestall Jessie's protests. "That's your life, kid. And how it should be." He looked away from his daughter and began tinkering once again with the sprinkler system. "There's a gal I've been talkin' to that works down at the courthouse. You know," he added with a shrug. "I'd see her on her breaks, that sort of thing, when we was working on the grounds."

Jessie nodded, her gut turning a bit as she suspected she knew where this was headed. "Alright."

Dobbs cleared his throat. "I know she's a widow," he continued. "Lost her husband to cancer, too. Five years ago."

Jessie nodded. "What's her name?"

He cleared his throat again, clearly uncomfortable talking about this. "Name's Elizabeth, but she goes by Betsy."

Jessie sat back on her heels again. "Are you interested in her, Dad?" she asked gently, able to tell he was really struggling to say what he needed to.

After a moment, he reached up and readjusted the brimmed hat he wore as the late summer sun beat down on them. Finally, he nodded. "Yeah. I was thinkin' of maybe asking her out to grab a bite to eat or something." He met Jessie's gaze, his own a bit sad. "But I ain't gonna do it unless you're okay with it, Jes. You know I loved your mama since I was fourteen years old." He removed the hat and ran his hand through his sweaty hair before plopping it back down. "I don't want you to ever think I don't love her."

"Oh, Dad," Jessie said, resting a hand on his arm. "I know how much you loved her when she was alive, and how much you still love her. But," she added gently. "She's gone now. Has been for going on nine years." He met her gaze. "You still have a lot of years ahead of you. I don't want to see you alone. If you don't want to be," she amended. "And hey," she said with a grin and a shrug. "If things go well with dinner or lunch, bring her to the barbecue so we can all meet her."

❧❧❧❧

Jessie stepped up to the doorway of Heaven's en suite bathroom, watching Heaven do her nightly ritual before bed. Jessie had already readied for bed in the hallway bathroom. They'd opted to not move her things into Heaven's bedroom until they had talked to the kids, and they planned to do so on the weekend.

"What?" Heaven asked, glancing at Jessie's reflection in the mirror above the sink. She was putting a material headband on to keep her hair out of the cold cream Jessie knew she was about to put on.

Jessie pushed off the doorframe and wandered in, stepping up beside Heaven. "I used to love watching you get ready," she said, picking up this jar or that tube. "No clue what most of this stuff is for, though." She set what she held down back in its place and walked over to the toilet, taking a seat on the closed lid.

"It's all to make women gorgeous," Heaven muttered with a little grin as she began to apply the nighttime goo on her face.

"But what if you already are?" Jessie countered. She raised a challenging eyebrow at the look she got, grinning at the rolled eyes. "So, you're okay with the cookout this weekend?" she asked, a subject she'd broached while she and Heaven had been working on dinner.

"Absolutely," Heaven said, looking at her face and making sure all the skin was covered with a thin layer of the white cream. "I think it's a lovely idea, actually." She smiled over at Jessie, who cackled. "What, not interested in sharing a bed with a friendly ghost?"

"Well, Casper," Jessie said. "I do work in a cemetery. I suppose I could have been followed home."

Heaven grinned before grabbing a face cloth reserved for this very purpose and began to methodically remove the cream. Jessie watched, though her gaze trailed down over the body draped in the silky spaghetti-strap nightgown Heaven wore. It was not shocking like the one Molly had been wearing that first night, but it was absolutely beautiful on the elegant woman who wore it. And, in Jessie's estimation, it was sexy as hell.

She tore her gaze away, still not quite feeling like she had the right to visually, let alone physically, have her way with this woman who made her heart race out of her chest. Something… something she didn't quite understand was holding her back. She looked down at her clasped hands, which dangled between her spread knees.

Her love for Heaven was endless. Her need and want for her was also endless. So, why was she holding back? Why hadn't she grabbed her and made passionate love to her, almost sixteen years in waiting? These were questions she was asking herself, and she could tell by some of the looks she was getting that Heaven was, too.

⚜ ⚜ ⚜ ⚜

"Ronin! Don't pull her tail!"

Jessie glanced over to the kids playing from where she stood at the outside grill, cooking lunch for everyone. She had to chuckle as Ronin and his cousins chased around the puppy the cousins had brought with them. The little beagle, Winnie, was absolutely adorable. She had no doubt that a puppy would be on the Christmas gift list this year.

The day was perfect, skies overhead blue as a robin's egg, not a cloud to be seen. Dobbs had brought his new lady friend, Betsy, who seemed lovely, though it was admittedly strange for Jessie, and she wanted more time to get to know her. But he seemed quite pleased with her, and that was what mattered.

Chloe had brought her friend Edna as her guest, and Heaven had never looked more beautiful. There had only been one surprise that had marred the perfection of the late-summer gathering for Jessie, and that had been the aunt Heaven had mentioned so many times over the months.

Said aunt was the mother of the three little ones running around their spacious backyard with Ronin, all stepping stones in age. She was married to Kingston Rawlins's half-brother Gerard, who, as it had been explained to her, was somewhat of a black sheep of the family. Not an heir to the Rawlins prestige or wealth and not a member of the political class, he was apparently a normal, hardworking family man. He was also the husband of the woman who was walking over to Jessie in that moment.

Jessie met her gaze before turning her focus back to the burgers and hot dogs that sizzled on the grill. "How are you, Mimi?" she asked.

"I'm really good," the pretty redhead said, though she looked so different now as a wife and mother in her mid-thirties than she had as a lost young woman of twenty. Her hair was coiffed in a much shorter and more practical style for running around after three children under the age of ten. "Busy." She gave her a small smile.

"Oh, I bet." Jessie returned the smile.

She felt decidedly uncomfortable. It wasn't just running into an ex—very unexpectedly—but also everything that seeing Mimi had drudged up. She had been in Jessie's life during its most painful time, while she was still in the Rawlins house, and after. Their last moments together had been ugly, Jessie pushing her away as she'd shut down fully after Molly's murder.

Knowing that Mimi had wanted something more substantial with Jessie left her very confused when she spotted the wedding ring on Mimi's finger, her hand wrapped around a glass of iced tea. "Your kids are adorable," Jessie managed.

"Thank you." The motherly love in Mimi's smile was evident as she glanced over to her two boys and one girl, all now playing in the sandbox Jessie and Dobbs had built for Ronin. "So, I'm sure you're extremely confused by my life."

Jessie met her gaze for a moment before returning to her task, flipping over the burgers and turning the hot dogs. "It's your life, Mimi," she said quietly. "You seem happy, and honestly, that's what matters."

"I suppose that's true," Mimi agreed. "I know it's pretty ironic that I ended up marrying Kingston's half-brother. But Gerard doesn't carry the Rawlins name, so I had no idea when I met him ten years ago." Her smile was soft and filled with affection. "We just clicked."

"I think it's wonderful, Mimi," Jessie said. "I truly do. As long as he's good to you and your kids, then it's a wonderful thing." She shrugged and let out a heavy sigh. "Women have to do what they have to do to be happy and safe." She met Mimi's gaze. "It's just part of it, unfortunately."

The redhead nodded and was quiet for a moment before she said, "I'm so glad you got your Heaven back. I know how much you loved her."

Her own soft smile spread across Jessie's lips. "Yeah. I guess things work out how they're supposed to." She met Mimi's gaze again. "One way or other."

Mimi held her arms out for a hug, which Jessie allowed. She squeezed the other woman to her, genuinely glad to see that she was okay. She certainly didn't judge her for her choices in life. She seemed happy, her children seemed very loved, and at the end of the day, that was what it was all about. She accepted a kiss on the cheek before Mimi walked away to join the backyard fun.

⁂

Jessie was quiet as she got ready for bed. There was so much swirling around in her head, and she wasn't entirely sure where to start. Heaven was also quiet, seemingly something on her mind as well. Jessie glanced over to the bathroom, where Heaven was rubbing lotion into her arms and legs.

Suddenly, she felt the need to be alone, needed some distance. Jessie rubbed the back of her neck nervously. "Um," she said. "I need some water." With that, she left the bedroom, closing the door behind her.

She trotted down the stairs in a pair of plain cotton men's pajama pants, as she absolutely hated nightgowns. She always got herself all rolled up like a burrito in the excess material. She also just felt plain uncomfortable. She also had started sleeping in the few undershirts she rotated as nightwear.

The house was dark and quiet, Chloe going home with Edna to have a sleepover and Ronin long ago conked out from an exciting day with cousins and lots of chasing a barking, tail-wagging Winnie around. She pushed on the light for the kitchen and grabbed herself a glass from the cabinet.

She was bothered. Really, really bothered. Glass of water in hand, she took a long sip of the cool, refreshing liquid before leaning back against the counter. She thought she'd dealt with everything, had had all her questions answered and ghosts exorcised, but clearly, she hadn't. Seeing Mimi that day had brought the worst of her pain back, pain that had been buried deep.

Glancing toward the stairs, she heard footfalls and knew they belonged to Heaven. Sure enough, she appeared in the kitchen a few moments later, walking out of the darkness and into the light like a beautiful wraith, her midnight hair and eyes stark against the paleness of her skin and her flowing nightgown. The angel of death, herself, come to seduce a soul to the grave with her beauty.

"Hey," she greeted.

Heaven didn't respond, simply walked to the

center of the kitchen and crossed her arms over her chest. Her face was relatively expressionless, though her eyes were filled with embers, ready to spark.

"Do you want to be here?" Heaven asked. "I know you love me, I know you love my kids, but I also know that you are a woman of integrity when it comes to perceived duty. I absolutely do not want to be duty or obligation to you, Jessie. My children and I will be fine, you don't have to worry about that. If I've learned nothing in these past fifteen years, it's been how to survive."

Jessie was surprised by the candid directness of Heaven's words. She was grateful, in a way, as they could get down to what really mattered without pretty words to try and save feelings.

"Why didn't you go with me?" The words gushed out of her mouth. The dam was broken. "Why, Heaven? You said you loved me and wanted to be with me. We dreamed everything into life, right?" She gestured at the house they stood in. "So, why?" Her profound hurt had fermented into anger, so repressed she hadn't even been aware it was still there. "We could have figured out what to do about my parents. I had an out for us— for me, you, and Chloe."

Heaven looked stunned for a moment, obviously not expecting the conversation to go in the direction it had. She cleared her throat and took a seat at the kitchen table. "He knew about us," she began quietly. "In fact, he used to hide in the house and watch us when I thought he'd left or wasn't coming home that week, whatever." She snorted. "Found that out later."

Calming a bit, Jessie also sat. "I know. I saw him one night, not long before I left."

Heaven nodded and indicated Jessie's glass,

which Jessie slid over to her. Heaven took a sip and then continued. "George Russ was very blunt about his expectations and what he'd do if they weren't met. Gotta give him that." She snorted. "Kingston, on the other hand, was all about games. Everything was a game to him. In so many words, he made it very clear that if I ever left him, he'd take Chloe from me and have you arrested on sodomy laws, as a homosexual woman. And me committed, a woman clearly wired wrong for loving a woman and not capable of being a mother."

Jessie sat back in her chair, her anger and hurt deflating so quickly it left her lightheaded. "My god. Yet again, trapped."

Heaven nodded. "Yet again."

"So, why did you leave now, then? The laws haven't changed."

"No, but his priorities have," Heaven said simply. "The kids and I have become an anchor around his neck. The only reason he put on any sort of act at all was to retain control to the end." Heaven looked down at her hands, which rested on the table in front of her. "I've never felt insecure of my place in your heart until now," she said quietly. She smiled ruefully. "It sucks." Her gaze finally met Jessie's. "I knew way back that Mimi had a thing for you when you were both working at the house. Seeing you two today, I know something happened between you." She cleared her throat and took a shaky breath. "Was it while you were at the house? With me and Chloe?"

"No," Jessie said easily. "Honestly, I must be pretty thick, because I had no idea she had a crush until she told me much later. After I'd been staying with Molly for a while, Mimi and I ran into each other as she was leaving her job, working for her uncle. I honestly had no clue she'd even left the house."

Heaven nodded, not looking at Jessie. "How long did it last?"

"A matter of months."

"Why did it end?" Heaven asked, her tone shy.

"One very simple reason," Jessie said, meeting Heaven's gaze. "She wasn't you."

Heaven studied her for a long time before she asked again. "Do you want to be here, Jessie?"

Jessie, realizing that the final bit of weight had been lifted, the final questions answered, final hurts healed, gave her the most loving smile she could. "With all my heart."

Chapter Twenty-Six

Heaven's entire countenance softened at Jessie's words. She took one of Jessie's hands and tucked the fingers against her face, her eyes closing at the contact. Jessie not only saw it in her relaxed body language, but she could feel the relief coming off Heaven in waves. She felt terrible for instilling such doubt in the woman that she loved so much.

Gently squeezing the hands that held her own, Jessie pulled away as she scooted her chair away from the table, getting to her feet as she urged Heaven to do the same. Both standing, she took Heaven into her embrace. She smiled as she felt the smaller body melt into her, Heaven's face buried in Jessie's neck.

Eyes sliding closed, Jessie allowed her fingers to enjoy the feel of the skin-warmed satin beneath her fingers. It all came into focus for her. She'd kept herself busy over the last decade and a half, worked hard, and had built a life for herself and her father, but she now fully understood just how much she had merely existed.

With Heaven's warmth against her, gentle fingers beginning to work their way into Jessie's hair, she was coming back to life. She almost felt the need to take a deep breath as she surfaced, the air fresh and exhilarating. She felt a kiss on her neck, a soft sigh falling from her lips.

Jessie's hands made their way up to cup Heaven's face as she looked up at Jessie. She felt like she was holding the most precious thing in the world. But, as she looked into Heaven's eyes, saw the determination and strength there, something that hadn't always been, she realized this was no longer the woman who had been so fragile in so many ways.

She'd been sheltered by a loving father and even by Jessie in some ways, always there to be her knight in shining armor to slay the dragon, real or perceived. But this precious woman had been left to endure and survive the psychological torture of Rawlins's sick games and emotional abuse of his neglect. She had been essentially forced into servitude to bear his children, locked up in the prison he and George Russ had created for her.

She'd not only survived it, she'd been the victor. Now she stood before Jessie, asking for one thing—to be loved. Jessie brushed her fingertips over Heaven's cheek just before her lips touched hers. They'd shared a couple brief kisses since reuniting, but this kiss was different in every way. Jessie wanted Heaven to feel her love for her, as well as her want and her need.

Heaven responded, the kiss deepening though remaining slow and exploratory. It was a reconnection with something lost so long ago, a rediscovery and reaffirmation of a promise made in that very room.

After several moments, Heaven pulled away, both of them left breathing hard. She caressed Jessie's face and met her gaze. "Let's go upstairs."

Jessie nodded. She took her water glass and dumped the contents into the sink before leaving it there to deal with in the morning. Heaven took her hand and, kitchen light turned off, together they made their way up the stairs. They checked on Ronin to make sure he was still asleep, and he was sawing logs, so they knew he'd stay asleep at least until the crack of dawn.

Heaven entered their bedroom first, and Jessie closed the door behind her, clicking the lock into place. Though currently their little guy was asleep, it was entirely possible he would wake up and surprise them, and that wouldn't be a good thing in the moment. As soon as she turned back from locking the door, Heaven met her. Now, her kiss was passionate and hungry.

Her body, her very soul was ignited, and Jessie pushed Heaven backward until they were on the bed, Jessie on top of her. Heaven's hands found their way up the back of Jessie's undershirt, her fingers like claws trying to pull Jessie even closer. Jessie's hand reached down, gathering the skirt portion of the nightgown in her fingers until she felt the softness of Heaven's thigh. She pulled it up, Heaven's other thigh raising until Jessie's hips were cradled between them.

Jessie pushed her hips down into Heaven, able to feel the immense heat between her spread legs. Heaven moaned into the kiss, her hips pushing up into Jessie. Leaving her lips, Jessie began to explore the soft warmth of Heaven's neck and throat. Hands left Jessie's shirt to find her hair, urging on her kisses and exploration.

She hummed into her task, loving the taste of Heaven's skin, the little whimpers and noises of pleasure she made, and the smell of her need. They'd only been together on two occasions when they were young. Granted, they'd made the most of both, but they had no experience save for what they learned together as they went.

Jessie was no Casanova, nor was her experience extensive, but her time with Mimi and the other woman she'd briefly spent time with had taught her a lot. She'd matured as a lover and wanted to share that knowledge with Heaven who, to her knowledge, had known no passion in her marriage and had essentially been a broodmare when the mood struck her husband.

Now, she slowed her movements and kisses and took her time. She wanted to truly taste Heaven, truly experience her, and show her how she felt through making love. She wanted to give that passion to her that others had been so generous to teach Jessie. Hell, even conversations with Molly about sex had opened Jessie's eyes to things she hadn't even thought of.

She slid farther down Heaven's body, pushing the straps of her nightgown off her shoulders. This allowed her to ease down the bodice to reveal gorgeous breasts. It was astounding to her that the last time she'd seen them, fourteen-year-old Chloe had been a nursing newborn.

Now, her mouth watered, as she knew how sensitive Heaven's nipples were, how much she enjoyed her breasts played with when they made love. And, as a breast woman, Jessie was happy to oblige. Heaven's groan deep in her throat as she arched her back made Jessie respond in kind. She could feel the hips beneath her begin to rock against her.

She could tell Heaven's need was growing, so she moved from giving equal attention to both breasts and farther down. She didn't even bother to remove the nightgown in that moment, simply got to her knees and pushed the material up, revealing incredibly saturated panties.

"Lift, baby," she murmured, pulling the material down when Heaven did as asked. She could see the confusion in the beautiful eyes looking up at her as Jessie tossed the panties aside and began to settle her shoulders between Heaven's spread thighs. She gave her a loving smile before lowering her mouth to where she knew she was needed most.

Heaven's head fell back onto the bed as a long, languid groan fell from her lips when Jessie's tongue made its first long, slow trail through the incredible wetness between Heaven's legs. Jessie's name floated on a whimper as Jessie continued to explore. She loved how Heaven tasted, loved how she felt, and loved the noises that she heard above her.

Jessie held Heaven's thighs open with her arms as her hips began to move faster, breasts heaving and whimpers nearly constant now. She knew Heaven was close, so she focused her efforts at the center of her pleasure, ruthlessly batting her tongue against a hard clit. The fingers in Jessie's hair tightened almost painfully.

Finally, Heaven cried out, her back arching off the bed with the intensity of her experience. Jessie held on, milking out every ounce of pleasure for the gasping woman until her head was weakly pushed away. Leaving a kiss on the inside of Heaven's thigh, Jessie moved away and, on her hands and knees, she hovered over Heaven, leaving light kisses on her face, murmuring words of comfort as the other woman tried to calm and come back to earth.

After a moment, Heaven's eyes opened and she met Jessie's gaze. She cupped the back of Jessie's neck and pulled her down for a deep, sensuous kiss. "Wow," she murmured, making Jessie smile. She looked into Jessie's eyes. "I want you naked."

"You first," Jessie said with a grin.

Heaven looked down at herself and burst into laughter. She left a quick kiss on Jessie's lips before sitting up. They both quickly scrambled out of their clothing, Heaven kicking the covers out of the way to the end of the bed. Jessie found herself flat on her back, Heaven on top of her. It felt amazing to feel her nakedness against her own, so warm and soft. She allowed her hands and fingers to trail over her back and shoulders and then cup a shapely behind.

"You know what I love about you?" Heaven murmured, resting her upper body weight on a forearm while the hand of the other tucked shaggy light brown hair away from Jessie's face.

"What?"

"I love that you are so hardworking, so strong and adorable in your trousers, usually dirt on your face somewhere." She smiled, fingertips brushing across Jessie's cheek, right where the dirt smudge often ended up being. "But then," she continued, those fingers trailing down the side of Jessie's neck, over her left collarbone and along the rounded side of her left breast. "Get you out of those baggy clothes, and you're absolutely stunning, all woman." She took her in a deeply passionate kiss as she cupped that breast. "So sexy," she murmured against Jessie's lips.

Jessie moaned into the kiss as nimble fingers tugged and lightly twisted her erect nipple, shooting delicious sensations straight between her legs, where she was already very needy. Her head fell to the side and eyes closed as Heaven's mouth drifted to her breast, replacing her fingers.

It felt wonderful to be touched, let alone by the woman she'd been dreaming of for so long. It was tempting to think that perhaps this was simply another dream, another morning to wake up alone. Opening her eyes, she watched as Heaven licked her nipple before sucking it into her mouth. It was real. They were together. And when she felt fingers move between her legs, where she was so wet, so ready to be touched, it was more proof that Heaven was indeed making love to her.

She groaned as two fingers easily entered her. Her hips rolled with the gentle thrusts. She urged Heaven to return to her, needing her mouth as the seed of pleasure had been planted and was steadily growing with every thrust inside. She was beginning to breathe too hard to continue kissing, and she was so aroused that it wasn't going to take long. Heaven continued her thrusts between Jessie's legs but stayed with her, looking into her eyes.

That look, so much deep love and desire, threw her over the edge. Jessie gasped and a quick cry erupted before she nearly held her breath as her body exploded around Heaven's fingers. Intense waves of pleasure crashed over her, her thighs slapping shut around Heaven's hand, trapping her inside as she rode out the waves.

"I love you so much," Heaven murmured as she cradled Jessie's head against her breasts.

It took a few moments, but finally Jessie snuggled into her. "I love you," she managed, her voice still a bit breathy. "With all my heart."

Jessie pulled Heaven down to snuggle against her, Heaven pulling up the covers before she settled in. It felt wonderful. She was home, finally home. She smiled as Heaven snuggled in even closer, raising her outer thigh to drape across Jessie's.

"You know," Heaven began, her head resting on Jessie's shoulder and hand just under Jessie's left breast. "When we were together before, it was also that ticktock in the back of my mind, knowing we were on borrowed time."

Jessie nodded. "Yeah. God, that hurt."

"It did. It just blows my mind that now that's not the case." Heaven raised her head, rested it on her hand, and looked down at Jessie. Her smile was radiant, and Jessie saw the young woman from the day when they found out Harv was going to give Jessie a job at the factory and help them achieve their goals and dream of a life together as "best friends"—though she knew in her heart that Harv had known better.

Jessie returned the smile. "You're stuck with me now. You said *I* need to be sure?" She quirked an eyebrow.

Heaven laughed, the sound like music to Jessie's ears. "Oh, baby, I'm hooked," she purred. Heaven squealed as she suddenly found herself on her back, Jessie atop her, hips resting between her spread legs.

Jessie chuckled. "Still hooked?" She adjusted her hips a bit so her clit was lightly pressed against Heaven's, whose eyes became hooded.

"Do you remember?" Heaven murmured, fingers running through Jessie's hair. "This was how we made love that final time, the morning I had to marry that bastard."

"I do," Jessie admitted. She left a kiss on soft lips.

"You know," Heaven said, her fingers trailing down Jessie's back and up to cup the backs of her shoulders. "I would swear on a stack of Bibles that you have some magic in there, because I just know that Chloe is yours and not his."

Jessie grinned. "I will happily take credit."

Heaven gasped as Jessie began to slowly move her hips, lifting her knees a bit closer to her body. Jessie's thrusts against her were slow and sensual, measured to keep them aligned perfectly. Their kiss was just as deliberate. The only sound in the room was the quiet creaking of the bed and then their breathing as it began to grow too heavy to kiss.

Jessie looked down into Heaven's flushed face, falling in love with her all over again. She could feel Heaven's nails trailing down her back as she moved between her legs, which sent chills through her. She raised herself to her hands and increased her thrusts, Heaven moving with her. Heaven's hands gripped Jessie's sides as they moved faster. Jessie's second orgasm was speeding upon her. Her eyes squeezed shut and her mouth opened as she cried out her pleasure, Heaven joining her a moment later.

Burying her face in a warm neck, Jessie ground her hips into Heaven, a second, smaller wave hitting her. She was panting as Heaven held her almost painfully tight to her as Jessie's arms gave way. They were nearly one as Heaven's legs wrapped around Jessie's hips.

After several moments, Heaven murmured, "If I get pregnant…"

Jessie dissolved into giggles.

❧❧❧❧

Chloe was quiet for a moment, her bottom lip tucked beneath her upper teeth just like her mother when she was in contemplation of something. Jessie and Heaven sat at the kitchen table quietly, waiting patiently for the young woman's thoughts or questions. Jessie glanced over at the woman whose hand she held. They'd decided to be very open with their affection as they talked to the almost-fifteen-year-old.

"So, you two are a couple, then?" Chloe said slowly, as though still working things out in her mind.

Her gaze flicked up to first her mother and then Jessie. "Like, a couple like a man and a woman would be."

Heaven nodded. "Yes, honey." She spared a glance to Jessie. "Truth is, we have been since we were teenagers." She met the girl's guarded gaze again. "But the way things were, I had to marry your father."

Jessie was aware that Chloe essentially knew the story of how her parents' marriage came to be, how it wasn't her mother's choice. So, she figured in that Heaven wanted to reiterate the reason why she and Heaven had to end their relationship so long ago.

"When we all moved in here," Chloe asked, eyeing the two. "Was that always going to be the plan? You two get back together?" There was no anger or accusation, simply an information-gathering question.

"For me," Heaven said. "Yes."

"I honestly had no idea what was going to happen," Jessie responded, deciding to continue the honesty. She felt if they expected this young woman to accept them and the strange turn of events in every way, they needed to answer her questions honestly and fully. "I knew I loved your mom, but I honestly had no idea what was going to happen."

Chloe nodded. "That's fair." She chewed on that lip again before asking, "So, you both were always homosexuals, then? It didn't just happen?"

Jessie hid her smile. "I think we're just born this way, honey. Like you said that night in the kitchen, God made us this way like He made you the way you are."

Again, Chloe nodded. "And, you two are going to share a bedroom now?"

Heaven nodded. "Yes. I want her with me, sweetheart."

"Do homosexuals have sex?" Chloe asked,

looking as though the question just popped into her head.

Jessie had to look away as her blush was fast and fierce. The previous night came back to her in living color. She felt a small kick to her leg under the table. Clearing her throat, she looked to Heaven, very happy to let her answer that question.

"Yes, sweetheart," Heaven finally said. "They do. They're just like a normal couple, only the same gender."

Chloe nodded, seeming to come to some sort of understanding within her own mind. She pushed back from the table and stood. "I guess at least you don't have to worry about any surprise pregnancies."

Jessie choked on her own spit and began to cough violently, Heaven patting her on the back with concern in her eyes. "I'm okay," she managed, words cut off by more coughing.

"Was it something I said?" Chloe asked, filling a glass with water from the tap and hurrying it over to the table for Jessie.

"No, Chloe," Heaven said, though Jessie could hear she was just barely holding back her laughter. "It's okay."

Epilogue

I lift my glass," Dobbs said, standing from the dinner table, those gathered looking at him and following suit. "To our new family." His smile was so warm, so genuinely happy, it nearly brought tears to Jessie's eyes. "A year ago, I never in a million years would have thought that not only would Jes and I not be spending Christmas alone, but also that we'd have our Heaven girl back."

Jessie glanced to the woman who sat next to her, their gazes meeting and communication sent. *I love you, too, baby.* She turned back to her father as he spoke again.

"And we didn't just get her back, but we added two amazing young people, too." He sent a doting gaze to Chloe and Ronin. "I now have the most important title that I've had in all my life, behind 'husband' and 'father,' and that is 'Grandpa.'"

Ronin beamed at his favorite person outside of his mother and his Jessie.

Jessie smiled when she felt Heaven's hand move to her thigh beneath the table. She placed her hand over it, their fingers automatically entwining.

"And," Dobbs continued, his voice softening. "I lift my glass to new people in our life." He smiled down at the woman who Jessie suspected was slowly moving into his heart. Betsy gazed adoringly up at him, the petite blonde with big blue eyes a wonderful addition to their little family. "So," Dobbs concluded, addressing the table at large. "Merry Christmas to those I love most."

A chorus of, "Merry Christmas!" responded.

"Baby?"

Jessie glanced over at the softly spoken word. "Hmm?"

"I need to talk to you about something," Heaven said, for Jessie's ears only.

"Of course." She lifted an eyebrow and said under her breath, "Are you pregnant?"

A loud bark of laughter escaped Heaven's lips, which garnered interest from those around them. She gave an apologetic smile to Chloe and Betsy before turning back to Jessie. "No," she drawled. "Though not for lack of solid effort."

Jessie grinned. "No worries, love," she said, growing more serious again. "Whenever you want."

Dinner had been eaten and the cleanup began. Heaven and Jessie insisted on taking care of it, allowing everyone else to enjoy their time together. In their household, it wasn't just about the "women folk" doing chores. Ronin had expectations put upon him as well.

At five years old now, he was more than capable of picking up after himself and helping carry dishes to the counter from the table. The older he got, like Chloe, the more responsibility he'd get. That was a valuable lesson Dobbs had taught Jessie, as he'd been a full partner to his wife and not an enforcer of gender expectations.

"So, what's going on?" Jessie asked, standing at the sink as it filled with warm, soapy water. "Everything okay, love?"

"It is," Heaven assured her, standing at the kitchen table working on what was left of the turkey to pick the meat off the bone. "First and foremost, I've been given the job of talking to you about getting a dog," she said, amusement in her voice. "They're pretty darn serious about it."

Jessie chuckled. "Oh, I know they are." She sent a smile Heaven's way. "I'm fine with it, baby. As long as Chloe and Ronin understand that they'll be responsible for a lot of the care. I think animals are wonderful for kids. Teaches them about responsibility, accountability, and honestly, compassion."

"I agree. Okay, next." Heaven sent her a slightly nervous look before returning her focus to her task. "I want to change the last name of the kids and me, for two reasons. For me, I was never a Rawlins, never *wanted* to be part of that man's family. And," she added with a sigh. "I'm truly worried that someday he'll end up in some sort of terrible scandal in politics, and I don't want that to boomerang to the kids. As it is, he has nothing to do with them, and frankly, few know he's their father. But…"

Jessie nodded. "I get it. So, are you thinking about going back to McGovern?"

"Well," Heaven hedged, sparing a glance back at Jessie. "No."

Surprised, Jessie turned to look at her. She knew how dearly Heaven loved her father when he'd been alive, and even now, so many years after his death. "Oh?"

Heaven didn't say anything for a moment before she walked to the sink and washed her hands, as she'd been wrist-deep in turkey meat. She turned off the water and took Jessie's hands in her own. "I want us to take Lowrey," she said, giving her a shy smile. "It was actually Chloe's idea, but I'd been thinking about it, too."

Jessie was stunned. "But McGovern is your family

name, baby," she said gently. "Attached to a long line of successful men."

"Who defines success?" Heaven challenged. "Look at you and Dobbs. You two have built your company since the summer, and now you're both considering leaving your jobs with the city because you're just too busy. And," she added, giving her a winning smile. "I'm very much looking forward to taking over the office and store duties in January."

Jessie grinned. "I can't wait to open our store. Anything and everything a person could need for their gardening or yardwork needs."

"Exactly." She squeezed Jessie's fingers to emphasize her next point. "But success is about so much more than money, a lesson I've had to learn over my lifetime. You and your parents were and are some of the best people I've ever known. So loving, giving, caring. You're honest, full of integrity..." She cupped Jessie's cheek with her hand. "Exactly the kind of name I want my children connected to. And," she said, looking deeply into Jessie's eyes. "I've always belonged with you."

Jessie placed her hands on Heaven's waist, profoundly moved. "If you're sure."

"I'm very sure." Heaven snaked her arms up and around Jessie's neck, her fingers finding their way into her hair. She smiled up at her with adoring eyes, so much love radiating off her like heat. "I love you," she said. "I want to be part of you."

Jessie grinned. "Oh, you are, baby." She initiated a slow, loving kiss. "Welcome," she murmured against soft lips. "Mrs. Lowrey."

Heaven's smile was radiant. "I like the sound of that."

About the Author

Kim has spent her life in Colorado and can't imagine living anywhere else. She's been writing since she was 9 and stumbled into her first book being published in her mid-20s. She's worked in the film industry as a writer, director and producer, but now enjoys the quiet, happy life of a professional author. She can be reached on Facebook and on her website at, www. kimpritekel.com

If you liked this book...

Share a review with your friends or post a review on your favorite site like Amazon, Goodreads, Barnes and Noble, or anywhere you purchased the book. Or perhaps share a posting on your social media sites and help spread the word.

Join the Sapphire Newsletter and keep up with all your favorite authors.

Did we mention you get a free book for joining our team?

sign-up at - www.sapphirebooks.com

Check out Kim's other books.

1049 Club - ISBN - 978-1-939062-97-0

Almost two hundred souls, one plane, six survivors, endless heartbreak.

When flight 1049, headed from Buffalo, NY to Italy falls from the sky, a firestorm of drama, pain, angst and sorrow ensues. Can an author, a business owner, a teenager, good ol' boy, veterinarian and ruthless lawyer survive? Better yet, can those left behind?

1049 Club is a story of survival, love, deep regret and miracles. Can the living make peace with the presumed dead? Can the presumed dead make peace with the lives and loves they thought they had before?

Blinded – ISBN – 978-1-943353-53-8

After a horrible explosion sends local television news reporter, Burton Blinde reeling both physically and emotionally, she walks away from her life and the dream job she was about to start at a major news network.

For six long years she hides out in a small mountain town, working at the local library, though is haunted by the life she had, including mysterious messages and gifts she was receiving before her life was turned upside down, a veritable bread crumb trail leading to the unknown.

Unable to resist, Burton begins to follow the clues,

which will lead her into the darkest places of human nature that she may not be able to return from.

Damaged - ISBN - 978-1-939062-45-1

Family. A group of people you are related to by blood or love.

Nora Schaeffer has come home to her family after twenty years working around the world as a photographer for National Geographic. She's welcomed into the open arms of her father and siblings.

Family. A group of people who support you, lift you up when you fall.

Shannon, the youngest of the four Schaeffer siblings, has vanished, leaving her five-year-old daughter, Bella, terrified and alone. To help find Shannon, Nora has no choice but to turn to the dark-haired specter who has haunted her for twenty years. Along the way, she finds her own long-dead heart and uncovers chilling family secrets beyond imagination.

Family. A group of people who will stick together to hide the rotten soul at its core at any cost.

Who will live? Who will die? Who will be the most damaged? And who will learn to love again?

The Gift - ISBN - 978-1-948232-47-0

The dead do speak. You just have to listen. Homicide Detective Catania "Nia" d'Giovanni is the only daughter in a large Italian family of six children. The backbone—a position not applied for nor wanted—she continues to create new glue to hold the dysfunctional group together. For Nia, family time feels more like herding cats than spending time with her brothers and feisty, aging parents.

Her heart has always been in her career with the Pueblo Police Department, especially since it will never be okay with her very Catholic mother to openly give her heart to any woman, until she meets a secretive waitress who has her at, Can I take your order?

And then it begins…

Three murders that are so gruesome, so horrible, they rock the small town to its core. Nia and her partner Oscar are left to piece together a deadly puzzle to find the key to unlock the monster they hunt.

Or, are they the hunted?

As they dissect the murder scenes where not one shred of evidence is left behind, more bodies begin to show up, each cleaner than the last, the shadowy specter that is the killer vanishing without a trace, making the woman Nia loves disappear right along with it.

When there is no evidence to follow, Nia must trust her instincts…or, is she being guided?

The Plan – ISBN – 978-1-948232-43-2

As the dark days of the Dust Bowl came to an end, the

midsection of the United States tried to rebuild and revitalize. In the small, dusty farming town of, Brooke View, Colorado, teenager, Eleanor Landry and her mother were dealing with her father, a self-appointment fire and brimstone preacher to his congregation of two. A plan to survive.

As the dark era of the robber baron comes to an end, giants of industry and innovation emerged with fabulous fortunes manifested in the mansions that dotted the landscape across the country. Lysette Landon, the teen daughter of the wealthiest family in Brooke View, was everything a good, proper girl of privilege should be. Only problem was, she wasn't dreaming of finding a young man to raise a family with. A plan to be free.

One look, one touch, all plans are off.

Secrets deeper and darker than the grave would bring Eleanor and Lysette together, their families connected by a web of lies and broken promises. A plan to escape.

Be careful because, life has other plans...

The Traveler Book One: The Hunted - ISBN - 978-1-948232-91-3

A story so epic one book can't contain it. BOOK ONE:

1977: In the era between flower power and the yuppie, Sonia Lucas is a young wife and mother, just starting out in life. Without warning, a strange presence and dark force enters her life, clouds building...

1917: ...and a storm brewing as the world reeled from the horrific events of World War I just before it was ravaged by a Spanish flu epidemic that would kill millions. Sephora Lloyd is a 16 year old girl lost in the responsibilities of an adult world helping to support herself and her mother. A beautiful young nun-in-training enters her life, bringing love and hope with her. That is, until a force bigger than either of them threatens everything Sephora holds dear.

Four women - three deaths - two words - one house
THE HUNTED

The Traveler Book Two: The Hunter - ISBN - 978-1-948232-93-7

A story so epic one book can't contain it. BOOK TWO:

1890: In the dying days of the Old West, Sally Little runs her booming brothel with the passion and tenacity the business of sex requires. Savvy and indulgent, there's one itch Sally can't let herself scratch. Afraid of hurting the woman she loves, she instead unleashes...

Present Day: ...her renovation crew and fixer upper TV show on a dilapidated mansion that has known nothing but death since a murder there in 1977. Samantha Leyton sees ratings gold in bringing the sagging old house to life, but instead she discovers only she has the power to unlock the mystery that hunted four women across time, leaving death and destruction in its wake. Can she release her sisters who came before her and finally be granted the gift of love that is stronger than any evil?

Four women - Three deaths - two words - one house
THE HUNTER

Finding Faith (Wynter Series Book 1) - ISBN - 978-1-952270-16-1

Faith Fitzgerald thought that if she got an education and became a high-powered attorney in Manhattan, maybe—just maybe—she'd gain the attention and respect of her absentee father. Considering he was the only parent she had left after her mother's suicide when Faith was just a child, she thought that's what it would take.

She was wrong.

What she dreamed would be glamorous and satisfying turned out to be grueling and thankless. Since she wasn't willing to play the game between the sheets, she was forced to stay in the cubicle jungle doing all the heavy lifting while the men got the credit and the rewards.

Deciding she is done, Faith packs up and, with the flip of the bird to the rearview mirror, leaves New York and heads home to Colorado. She has nothing there: no job, nowhere to live, no relationship with her father. Truth is, she barely has a relationship with herself.

On the drive home, she finds herself in Wynter, a tiny mountain town at the foot of the Rockies. Looking more like it belongs in a made-for-TV Christmas movie than on the map, Faith is utterly enchanted. When she tries her luck and buys a raffle ticket at Pop's, Wynter's charming café, her prize is far more than meets the eye—or the heart.

Enter Wyatt, a feisty, sexy southerner and waitress at Pop's, who just happens to be married to a local sheriff's deputy. All is not as it appears with the All-American boy and his Georgia peach.

A colorful cast of unforgettable and charming characters will teach the jaded attorney that sometimes to find yourself all you have to do is go back to the basics…and have a little Faith.

Taking Liberty (Wynter Series Book 2) - ISBN- 978-1-952270-24-6

A victim of a massive corporate downsize, Liberty Faulkner suddenly finds herself without a job, without a home, and without a plan. Though certainly not part of her vision, Libby decides that the familiar is the safest path back to her life goals. In this case, the devil she knows is home: the tiny mountain town of Wynter, Colorado, a close-knit place where everybody knows everybody and everybody's business. Seems like the perfect place for the twenty-five-year-old to start over and figure out who she is without being noticed…not.

Sergeant Grace Montez escaped her dead-end job and toxic relationship in New Mexico and moved to Wynter to help build their police department from scratch. Now an established figurehead in the community, she's got her professional life dialed in and even mentors new recruits on the force. After a challenging childhood and lifetime of abandonment and disappointment, Grace hasn't been interested in another relationship—especially because no one has caught her eye since a certain quirky college student who used to make her caramel macchiato at the local coffee shop moved away three years ago.

Now that quirky college student has returned as the beautiful, mature woman Libby has become. Can Grace keep her distance, or will she finally take liberties with what is being offered?

Justice Won (Wynter Series Book 3) - ISBN - 978-1-952270-36-9

In 1890, seventeen-year-old Justice Kilkoyne and her mother, Ninny, are one bad decision away from living on the streets of Azrael, Pennsylvania. Ninny's propensity for the bottle has left Justice to play the adult, her androgynous good looks helping her pass as a young man to gain employment and keep them—if just barely—above water.

Determined to find a better life for them, Justice saves every penny to get them on a train headed west to the sunshine of California. Before they can leave, the bigotry of one shopkeeper sends Justice on the run, chased by the police for a crime she didn't commit and straight into the unwitting arms of a stunning young prostitute, who, after an unexpected connection, becomes Justice's Angel.

The day arrives to leave Pennsylvania for good. As

Justice and Ninny get settled, they're surprised by the appearance of Angel, also wanting to start anew. When the trip is violently interrupted in Colorado, Angel just may be lost to Justice forever.

Can Justice find a new life when she makes her way to the fledgling mining town of Wynter, Colorado? Can her heart ever be whole again?

Curtain Call - ISBN - 978-1-952270-42-0

What do you do when you come from a long line of dancers that spans the globe and generations, yet you can't tell your right foot from your left? You fall in love with a dancer, of course!

Gray Rickman is an awkward seventeen-year-old when she first sets eyes on Christian Scott at the dance studio/theater Gray's parents own and run in Denver, Colorado.

Though only a handful of years older than Gray, Christian carries herself with poise and wisdom far beyond her years. A woman of few words, she speaks volumes with her body.

Before Gray even really knows what her type is, Christian stars in endless daydreams and even fulfills a couple of her fantasies before vanishing out of thin air, leaving Gray in an empty bed with nothing but bittersweet memories and broken dreams.

With no choice but to move on, Gray attempts love, even moving with her college girlfriend to New York

City to pursue a career in journalism. But her standard has been set, the bar way too high for any other woman to reach or clear. It's an unexpected encounter in an obvious place when Gray sets eyes on her dancer again. Will the bright lights of Broadway illuminate the way back to the woman of her dreams? Or will they blind her to any other possibility of happiness?

Break a leg, Gray. The Great White Way calls.

Encore Performance - ISBN - 978-1-952270-52-9

Grey Rickman, a journalist for The New York Times, is offered the opportunity of a lifetime and a huge boost to her career—ghostwriting a memoir for one of the world's most beloved actors. She is deeply in love with her girlfriend, dancer Christian Scott, and her world couldn't be better.

Christian, though proud of Grey and all that she's accomplished, is facing her own career dilemma. All she's ever wanted to do is perform and create, her body her kinetic canvas. But, in one of the few industries where youth matters above all else, her time is coming to make decisions that no woman in her mid-thirties should have to make: is it time to retire?

As the career of one begins to explode into the stratosphere and the other's implodes after a career-ending injury that makes any retirement discussion irrelevant, Grey and Christian begin to drift apart. Changing priorities and newly built walls lead to fears and accusations, further tearing at the fabric of the love they've worked years to create.

Will cooler heads prevail to warm up the hearts of the deeply passionate couple in time to create a new dream for their second act?

Swann Song - ISBN - 978-1-952270-63-5

Christine Swann is a world-famous singer/songwriter and lesbian icon, known for her edgy style and heart-pounding songs. Gorgeous, rich and miserable. Her music has always been her life, her escape from an unimaginable childhood, and choices no thirteen-year-old should have to make.

Now, pushing thirty, she wants out. From all of it.

Willow Bowman lives in the farmhouse her beloved grandmother left her, with her husband. A pediatric nurse and small-town girl, she relishes in the safety of her marriage that keeps difficult questions at bay and keeps her life quiet and peaceful, because that makes sense to her.

Until one night when Willow is driving home and is about to cross the old, rickety Dittman Bridge not far from the farmhouse, and she sees a figure jump off into the cold waters below.

The moment she jumps in and pulls the woman dressed in leather pants out, both their lives change forever.

Keeping Hope (Wynter Series Book 4) - ISBN - 978-1-952270-78-9

Twenty-four-year-old Hope DeSilva has been released from a three-year stint in a Georgia prison. After returning to her family property in a tiny Georgia town, she decides she's had enough of the poverty, violence, and progound family dysfunction. It's time to get out on her own. She buys a $400 car and heads to find work out west.

After the car breaks down in Colorado, she's given a ride into a mountain town called Wynter where she runs into brash, aggressive police officer Samantha Gains, who has not one ounce of patience or sympathy for a felon in her black-and-white world of right or wrong, good or bad.

But, running from her own family trauma and inexplicably bewitched by the young newcomer Hope, Samantha begins to realize that maybe her strict worldview isn't as simple as it seems. When a freak accident brings the two women together, it will take both of them letting go of their pasts to truly move on.

Take another trip to Wynter and revisit old friends as they work their magic to help Hope and Samantha find their footing—and ultimately bring them home.

She Who Would be King - ISBN - 978-1-952270-89-5

Cateline is the seventeen-year-old daughter of a nobleman in fourteenth-century France. It's a time when children aren't seen as those to be loved and cherished, but instead are used as pawns and bargaining chips on the chessboard of control and privilege.

She is married off to a prince in the country of Sursha, a Gaelic-speaking island nation near Ireland. Fergus, her betrothed, is next in line to take over once beloved King Carthac dies. Or is he?

Fallon, the youngest royal child and only girl, has been raised as one of the king's sons her entire life, for reasons she has never fully understood. A natural fighter, she was raised to be a warrior and head the Crown's Elite Guard assigned to protect her boorish brother Fergus.

Forced to fill in for her brother in an unexpected way, an instant attraction between Fallon and Cateline forms. In a game of thrones filled with deception and betrayal, even the most secret love can mean death.

Control - ISBN - 978-1-959929-01-7

Keller Mitchum has already lived a lifetime in eighteen years. Fully responsible for her five-year-old sister Parker, Keller has seen and experienced things in life that should exist in the most intense fictional plot. Wise beyond her years, she will do absolutely anything to keep Parker safe.

Garrison Davies is a twenty-three-year-old pilot in Massachusetts, working with her father in a small, family-owned cargo business. Independent, feisty, and brilliant at what she does, she makes little time for anything outside of her beloved planes and dogs. Her simple and structured world is turned on its head when a difficult situation lands two unexpected guests into her life and her house.

Garrison tries to make a safe space for Keller and Parker, only partially aware of the horrors they come from. As time passes, it becomes clear that it's not only the past that keeps the two sisters at arm's length. Can Garrison break through Keller's defenses and help her regain control?